April Fool's Day

Books by Josip Novakovich

Novels
April Fool's Day

Short Fiction
Salvation and Other Disasters
Yolk

Essays
Plum Brandy: A Croatian Journey
Apricots from Chernobyl

As Editor
*Stepmother Tongue: Stories in English
as a Second Language*
(with Robert Shapard)

April Fool's Day

A Novel

Josip Novakovich

HarperCollins*Publishers*

HarperCollins books may be purchased for educational, business, or sales promotional use. For information, please write: Special Markets Department, HarperCollins Publishers Inc., 10 East 53rd Street, New York, NY 10022.

Sections of this novel, in slightly different form, appeared in the publications noted: chapter 4: *The Paris Review,* #113; chapters 5 and 7: *Fiction,* vol. 11, #3; chapter 13: *Witness,* vol. 5, #1; chapters 14 and 17: *Manoa Magazine,* vol. 9, #2; chapter 15: *Antaeus,* #70.

FIRST EDITION

Designed by Nancy Singer Olaguera

Printed on acid-free paper

Library of Congress Cataloging-in-Publication Data

Novakovich, Josip
    April fool's day : a novel by Josip Novakovich.
        p.   cm.
    ISBN 0-06-058397-5
    1. Political prisoners—Fiction. 2. Yugoslavia—Fiction.
3. Young men—Fiction. 4. Soldiers—Fiction. 5. Croatia—Fiction. 6. Serbia—Fiction. I. Title.

PS3564.O9148A86 2004

813'.54—dc22   2003067656

04 05 06 07 08 ❖/RRD 10 9 8 7 6 5 4 3 2 1

For Eva and Joseph

Acknowledgments

Thank you to Terry Karten, Andrew Proctor, Jeanette Novakovich, and Anne Edelstein for the help, inspiration, and guidance in making this book; to Bill Cobb, Jamie Kembry, Toby Olson, and Lucy Ferriss for insightful feedback; and to Anne Stringfield and Boris Fishman for urging me to send the novel out. Also thanks to the National Endowment for the Arts, the Guggenheim Foundation, the Yaddo Corporation, and the Lewis and Dorothy B. Cullman Center for Scholars and Writers at the New York Public Library for their generous support.

April Fool's Day

Ivan falls in love with power as
soon as he learns how to crawl

Ivan Dolinar was born on the first of April in 1948. Since his parents did not want him to go through life as a Fool's Day joke, they registered his birthday as the second of April, in the Nizograd Birth Registry in Croatia. His surly father gave the baby the first name that popped into his head—the most common name in the region and, for that matter, Europe. Nobody else in the family tree, however, bore that name, from what Milan could tell, and that was a further advantage to choosing it, since he didn't feel particularly grateful to the tree.

That Milan Dolinar was surly was not personal but historical. On his wedding day, the sixth of April, 1941, Belgrade was bombarded. The king, having signed the pact with Germany, had already fled the country (taking along all the gold that could fit on his plane and dropping some to enable the plane to attain sufficient altitude to fly over the Bosnian mountains toward Greece—to this day people look for the gold in Bosnia), and a variety of armies, domestic and imported, began to crawl through the country.

Ivan's father was drafted into one of them. He distinguished himself by courage on the battlefield and would have received the highest honors had he not changed armies several times and joined the winning side too late. He was not the sort of medal-winner who hides in a bunker during battles, who is the loudest once the battle is over, and who carries with him enough brandy to give to his superiors. Ivan's father rushed to the front lines and threw hand grenades at the enemies from up close; he shot from his machine gun, shivering with joy when his bullets ripped a soldier's guts, blood spurting into mud in the heart's rhythm.

One white wintry day, a green mufflerless truck dropped Milan Dolinar off at home, maimed. Milan carried his severed arm and leg in a potato sack, because he had heard that science could put his limbs back on. After several weeks the ice thawed, and the hand and the leg rotted, despite Milan's keeping them in the coldest corner of his basement. Yet he kept even the bones, thinking that science would one day be able to restore his limbs. He read all the medical books he could lay his hands—or, rather, hand—on, and he claimed he knew more about illnesses than all the doctors in the county combined. When he sat near the town center kiosk, under chestnut trees, and smoked his pipe (which was good for his sinuses in the wet climate), many people stopped by and asked him how to treat their rheumatoid arthritis and varicose veins. Sometimes lighting his pipe was the fee for the advice. He was prophetic indeed about the beneficial influence of red wine on the blood vessels and memory faculties, so every afternoon his nose turned red, and he related his war reminiscences to random young listeners in horrifyingly vivid detail. And when Ivan was born, his nose positively beamed. Several months after Ivan's birth, Milan Dolinar died in delirium tremens.

From early on, Ivan wanted to distinguish himself, as though he knew that he suffered a handicap. He fell in love with power as soon as he learned how to crawl. He screamed for milk even when he didn't want any, just so he could command his mother's attention. He was breast-fed for almost a year; he wouldn't have cow's milk as long as he could sink his face into his mother's smooth bosom.

Then his mother, Branka Dolinar, gave birth to Bruno, the son Ivan's father had conceived before his death—red wine was good even for that. Ivan was pushed away from his mother's soft breasts, although she did have two. No matter how much he screamed, he got only cow's milk. As for pacifiers, after the war there weren't any, and he had to make do with his little fingers.

Several years later Ivan took revenge for being displaced from his mother's bosom: he continually tortured his younger brother—pulling his ears and nose, and bopping him on the head. There was nothing more melodious to him than the boy's crying. Ivan was not vicious—he merely treated his brother as a temporary musical instrument, an organ, on which he was learning to control the keys, and after all, isn't music all about the beauties of control and order? The rest of the day he would spend hugging Bruno, making him paper airplanes, and giving him chocolates he stole from the local store. But as Bruno was about to grasp a bar of chocolate, Ivan would withdraw it and tease him to grasp it again—in the meanwhile, he would back his way up toward the dark attic, and Bruno would follow, reaching up toward the alluring bar. And once his brother passed the threshold of the attic, Ivan would lock him in to scream in the dark. Ivan enjoyed the high pitch he thus elicited from his brother's windpipe—but soon thereafter he would open the door and apologize, promising they would go fishing together.

They often went to the little river, which passed through the town, and sat on the clay bank below weeping willows. Ivan found the fish they caught too slimy to touch, while Bruno enjoyed getting the fish off the hook and spearing it on a branch and grilling it over the fire Ivan made. Under the tree's canopy, they were like little Indians; they ate, and they smoked dry willow leaves. Bruno caught toads with his bare hands and laughed at how they looked like bald, fat old men.

When Mother went shopping, she ordered Ivan to babysit, and often he did it quite literally, sitting on his crying baby brother. Mother beat Ivan for beating Bruno, and the resentful Ivan would beat the boy again and then offer him pencils, with which Bruno drew frogs and fish.

Fearing that Ivan might be slightly retarded, his mother enrolled him in school a year later than usual. Ivan was one of the largest boys in the class, and he wanted to be the strongest. He choked other boys—he did that intelligently, as a diagnostic test: if a boy's nose bled, he warned the boy that he suffered from anemia, and suggested licking rusty pipes for therapy. Sometimes, if he felt particularly concerned for the boy's health, he'd drag him to the rusty pipe that ran along the school wall, and force him to lick it there and then. If the boy wheezed too long after the stranglehold, Ivan informed him he had asthma and recommended diving, to strengthen the lungs. He showed talent for medicine early on, and in a way his methods of diagnosis and therapy were on the par with the quality of medical care one received in Yugoslavia. He experienced that care: during an outbreak of hepatitis in the neighborhood, a doctor stabbed his right buttock with a huge needle all the way to the bone while a nurse held him down with her palm over his mouth so he wouldn't alarm the people in the waiting room. When the needle reached the bone, the doctor still kept pressing; a deep pain lingered in Ivan's buttock for a month afterward. Ivan imagined that he was actually good to the boys. He'd offer them sweets (his cough medicine), tutor them in math, and whisper the right answers to them during exams.

Longing to prove himself with something big, he put stones onto the railway tracks and, hiding in thorny bushes, waited for the next train, which came from behind a curve, panting out clouds of steam. Ivan's breath quickened; he expected the train to crash in the gravel ditch and crush all the passengers who were now waving white and red handkerchiefs. He felt sorry for them—it was too late to take the stones off the track. The train only shook. That was almost enough for him; he shivered, proud that he had so much influence. After the iron wheels rolled on, white dust, like flour, remained on the tracks.

He balanced ever larger stones on the rails, making the trains shake more and more, until one noon a policeman caught him and slapped him so that his handprints remained on the boy's soft cheeks for the whole afternoon (the handprints were so clear that a fortune-teller could have read in them how many wives, children, years, and money the cop would enjoy and suffer). To avoid another set of handprints—his mother's—Ivan stayed away from home. He crawled into a World War II bunker, some twenty yards up the hill from the tracks. Cobwebs from above and nettles from below made his entry uncomfortable. Inside it was cold and totally dark. As he felt his way along the wall, he got a cut on his forefinger from a river-shell fragment, which was part of the concrete mix. He shivered, fearing snakes and human skeletons were scattered around him in the dank darkness.

After a while, his fear dissipated. He took one skull with a hole in the pate and carried it home wrapped in newspapers like a watermelon. He hid the skull in the attic, imagining it would work as a ghost-receptacle. The executed man's ghost would visit what remained of his body and would perhaps come out of the skull at night to smoke cigars and sigh with sorrow.

In the evening, while visiting the skull, Ivan lit a cigarette butt he'd found in the gutter, and smoked and coughed. There was no sighing of the ghost, and Ivan felt brave indeed. Maybe there were no ghosts, only souls, and souls went far away, to heaven or hell. What would happen in resurrection? He savored the mystery surrounding the skull.

Confident, he took a bet with several boys from his class that he could lie down on the tracks under a passing train. A quarter of an hour before the train was scheduled to pass, he went to the train station and checked the coaches for any metal objects that might hang from it and, finding none, he felt assured enough to lie down on the tracks.

When the train appeared around the curve, it struck him that another coach could have been added, with a metal hook hanging so low that it would crush his skull. He jumped off the tracks into the ditch a second before the train could reach him. The boys laughed at him. Ivan chased them because he hated appearing ridiculous, which made him look all the more ridiculous.

Ivan loves the state apparatus

Adoring power, Ivan was ready to love the army, the state, and the president himself. A block away from his home in front of a green garrison, guards stood stiffly in their shacks. They opened and unloaded a rifle to let him take a look at his street through the barrel: the street rolled inside, like tobacco on cigarette paper, and shone, diminished and oily, with people hanging upside down, like tiny bats in an icy cave. The soldiers placed a green cap atop his head, with a star made of yellow metal and red glass—*partizanka,* named after partisans, though probably no real partisans had ever worn the dandy Socialist Realism cap. The cap sank over Ivan's head, his large ears notwithstanding. Then the soldiers put a rifle over his right shoulder. Ivan marched with such hatred of the invisible enemy that in lifting his legs high and slamming them on the cobblestones, he looked more like a caricature of a Nazi youth than a partisan. The wood on his rifle dragged over the cobbles. Even the forbidding captain with a thick Stalinesque mustache laughed. He put Ivan on his left knee and bounced him up and down in a fatherly fashion, then took off Ivan's cap, straightening one disobedient cowlick. Pride had startled Ivan's hair, and he imagined that the captain was just like his father used to be.

The captain put Ivan on his bay horse. The trouble was that Ivan suffered from a horse phobia: once, when he was three, he had been stranded in a narrow passageway where a pair of horses were pulling a cart loaded with firewood. He had attempted to disappear into the wall as the huge beasts trampled forth—sparks flying out of the stone beneath their hoofs, foam dripping from their mouths—while the cart driver had shouted obscenities. To Ivan, the horses had been elephants that would squash him like a pumpkin. Now when the captain tossed him onto the back of the warm horse, Ivan shrieked with such terror that the crowd of soldiers burst out laughing. Red, sausagelike excrement slid down Ivan's patched-up pants and dropped on the ground, showing that Ivan had recently eaten tomato soup with rice and pork-blood sausages. The scarlet cattails steaming on the cobbles—it was a cold November afternoon—threw the whole company on the ground, some on their knees, others on their bellies. They rolled and screamed with laughter. The one who cried most was Ivan; everything refracted through his tears into a bright shame.

Still, Ivan continued to admire the power of the state, and he wanted to glorify Yugoslavia. For the Day of the Republic every student was supposed to contribute a starry paper flag to decorate the school. You could buy a flag for an aluminum two-dinar coin in the town's only bookstore. Ivan and a friend of his, Peter—the best soccer player in their class, bony, with large bumpy knees that seemed to give him extra balance—wanted to surpass everybody in Yugoslav patriotism. They could neither persuade their mothers to give them enough money for several flags nor steal any coins, let alone banknotes—featuring muscular workers and large-breasted women harvesters—which were so colorful that they, too, looked like paper flags. On the way to the soccer field the boys saw hundreds of paper flags hanging from electric wires between lampposts. They kicked a soccer ball all afternoon, aiming at the wires, and whenever they hit the target, two or three flags zigzagged to the ground.

At dusk they had about eighty flags each; Peter, to Ivan's chagrin, had several more than he. Nevertheless, the slight inequality didn't harm their friendship. Ivan accompanied Peter home, and at Peter's doorstep they talked about what a great thing it was to be free, thanks to Tito and the Party. Then Peter, feeling bad that

Ivan would have to walk alone, accompanied him home. Ivan walked Peter home again—laughing whenever they saw a street with an electric blackout. They walked like that until two in the morning—when their mothers, who didn't have telephones, ran to the police station. For children at that time, Yugoslavia was such a fabulously effective police state that the towns were safe—it was normal to walk in the streets till midnight, but any later and some parents with nervous constitutions would wonder where their children were, worried not so much whether they were safe but whether they had run away from home.

After being whipped at home (just a few friendly whacks, more for the joy of being reunited as families than for genuine punishment), the boys were anxious to deliver the flags to the teacher, expecting praise.

The teacher entered the classroom, slamming the door behind her. She wore a shiny reddish perm, which looked like bronze on a freshly minted sculpture. The students stood up to welcome her, saying *Zdravo, drugarice* (Hail, comrade), and when they sat down she spoke: "This is the day when we should sing because we are free, we have a country, we can live in brotherhood and unity, all of us southern Slavs. Our fathers and grandfathers shed their blood against the Nazis—Germans, Italians, Austrians, Hungarians, Bulgarians, Romanians, and the domestic Nazis." She raised her voice to a high pitch. "The domestic Nazis were the worst of all: they built a concentration camp, killed pregnant women, burned villages, and now live in Germany, Argentina, and America, conspiring to destroy us." She paused and scrutinized the hushed class, clenching her eyes into a line bisected by her thin nose. "But some of them have stayed right among us. Soon they will plant bombs to blow up babies and old men as the soulless Germans did during the war. We must stop them before it's too late!" Her voice was shrill again, and two tears rolled down her cheeks, leaving dark and crooked paths. Her red lipstick was smeared on the side of her mouth like fresh blood, and the particles of her spittle sparkled like snow powder.

She whispered about the blood and love that gushed out of the open hearts of the partisans and Tito for all the good Yugoslavs and particularly for children. "Yet," she shouted, "some among us conspire against it all! Yes, yes!" and the *s*'s hissed. "Right in this classroom!

"They tear down flags, spitting on them and trampling them underfoot. Just take a walk through the center of the town. The flag ropes look like the gums of a ninety-year-old man—bare, no flags! And why?" She narrowed her eyes again and scanned the classroom, putting her thick wrists on her waist. It was so quiet at that moment that the buzzing of a fly not only could be heard but was heard.

Ivan and Peter were past being pale; they had turned green.

"Yes, they are here. Two of them. Let them turn themselves in, and we'll be lenient. If they don't, if they do not . . ." She grabbed the long geography stick that was used to point to all the regions in the world—Siberia, Madagascar, Tasmania, and perhaps Tunguzia, the cynical El Dorado of the Slavs ("guz" meaning buttocks in most Slavic languages)—and swished it.

Ivan and Peter imagined that they would be taken out—white cloth over their eyes—stood against the wall, and shot by soldiers, some three dozen bullets tearing through their chests.

After an hour of being intimidated, Ivan and Peter had not "volunteered" to admit their guilt. When the school principal (an avid beekeeper) appeared, the teacher ran to the bench where Ivan and Peter sat, snatched the flags from their drawers, and held out the colorful pile. Ivan and Peter tried to say that they had gathered the flags to celebrate the very same Communism they were accused of subverting, but their throats were so dry that they could only squeak.

"There, you scum!" shouted the teacher with saliva trickling down her chin. "Don't tremble, you pitiful cowards. I won't touch you! Why would I touch sleazebags like you? Virgin Mary forbid! And . . . ah . . ." She faltered because she had departed from her chosen jargon.

Her pen kept tearing the paper as she scribbled her instruction to the parents to reeducate their children. She wanted the parents to sign the notes, and if Ivan and Peter failed to bring the signatures back to school within two hours (she generously allowed time for beatings), they would be expelled from the school. Ivan had forged the signatures of many a parent whenever his schoolmates wanted a day off. But now the idea of forging did not cross his mind.

At home Ivan's mother had just finished making honey cookies, and her fingers were so sticky that after reading the note she couldn't free herself from it. She opened the Bible and read that thou shalt give Caesar's to Caesar—meaning that you should respect God-appointed rulers (Tito, the atheist Communist Party, the flag)—and that thou shalt not spare thy rod on thy son's back.

She took out a stick from behind a cupboard. (She had undergone the world war in hunger and fright, and she feared the police state. She didn't want to be close to the state, but she didn't want to alienate it, either. To her, the main virtue was to be as inconspicuous as possible. Clearly Ivan had violated that kind of sensibility and had begged for too much attention and now he was getting it.) Ivan tried to run out of the room, but tripped over the trash can, spilling the head of a holiday goose. She whipped Ivan. It seemed to him that one of his arms and some ribs had been broken, and they would have been had the rod not broken first—the splintered end flew across the room and bounced off the floor. Ivan did not cry, out of pride. Hatred for all authority, maternal as well as paternal, rose in his throat as bloody phlegm. Yet he had to go back to school, because, though he detested it, he was afraid of what would happen if he did not go.

He was barely able to walk as sweat salted his wounds, but as soon as he got home again from school, his mother was about to send him into the streets. The old wooden radio—its dark yellow cloth cover shivering over the speaker—announced that the Soviets had occupied Budapest. Ivan's mother was addicted to listening to the radio precisely for news like this, which immediately sent her into a panic attack. She leaped from the chair and rummaged through a Czech Bible in the cupboard. She gave Ivan bills larger than he'd ever seen before, and sent him and Bruno to the store with a small wooden cart, a miniature likeness of a horse-drawn carriage, to buy fifty kilos of flour, twenty liters of oil, and five kilos of salt, supplies that could last several months in case of a Soviet invasion. The boys ran and arrived at the corner grocery store among the first shoppers. The shop assistant laughed at Ivan. "What do you need that much food for?"

"The Russians are coming."

"The Russians are always coming. Why should we care? We have Tito," he replied.

Outside, a long line quickly formed, dozens of pale people, all wanting to buy flour, oil, and salt.

"Will the Russians kill us all?" Bruno asked.

"Yes, I believe so," answered Ivan.

Bruno cried.

"If they come to our house, we should set a trap for them," Ivan said. "Let's hide the oil and tell Mother that the shop ran out of it, she'll believe it—just look at all these people, they all want oil—and then we'll pour oil and gasoline everywhere and light a match, so all the Russians will burn to death."

"What about us?"

"We'll burn with them."

"I don't want to."

"If the Soviets come here, we'll have to study sixteen hours a day."

"That might be good. We could become airplane engineers."

"Tractor engineers. I'd rather go to hell."

Just then Tito's voice came from the street corner, where loudspeakers were placed. "We have defeated the Germans, and we will defeat you Soviets if you come here. We have the best-trained and most disciplined army in Europe. We are ready to fight to the last man. Long live Yugoslavia!" Tito addressed the Soviets directly as though they could hear his message in the streets—he probably imagined that the country was full of Soviet spies, so this was as good a way as any for communicating with Moscow.

Ivan writes a touching letter to the president, filling it with praises of the highest quality

Ivan wanted to express his admiration for the president. Tito had stood up to the Soviets and after a standoff of a few months, the multinational sea of Soviet soldiery rolled back its tanks, and Yugoslavia stayed free, or at least free from foreign rule. Actually, the admiration for the president had been institutionalized. All the schoolchildren throughout the country had to write to the president for his birthday, "Day of Youth," May 25. Each school chose the three most lyrical epistles, each district half a dozen, and each republic a dozen. For several weeks handsome female and graceful male athletes relayed the letters through the country's six republics and two autonomous regions, stopping in every town for a jubilant reception of more letters in town squares—usually named the Marshal Tito Square. On Tito's birthday a hundred thousand people filled the Belgrade Partizan stadium, where the bodies of dancers and athletes, dressed in the flag colors, formed DRUZE TITO MI TE VOLIMO (Comrade Tito, We Love You). Girls lifted their legs high, like cheerleaders—though with more discipline than cheer. Afterward, several blushing girls and boys, tiptoeing to reach the microphone, read nearly a hundred letters to the stoical president. Then Tito delivered a speech, though nobody could tell for sure in which language: whether Croatian with a Russian accent, or Slovenian with Serbian vocabulary, or Ukrainian with Serbo-Croatian vocabulary. No (Slavic) national group could feel neglected. Tito's peculiar speech gave rise to rumors that he was a Russian pretending to be a Croat; that he was a Ukrainian actress, Lenin's mistress; that he was a robot designed by Soviet space engineers.

Marshal Josip Broz Tito spoke slowly—pausing often, as if reconsidering each word—without trying to create a delirium, as Yosifs, Josefs, and other variations on the name were fond of doing. A delirium followed nevertheless; people failed to comprehend how they could be so lucky as to be in the same space where the president was, an honor greater than being in Mecca for a Muslim.

Ivan loved reading about Tito's courageous acts: during World War II Tito had lived in a large cave, where the Germans couldn't find him, and when they finally did, thousands of soldiers died defending the cave until he escaped in disguise and sailed off to the most remote island in the Adriatic, the island of Vis, from where he conducted the successful military campaigns while cultivating the most fertile vineyard with grapes as large as eggs.

Ivan was inspired to write the best letter. After all, he understood prayers from the local Calvinist church (his mother dragged him there every Sunday morning), where the basic point was to address God as flatteringly as possible. He looked around the classroom superciliously, and wrote. He was sure he would win.

Our Most High President:

Hallowed be thy name, thy will be done abroad as it is done at home, give us our daily bread and soccer balls of leather.

Our most high, omnipotent, omnipresent, and omniscient President, we love you beyond the power of reason. No words are good enough to express how omni-wonderful you are. We are honored that as worms we are allowed to crawl on the dusty road of socialism. We love to pronounce thy name while we know that thou couldst with one little finger of thine—but even thy little finger is large—grind us into dust the way salt melts snow. Thou hast led the strong brave heroic partisans against the heathen soulless robots, the capitalist Germans, who even now lead our folk astray, to work in their factories. Thou hast given us truest equality, shedding your blood in numerous battles, and thou hast always fought so bravely against the German troops that they never managed to capture thee—so that none of us would perish but would all live in the wonderful, beautiful, lovely, astonishing, amazing grace to sing thee praises for ever and ever or as long as our throats last.

Thanks a lot. Glory to thee, glory that beats all human and divine reason.

Death to fascism and freedom to the people!

Your wormly comrade,
Ivan Dolinar.

Triumphantly he handed the letter to the teacher, who read it without delay. She turned red and shrieked out: "Rascal, come here! How dare you write this ridicule! What cynicism! Who would expect it of a child!"

"But I am sure it's the best letter in the whole Socialist Republic of Croatia. The president will like it."

The teacher tore up the letter and ordered Ivan to kneel in the corner on corn kernels while other students practiced simplifying fractions. She wrote another letter to Ivan's mother. But this time Ivan signed it. On his way home he passed by shops, banks, Turkish baths, and pubs, and from everywhere pictures of Tito gazed at him sternly, while soldiers and police, smelling of tobacco, strolled.

Ivan finds out that the world
is a huge labor camp

Taken aback by the cruelties of the adult world, Ivan retreated into the shadows of trees. He tested his courage by leaping from branch to branch and from one tree to another. Whenever he walked into the town park, he breathed deeply, enjoying the moist fullness of freshly photosynthesized air. He strode through the chirpy green tranquility of the park past a partisan monument. The partisans' noses were sharp, lips thin, cheekbones high, hands large and knotty; everything about them was angular—a combination of Socialist Realism and folk art. This type of sculpture was common in most Eastern European towns; the larger the town, the larger the proportions of the custom-made sculptures. However, there was something unusually fierce about the Nizograd version; the faces evinced a startlingly enthusiastic hatred. The sculptures were ugly, Ivan was sure, but he admired the power expressed in them, and sometimes for dozens of minutes he stared at the bronze muscles, wondering whether he would ever manage to grow such big, well-defined musculature.

The monument was done by Marko Kovacevic, a sculptor educated at the Moscow Art Academy, who had been a Communist before WWII, when it was dangerous to be one. In the war he fought against the Germans, and earned several medals. After the war, the Party commissioned him to erect a monument to those who had fallen. He received so little money for it that his expenses were barely covered.

Communists from the neighboring town wished to have an exact copy of the monument. Marko asked them to pay in advance, which they did. After the monument was completed, the mayor uncovered it in front of a crowd. The bared partisans were as small as dolls. The people booed Marko, but he said, "Comrades, little money—little partisans." Marko excommunicated himself from the Party, flinging the red book of membership into the garbage.

Since in a poor Socialist society nobody, except for the Communist government, could afford sculptures, he could not make a living as a sculptor. He became a tombstone maker, specializing in tombstones of deceased Party members; he did not mind them dead.

Kovacevic moonlighted as an art teacher in Ivan's class. He was tall and heavy-boned, with a massive hooked nose like Rodin's and bushy and horned eyebrows like Brezhnev's. His hair, the color of steel, was cut several times a year to a centimeter's length so that it looked like hedgehog bristles. The hair grew quickly, obeying no conventions, leaping into several shocks and cowlicks. Even when it was long, his ears stuck out, with hairs of their own.

When he entered the classroom—a room with greasy maple floors, thick walls, high ceilings, and chandeliers—he shouted out the assignment: to draw a tree whose branches scratched the windowpane in the wind. Those who did not do that assignment had to print inscriptions, HEREIN LIES IN PEACE . . . The ones he liked best, he would use on tombstones.

Then he pulled four chairs together, took off his boots, put one beneath his head, and soon the room resounded with his snoring, whereupon the children sneaked out of the classroom into the park to climb trees and dig with branches into the soil for small Roman, Byzantine, Turkish, Hapsburg, Hungarian, Croatian, and Yugoslav coins. Waking up half an hour later, he shouted out the tall windows, calling the kids back inside.

Before the end of the two-hour lesson, he strolled down the aisle, looking at the drawings. Ivan slouched.

"What's that?" Marko asked him.

"A tree," Ivan answered proudly. He had paid painstaking attention to the details.

"I don't see it. A tree lives, has a soul. Yours is a bunch of doodles."

He took a pencil and drew a line down the tree. The graphite pencil-tip broke and flew off, hitting the windowpane. Marko continued to draw the line, unperturbed, to the core of what the tree should have been, and sure enough, it now looked like a firm tree, irrepressible, ready to resist howling tempests.

"See, you give it marrow. This is no beauty salon. First you make a tree, and what you do with it later—whether you put lipstick on it, eyelashes—that's incidental. But let it stand, for heaven's sake!"

He gave the tree a distinct character, his: grand simplicity. How, Ivan wondered, does one learn to impart character with one stroke? Maybe one can't learn to impart character like that unless one becomes a strong character first. And how do you do that?

Marko walked back and stared out the window, abstracted, and let the children raise hell. But when Marko saw a girl crying at the end of the second hour, he asked her why, and she pointed at Ivan and said, "He slapped me."

"Comrade," Ivan said, "she spilled lemonade over my watercolor painting!"

Marko jumped over the table, grabbed the hair on the back of Ivan's head, and shouted, "Painting you call it! Even if it was . . ." And he struck Ivan with his fist. Ivan heard thunder and saw lightning even though his hands covered his ears and his eyes were closed.

"That'll teach you. I am beating a beast. You aren't the beast, you are a fine boy. But there's a beast in you. The only way I can reach it is through your skin. Let's hope some of the pain gets to that beast. Nothing is efficient in this life, I know, a waste of energy and pain, but . . ." Another slap. "Now, repeat after me, Girls are to be kissed."

"Girls are to be kicked," Ivan echoed. Whereupon Marko kicked him with his ox-hide boots. Ivan flew down the aisle, landing in a heap.

In the meanwhile, Nenad, a friend of Ivan's, fired his sling-shot from the window and shattered a lamp on a post.

Marko shouted, "Come here, beast!"

"No, comrade, it wasn't me," Nenad said.

"Come here, animal, I'll show you your God!"

The boy leaped to run away, knocking several benches over. Marko grabbed a coal shovel and hurled it. The weapon struck the wall half a foot above Nenad's head, making a hole in the loose mortar, as he rushed out the door.

Marko was mostly pacific, ignoring the children the way a bull ignores flies. Of course, a bull's tail now and then whips horseflies away. At the end of the class period Marko shouted for silence and stood on the table. In the posture of the partisan on the pedestal who was doomed to shove his rifle into the air as long as the bronze lasted—or until a new regime came to power—Marko pulled out his front teeth and shoved them toward the gasping children. "Comrades! I'm a new man. I have new teeth. They will not give me pain. If I get tired of them, I put them in a glass of water. When I need to chew or give a speech, I put them back in. Progress! That's called progress!" Then he fitted the upper teeth back into his mouth and grinned, flashing the pink and white, closed his mouth, and masticated so that muscles on his jaws kept popping, making a seesaw pattern, his jaw clanking. The kids watched silently, their eyes popping.

Marko took a bite out of a red apple, grinding his teeth sideways, the way a bull ruminates, turning his head a little to the left, a little to the right. "That's art, my children. It makes life good, that's what art should do. Now you may go home. You've learned enough for today."

He pointed at the three largest boys in the class, Ivan among them. "You go to the junkyard, ask for Marko's cart, and pull it to my place. You need some real life."

As the boys pulled the laden cart, they heard the chilling screams of pigs being slaughtered at a nearby slaughterhouse. The cart squeaked under the weight of chains, parts of engines, axels (bones of old school buses) whose blue rusty bodies lay outside the yard, like tired elephants. Panting, the boys hauled the metal uphill, through and beyond the town, where the park turned into forest, to Marko's home.

The redness of his house's bricks cried against the green forest. The massive house cast a long shadow over the backyard, vanishing in the darkness of the underbrush. What was in the shadow attracted even more attention, so much so that the bright house seemed pale, while the darkened objects in the backyard—planks of wood with bent nails sticking out, rusty train wheels, oily cats, tin cans, tires, winding telephones— began to glow. The top half of the house was finished while the bunkerlike downstairs still had rusty rods sticking out of the exposed concrete. A side door opened a little. A woman of worn-out countenance peeped out. She wore black, as if her husband, Marko, were dead.

Ivan used to wonder what the point of hoarding rusty junk was, but now he found out: Marko had erected two pillars carrying a steel beam and a pendulum connected by chains and a whole series of cogs to a smoke-emitting motor. Ivan thought that Marko was building some kind of modern sculpture, something he had learned in Russia.

Marko placed a large whitish stone beneath the steel base of the pendulum. With a chisel he cut grooves into the stone to fit the blade, switched the motor on, and the blade roared on the stone. Now and then he poured water over the stone, as if baptizing it, though it was too late for baptism: he was working on a tombstone. His cats ran away into the woods, but returned, and, transfigured into hedgehogs, stared at the monster who consumed stones.

While the other boys left, Ivan stayed. Marko said, "Could you pour water over the stone every third minute?" and handed him an aluminum cup and a bucket.

"What do you think of Plato's ideas?" Ivan mentioned the philosopher because, now that he was twelve, he wanted to appear precocious. Marko motioned for Ivan to sit on a pile of logs. He sat down, too, and said, "You know why his Socrates died? He raised his voice against tyranny. That's how it was then, that's how it is now. Nothing's changed. Our government is a bunch of tyrannical crooks."

"But there is more to Plato . . ."

"There's less to Plato," said Marko. "He wrote with tyrants around him. You must learn how to read it—it's politics, not philosophy."

Marko spoke so loudly that Ivan turned around suspecting they'd both be jailed.

"But you say whatever you want, and you are not in jail."

"I was about to become minister of culture, but I spoke up against their Mercedes-Benzes and champagne. Since I had contacts in the Soviet Union, they treated me as an informer. They sent me here, behind God's back. This is my Siberia. But enough of this, there's work to be done; I must support the old hag and the young hag." He spoke with acerbic, Serbian bitterness.

To Ivan, minister of counterculture, if one could officiate anything like that, it would seem more suitable.

Marko walked up to a stone. He hit the broadened head of the chisel with his heavy hammer over and over; the metal rang dull in a mesmerizing rhythm. Bluish steel cut into bluish-gray stone, stone dust flying everywhere. With his gray hair and bluish, stubbly cheeks, he blended into the grain of the stone, and all Ivan saw after a while was a rock with a pair of upwardly curved eyebrows. Ivan stared at the tombstone of a yet unnamed man, with a face of eyebrows and stone—no nose, no eyes, no ears.

"Is there eternal life?" Ivan shouted out of the blue. This was an important topic, on which he had reached no conclusion. He attended the Calvinist church, where, throughout his early childhood, the organ had terrified him. A dried-up German woman played with terror in her eyes as if at the next step she might be ambushed by partisans. Considering the noise that was coming out of the organ, her fear was justified. Ivan found going to church embarrassing. The townspeople spread rumors that Calvinists held orgies. These rumors enticed some older men into the church; disappointed that there was nothing of the kind, they spread rumors that Calvinists copulated with sheep. Many children at school called Ivan "the Calvinist sheep-fucker." But far more serious than the embarrassment was the threat of eternal damnation. The minister said Christ could come any day, and he read thunderously from the Bible: "And there followed hail and fire mingled with blood, and they were cast upon the earth: and the third part of trees was burnt up, and all green grass was burnt up . . . and the third part of the sea became blood . . . And, lo, there was a great earthquake; and the sun became black as sackcloth of hair, and the moon became as blood; and the stars of heaven fell unto the earth, even as a fig tree casteth her untimely figs, when she is shaken of a mighty wind. And the heaven departed as a scroll when it is rolled together." Those who were not saved would remain on the desolate blood-charcoal earth, frozen without the sun, starving, and praying for death, but they couldn't even die.

Ivan asked again, "Is there eternal life?" Marko turned around and looked at Ivan as if he had seriously misunderstood something.

"Why do you always work?" Ivan asked as if Marko had misunderstood.

"God works six days a week, and who am I to work less? The whole creation travails, works—and so must I."

"But work is punishment, can't you avoid it?"

"If you don't work, you grow weak, slothful, and a thousand vices and vipers poison you."

"But still, couldn't you rise above that?"

"There's no rising above. Nobody can rise so high as to oppose God Almighty. By the sweat of your brow . . . that's how you must live. If you fail to accept your punishment, God will destroy you." He looked like a bleak judge giving a life term in the Siberian labor camps.

He grabbed a shovel. He strained his seesaw jaw muscles. Ivan felt a void in his rib cage. "But isn't God love?"

"That's right, He wants you to stay out of the reach of the devil, and you do that by work. Love is work, not sloth."

Ivan was more dejected than the rich young man who asked Jesus what more he should do to be saved and was told to give up his riches to the poor.

"Is there heaven? Hell? Is that why you work?"

"God will not burn you in hell the way Italians grill frogs. God is no Italian cook. There is no hell. There is no heaven either."

"No eternal life?"

"The Creator learns from what He creates and from what His creation creates. The more you work and create, the more He learns through you. Your eternity is in the knowledge of creation, which survives in God. As that part of Him, you live on. But you don't live on alone, not even now are you alive alone, with your own life-powers, those all come from Him as a loan, and as individuals we aren't actually alive."

"You mean we are dead?"

"No, we aren't capable of that either."

Marko chiseled away some rough edges from the stone. His nails were blue; perhaps he had hit them with the hammer. His tendons went prominently into his fingers. His veins, like blue snakes, twisted around each tendon into semblances of the symbol of medicine. When he opened his palm his skin looked like the skin of Ivan's foot after the end of a summer spent barefoot. Layers and layers of blisters, one atop the other, burying one another, the dead burying the dead. The calluses were tombstones to the once-living skin. The palm was his biography of labor. Chiseling into the stone, Marko wrestled with time, wishing to mark and catch it. But time evaded him by martial arts methods, luring him to cut into the bones of the earth, into rocks. Time would let him exhaust himself. He was being spent in epitaphs. Gray widows would stare at the outlines of the epitaphs to find the ghosts of their loved ones in the bleakness of the stone above candlelight, expecting that something in the stone would begin to flicker into life.

The idea of work disturbed Ivan even more than the idea of

mortality. "Still, don't you take time to relax and enjoy?"

"Sure." Marko ground his teeth, took them out, washed them in the aluminum bucket of water, and put them back in. "I've just enjoyed myself."

"What's there to life if you just work?"

"This: work, eat beans, screw, turn to the wall, fart and snore; work, eat beans, screw, turn to the wall, fart and snore; work . . . That's the logarithm of life."

"How about music, art, literature?"

"A fiddle is of no use in the mill. This is enough music for me." He pointed to the stone-cutting machine.

"But you must enjoy painting?"

"Paint-smearing: a waste of time. Literature: garbled words of sloth-ridden people who want to talk their way out of work."

As for the radio, TV, and newspapers, he said he had no use for brainwashing.

"How do you keep up with the news then?"

"I read history. There's nothing new under the sun. You can find out what is going on by reading about a thousand years ago."

"What if a war broke out?"

"That would be nothing new."

"But you might find out too late to flee for the mountains."

"In the war, there's no running away. Anyway, war would be good for my business. Tombstones would be in demand."

And he resumed working. Ivan walked away pensive.

5

Formaldehyde helps Ivan transcend his
fear of other people's death

When Ivan turned nineteen, he wanted to become a doctor, for if he was not well suited for the army, or politics, or arts, or sports, he could still fulfill his ambition to gain power and distinction—as a physician, a master of people's hearts, genitals, and brains. Ivan read basic chemistry and biology books all summer long, and then, on the day of the entrance exams at the Zagreb University Medical School, he grew terrified that his townspeople, who gravitated toward Zagreb, would read the results of his exam failure on the med school billboards. So, instead, he took and passed the entrance exams in Novi Sad—in the Autonomous Province of Vojvodina—in Northern Serbia.

On the way to his studies in Novi Sad, he gazed into his deep-set brown eyes in the mirror of the train toilet, shaved, plucked the hairs out of his narrow nostrils, and thought that he looked like a sharp adult. He went to sleep on a wooden bench, lying sideways, with his sweater and coat. He woke up with a crick in his neck and itchy sweater lines imprinted on his face. He looked through the window, his forehead against the vibrating pane, his breath clouding up the images of flat muddy fields and the hazel Danube. Low, long houses bent under dark red mossy roof-tiles. Mortar on the houses was cracked; raw bricks melted and eroded in the rain; geese ran in the ditches; peasants sat on benches in front of their homes, drinking brandy for breakfast. Then the streets widened, and colorless high-rises stood solitary; wet pink and white linen hung from cramped terraces like flags of surrender, unmoved by the wind. Dispirited by the desolation, Ivan swore he'd transfer out of Novi Sad as soon as possible.

At the train station, which stank of diesel and roasted pork with onions, people looked sternly unhappy. Ivan walked to the restroom, but a washerwoman wouldn't let him in unless he paid five dinars. He handed her one thousand, as he had nothing smaller. She didn't have the money to give him change.

"Can't you let me in, anyway?"

"No, the rules is the rules. Five dinars."

"You can't have such rules unless you have the change."

"Go buy a newspaper, and you'll have the change."

They shouted before he yielded and bought a sports newspaper. In the dimly lit toilets he analyzed the chess diagrams on the back page. The stench of industrial soaps and nitrogen filled his nostrils. On the way out he felt ashamed—how can you be rude to somebody who's desperate enough to clean bathrooms?

Ivan came to the university offices too late to get a room assignment and a key that day. The following day, after freezing during the night on a park bench, Ivan timorously scrutinized his future dorm. Red bricks peeped through the blue mortar like the knees of a poor man through his work clothes. Papers flew out of the windows, zigzagging, like leaflets from a conquering air force.

Somebody shouted, "Hero, where are you going?"

Ivan turned around—he stood between two parallel buildings resembling two magnified matchboxes on their longer sides—and wondered whether the echo could deceive him. Suddenly palms went over his eyes, and a voice said, "Guess who!"

Ivan turned around and saw a ruddy stranger in a clean white shirt.

"Why, I don't know you."

"So what if you think you don't know me? My name is Aldo. You need a cup of coffee? Jump through the window!"

Ivan did. It was a small room, with three beds, a parquet floor, and a gray shredded carpet. "I don't drink coffee."

"What a queer fellow, doesn't drink coffee. Anyway, what are you studying? If you want to learn, you must smoke and drink coffee."

"That's preposterous. I don't need to stress out my system with these banal substances which serve merely as a tool of conformism, everybody imitating everybody, smoking the same cigarettes, in the same style, drinking the same kind of coffee in the same manner."

"You're a funny bird. But look at this coincidence: the world was stuck in the Middle Ages until people began smoking. Smoking got them thinking. But once they got coffee, they could really think, and they started inventing things all over the place. Before coffee, people started their days with ale or wine, and coffee got them out of that bad morning habit, and it gave them acceleration during the day, firing up their brains. Just imagine what we'll be able to do when people chance upon even better drugs."

"Is that your theory?"

"My economics professor told us that. See, you learn all kinds of things at a university. You'll have fun, but promise me, just for our friendship's sake, that you will have one cup of Turkish coffee with me now?"

That coffee theory of Industrial Revolution made Ivan take the stranger more seriously than he had been inclined. After coffee, which he found thick, burnt, and both sugary and bitter, Ivan grew sleepy, and he lay down in the most indented bed, and coiled up like an embryo in an egg cut in half, his mouth half open and his eyes half shut.

Since Ivan was among the last ones to apply for a dorm room, he got a bad one, and the following morning, he was despondently looking around the room, crowded by four beds and two large cupboards.

A knock on the door. Ivan opened it, and a pale yellow, tall, bony young man walked in. "Oh, my own bed! You have no idea what it means to me. Which bed do you want?"

"Makes no difference to me. They all look equally ugly."

Yellow lay down in a corner bed, and instantly fell asleep.

Air bassooned through Yellow's nostrils gently, subtly, rolling like a purr. Then the breathing stopped. Just as Ivan was ready to feel for Yellow's pulse because Yellow's chest did not shift, a bomb of sorts fell between them. Yellow sucked air so desperately that it sounded like the roar of a starved lion and the shriek of a dying zebra.

Another knock. Ivan opened the door carefully as if he were turning back the cover of an ancient apocalyptic book to take a look into the future. Whoever came in would be his company for nine months, night and day. A sturdy fellow named Jovo stepped in, with bushy eyebrows and stubbly, pentagonal jaws. They exchanged several sentences by way of introduction, and Ivan said, pointing at Yellow, "He snores."

"So? Even beautiful women snore."

Abruptly, another slaughtering sound tore out of Yellow's throat.

"Mother!" Jovo said. "This is going to be a rough year. Have you heard, last year sixty percent of the first-year students failed human anatomy!"

Aldo volunteered to be their fourth roommate. In white overcoats, Aldo and Ivan walked into the hall of the international food fair, Novosadski Sajam, and stole a big crate of red apples and carried it out, past the police. Ivan wished to impress his new friend by not flinching from adventure. They repeated the process several times and filled up their cupboard with apples.

"This could last us till Christmas," Ivan said.

"It could," Aldo replied.

They gave some apples to their roommates, then some to the neighbors, and it turned out there were many neighbors. In twenty minutes their fall supply was gone, and the reverse of the Sermon on the Mount happened (where two fish and two loaves fed a multitude). Here, a mound of food flattened while crowds of hungry people of various religions clamored so loudly that one could not preach anything to them.

Next, Ivan and Aldo stole a chain of sausages, long enough to encircle the dorm. Ivan enjoyed the sense of comradeship and ever-growing courage that stealing together gave them. "That's Communism," Aldo said. "I don't get enough financial aid, though I am a Party member and a veteran. So I correct that. We people have to make up for bureaucratic omissions."

Late at night, having eaten a stolen sausage and pleased with the intricacies of the *nervus vagus,* Jovo opened the door and made such an explosive fart in the empty corridor that the windowpanes vibrated. Soon afterward, a door creaked at the other end of the long corridor, and a reply in kind was made; a little attenuated, it sounded like Jovo's echo, yet it was still mighty loud. "Hey, brother, good night!"

The compatriots walked out in the corridor in their underwear, shook hands, and made a date for a dinner of bacon and beans. It turned out they were from the same region, a Serbian village near Bihac in Bosnia.

In the mornings, Ivan went to the anatomy practicum. The assistants gradually sliced a man, throwing thick, loose skin with subcutaneous yellow fat into aluminum buckets on the side of the marble table; they cut out muscle by muscle, organ by organ, and pickled the viscera in bottles with Latin labels; they bleached the skeleton in acids and hung it on a peg; its bones, connected with wires, rattled in draughts. Nothing would remain of the man to return to the grave. Achilles wasted most of Troy to bury his friend Patroclus; how could they leave a dead man out, homeless?

In the afternoon, when Ivan climbed the stairs back to his room, he looked for his bed, never knowing where Aldo would push the beds and how he'd angle them. Aldo was obsessed with interior design and with finding the least acoustic spot for Yellow's bed. The beds circled around the table like planets around a star. Aldo never ran out of permutations but despaired about the air. Even when the temperature was below freezing, he insisted on keeping the window open. "You can eat shit, but you can't breathe shit," he said.

The roommates got used to the cold room. The winds blew straight from Poland through Hungary into their room on the northeast side.

When Ivan finished studying, he wanted complete darkness— he thought that even sparse photons hurt him, drilling into his brain through his optical nerves. He wrapped a T-shirt around his eyes, and yielded to the floating sensation of a sleep of sorts, unsure whether he vividly remembered or hallucinated the stringy whiteness of nerves and the purple hollowness of veins floating around him in cobweb formations.

Yellow, whose quirks were sufficiently expressed in his sleep, wasn't free of them in wakefulness. His eyes bloodshot, his cut lip twitching, he recited Baudelaire; his face contorted with longing, yearning, hankering (he knew the distinctions among the three), wishing, desiring, hoping, fearing, despairing. His Adam's apple, sharp like an axe, traveled in his neck. The roommates chuckled at Yellow's recitations and subdued their laughter in the down pillows of various slain birds. Listening to *Les fleurs du mal,* they laughed through the grief of bled ducks. Whenever a line struck them as particularly subtle, they repeated it two octaves higher than normal. Yellow did not mind that the swine did not find the pearls edible; he laughed along with them, as though Baudelaire was a comic poet, after all.

The university bookstore had run out of the books Ivan needed. Ivan borrowed *The Abdomen* from a second-year medical student, Selma, from the local Calvinist church. He went to church every Sunday morning, looking forward to the end of the boring sermons, to talk to her. She talked in a whispering way, telling him that everybody falls in love two times; the first time in youth was a rehearsal for real love, which overcomes women in their thirties. In her mid-twenties, she was looking forward to real love. She dated a Montenegrin medical student, and one morning she introduced him to Ivan at her home. Ivan talked about all the virtues of sexual sublimation. Crude sexual energy, unused, becomes refined spiritual intricacy of imagination and creativity. "Therefore, if you want to become a great surgeon, you should not have sex at all."

The Montenegrin claimed that only when you were relaxed could you concentrate; and he looked toward Selma, to exchange liquid glances. She sat supplely, displaying the curve of her waist, hip, thigh, all a continuous luscious grace.

Ivan left, mad.

Still Ivan continued to visit her. Her room was in a small orange house, which languidly exuded a smell of wet clay on a narrow cobbled street. The cobbles were so uneven that you had to watch your step. Ivan and Selma now skipped church and talked nearly every Sunday morning. She told Ivan that she was raised as a secular Muslim in Tuzla and that Calvinism was her first contact with religion. She lay on the sofa and looked at him with seductive sincerity, pervaded with a playful, challenging sarcasm. But quickly that appeared too direct to her, and she retreated. "You see, if I lie down, blood pressure in my veins drops. You know, the pressure in the veins depends largely on gravity." After talking about the physiology of veins for ten minutes, she said throatily, "You must be good to your veins," and, touching him lightly on the top of his hand with the tips of her nails, she made him promise that he would be good to his veins.

Selma gave him a huge Russian anatomy atlas in three volumes and told him to feel free to consult her, because she loved to refresh her knowledge of anatomy. When they stood in the door, and her bosom seemed to invite him, she shifted her legs, as though dancing, and said, "Shifting legs tightens your muscles. The muscles massage your veins, keeping them narrow, so not too much blood can stay in them." And his impulse to take a plunge, to clasp her in his arms and press her breasts against his ribs, was dispelled. Several times they stood like that, awkwardly, on the verge of a kiss, but before Ivan could overcome his anxiety and fear of her powerful femininity, she'd withdraw, and he'd walk home swearing at his lack of strength, at his self-consciousness.

Now the three medical student roommates had all the books for human anatomy, the course that mattered most in the first year. Physics and organic chemistry did not intimidate the roommates, but the vast Latinized anatomical descriptions did, especially because their professor was an imposing figure—tall, with a strong jaw, a resonant bass voice, and a constant frown. Besides being the professor of anatomy, he worked as a brain surgeon. He seemed to despise all the students.

He was a Montenegrin Serb. Jovo said to Ivan: "He'll fail you. I am sure he's allergic to Croats. If I were you, I'd study hard."

A dozen assistant professors ran the anatomy practicum and conducted the six colloquial exams. Radulovic, the professor, had sworn that whoever passed all the six colloquial exams, would not fail the final one.

Partly because he hadn't had the books right away and partly because he had spent too much time at Selma's, Ivan wasn't ready for the first exam. A woman assistant professor of anatomy tested him in front of thirty students. She sat in a chair in front of him, crossed her smooth suntanned legs, her skirt slid up, and she asked him a question, mostly in Latin. To illustrate the point, she took his hand into hers, placed the back of it on her naked knee and slid it toward her skirt over her fuzzy hairs; she poked her polished nails into the tendons of his wrist, touched different palm muscle groups with her fingertips strokingly. She kept his hand on her thigh even when she asked him a question about the elbow; her skirt slid farther up. She looked calmly into his eyes, waiting for his answer. He couldn't recall the exact Latin names, so he hesitated. Her steady, dark blue eyes analyzed him. Trying to stir his memory, he was afraid he wouldn't recall the Latin names—and he didn't. He leaned forward to hide his erection. A slight mocking smile curved her lips. His hand twitched in hers, and he blushed. She gave him an F, quite coldly, without waiting for him to recover.

He had lost his chance to pass anatomy safely, step-by-step. His roommates passed their first exams, and he didn't tell them that he had failed.

When Yellow snored late at night, Jovo would fling *The Arm,* the lightest book, into Yellow's ribs. If it was worse, he'd resort to *People's Defense* (they took a military-training course). In severe cases, he threw *The Head*. But when not even that stirred Yellow, Jovo flung the Russian anatomy atlas, about thirty pounds of paper bound in hard covers—imperviously hard, as if the information had to be protected by the Iron Curtain. When the reference book struck Yellow, he must have beheld all the colors his liver was capable of secreting radiate like a planetarium. His body flew high up off his bed, evenly, like a magician's. He hung suspended in the air on a magic carpet of his pain, his eyes wide and translucent. He crashed back onto the bed. He would not snore, and he wouldn't groan either.

With a broomstick, Aldo poked Yellow's ribs as though they were spent embers. "My God, if I could only know what's wrong with him—just for that I'd study medicine for five years!" And then, Aldo asked his roommates—Yellow was now awake—why they studied medicine. Yellow wanted to alleviate the miseries of the world as an anesthesiologist. Jovo wanted to earn money. Ivan's reasons were philosophical—at least he expressed them in complicated terms, in such a way that it wasn't clear what his reasons were. Aldo argued that they studied because they were sexual maniacs. "I am not too old to study medicine. But twenty-seven is too old!" He pointed at his receding hairline. "Besides, a bald gynecologist would look obscene. I might just as well become an economist."

"If I could see my mother right now!" Aldo whined the following evening as soon as he opened his economics textbook. "What wouldn't I give if I could hug her and drink cold spring water! I can't take it anymore." He grabbed his hair to tear it but remembered in time that he didn't have enough to spare. Then, changing from despair to joy, he jumped. "I can still catch the midnight train. I have no money, but so what? I can travel in the toilet!" And he ran to the train station.

Back two days later, he said: "Life is wonderful. I've seen Mother. I am alive again!" He pulled out some fresh bacon. "Here, let's enjoy."

"I can't eat that stuff. It's got too much cholesterol and saturated fats."

"Come on, don't listen to all the doctors say. You've got nothing to fear from your heart."

"How would you know?"

"It's a good one, I know."

Aldo sliced the parts with more meat than fat for Ivan, and they chewed the bacon with onions and dark bread. The two of them had become thick as thieves, so that in times of trouble Aldo always looked for Ivan.

For example, late one night Aldo shouted as he entered the room in pitch-darkness where Ivan slept alone, because the other roommates had gone home.

"Ivan! I hope nobody ran after me. I ran so fast I couldn't look."

"What the hell?"

"Listen. Today I met a woman on the bus. I arranged a date with her at her apartment. I rang the bell, and for a long time she didn't show up. When she opened the door, she was out of breath, and she said she was alone, though I didn't ask her. When we entered the room, she moved backward to the door, turned the key in the lock, and put it into her skirt pocket. We chatted, straining. The dim room smelled of wax. The cupboard creaked. I opened it, and saw a pale purple leg—whether alive or dead, whether cut off from the body, or whether the whole man was there, I couldn't tell."

"But you heard the creaking. He must've been alive."

"The body could have been losing balance. Nothing moved when I opened the cupboard. I grabbed her arm, twisted it, snatched the key from her skirt, pushed her onto the floor—she didn't make a sound—and unlocked the door, jumped one flight of stairs straight, and another, and ran."

The lights weren't on in the room, and the story drew conviction from the darkness and the silence that followed.

"I saw something suspicious in the courtyard—a pathway leading to a little house, but where the door should have been there was a wall, and it smelled of fresh mortar. Why should a house be walled in, without windows? There could be torture chambers there. Maybe they kill people to make sausages out of them."

"You are paranoid."

"Just a week ago I heard of such a case in Tuzla. A couple killed a man, cut him to pieces, and put him in a deep freezer in their basement. Humans don't know how their own flesh tastes. They could mix people meat with horse meat and sell it as venison."

"But out of seventy kilos of human body, you wouldn't get much meat."

"I need to buy a gun. You have a gun?"

"No."

"That's foolish and naive of you—and of me. Almost everybody out there has guns—you know that?—and we walk like babes in the woods. All we have is our dicks, which lead us into trouble."

6

Ivan applies his knowledge of the nervous system

Ivan enjoyed Aldo's quirks and freedoms. Aldo wished to have authority—he joined the Party and planned to work for the government. Women-chasing, however, was a serious obstacle to his career. He boasted about his amorous adventures, classifying them according to nationalities (Macedonian, Albanian, Tunisian, Slovenian) and topography—under the bridge, on the bridge, in the mayor's wine cellar, on the riverbank, sliding into the Danube, on the Tomb of the Unknown Soldier, in a cargo train in a heap of hot peppers. And he claimed he was nothing compared to his big brother.

One day Aldo announced that his brother might visit. Aldo cut sausages into thin slices. He did the same to the cheese, making it look like patches of silk, spreading it in a variety of geometric shapes. By the way he set the table, you'd think Euclid himself was going to visit.

The floor of the room was waxed, the beds carefully made, the windows washed. Even the cracked cupboard looked healed. There weren't even clouds in the sky, as though Aldo's broomstick could reach there. No sooner did Aldo put the finishing caress on the food design than there was a triple authoritarian knock on the door. A bulky man in a blue business suit acknowledged the students with a slight bow, handed his coat and his hat to Aldo, and then ate with gusto, his eyes watering. If Brother extended his left palm, Aldo put paprika into it.

"Aldo told me about you," Brother said. "Student life—such freedom, such naiveté! Anyway, at the bus stop I met a pretty darling. I should've brought her here, and all of us could've had fun."

Aldo, Jovo, and Ivan stared at him with gratitude, as if he'd actually given them a present.

"Then we'd be so relaxed we'd discuss elevated matters, but now that we are horny, it's hard to, isn't it, my brothers?"

Big Brother took several minutes to stand up and stretch enough to settle into the right posture to receive the coat Aldo held between thumbs and index fingers as if he'd defile it. His belly, pouring over his belt, contributed to his Belgrade political look. Aldo seized a disk of butter from a pot of cold water, where it had swum among grape leaves like an albino hippo among pond lilies, and polished Brother's black shoes until they shone like moonlight on an icy lake. Aldo glistened with happiness on all fours, like a dog looking up to his master, about to go hunting. He would have wagged his tail if he'd had one.

Walking down the corridor, Big Brother produced a set of firmly resounding big steps, and Aldo produced another set of sharp quick steps, sounding like a big drum and a small drum. The big drum kept the rhythm on a large scale, while the small one improvised, inventively filling the spaces with a variety of brief syncopations and rushes. Aldo managed to cover in the same walk at least three times the distance Big Brother did. Aldo walked around Him, now to the left, now to the right, behind, ahead—like a tour guide, a bodyguard—although he looked like a growing son next to his father and like a servant, buying Him evening papers, cigars, matches, toothpicks.

After following them for a while in sheer fascination, Ivan walked back to the dorm. He and Jovo opened their Russian anatomy atlases and climbed over the hills into the valleys, streams, forests, lakes, icebergs, rocks, cliffs, and bogs of the human body, but they found no carnal knowledge there. At midnight, Big Brother and Aldo showed up with a girl of slight build.

"Comrades! This is the fair maiden I recited poetry about. What luck—I encountered her on the promenade near the Palace Hotel."

The girl vanished under the covers with Big Brother. You could not be sure there was anything there except a wrinkle in the blankets. Aldo switched off the light, and Ivan listened to the sounds of the mystical knowledge of human anatomy he couldn't find in his books. Sleep visited no bed, judging by the squeaks that came from them all. Panting arose from the politician's bed, a slow bass with a chirp above it. Later there were sounds of larger birds.

In the morning the girl was still in the politician's bed. Ivan wondered what had happened to the promise—or, rather, threat—of sharing. Aldo did not say anything, and, for once, he did not exercise upon getting up.

Ivan was glad that he wasn't introduced to love-making in a sordid manner.

"And your brother is a politician? Is that what they are all like?"

"More or less," Aldo answered. "You must have a lot of testosterone to make it in politics. And if you have it, that's what you do, you get laid all over the place."

"No wonder our country is so screwed up. How do you ever get anything done if your gray matter is made out of sperm?"

"Whose isn't?"

"Mine. I must have enough self-discipline to become a doctor."

The following week, Ivan couldn't concentrate. Whenever a pretty woman passed by, he was wistful; why did female beauty distract him? What good was sex to him—he had no access to it, and yet it had full sway over him. He decided to shake off such lack of self-control—he would study with concentration. He went to the park to oxygenate his brain and to read up on the anatomy of the nervous system. He was particularly interested in the various interconnections among the nerves, such as between the pubic area and the inner thigh. It seemed that there was a direct connection between the two, and thus, if you touched a woman's inner thigh, her genitals might receive some of the stimulus immediately, without the impulse first having to go up the spine and back to the pubic area. The inner thigh must be a highly erogenous zone, judging by that. He was eager to substantiate his theory, but he didn't have a girlfriend, and he couldn't just walk up to a woman and ask her whether she'd like to participate in a pleasant experiment. Maybe he could ask Selma? After all, she had a scientific streak in her, and she might not mind experiencing some pleasure for the sake of science. No, Selma was too much of a lady, and therefore he couldn't ask her—or could he?

He walked around the park, trying to draw pleasure from looking at huge oak trees. He enjoyed nature, and he enjoyed even more the idea that he enjoyed nature, while, in fact, staring at trees was a little too tranquilizing and after a while boring, although at that moment they were beautiful with all the rusty foliage. When he wanted to sit down he found no unoccupied benches, but they were long enough that if someone sat even in the middle, you could comfortably sit on the edge with at least a yard between you and the other person. He had various choices—to sit with a decorated war hero who snored, or with a long-nosed soldier who read the sports pages, or with a mother whose blue breast was nursing a red baby, or with a young woman dressed in pastel tones who was sunbathing her face. She had tossed her head backward, her long brown hair hanging loose behind the back rest, and with her eyes closed, she faced the sun. Her skin shone with a wonderfully clean complexion. Her lips were red, and he wasn't sure whether that was a natural hue or whether lipstick played a part in the freshness. He sat down next to her and read about the places where facial nerves were closest to the skin—one on each side of the chin, in the mental foramen: a little hole through which a bundle of nerves surfaces. If you press them, the footnote in the book stated, you will feel pain. Then, near the prominence of the zygomatic bone and a little inside of it, the same thing—a bit of an opening, the infraorbital foramen, where you can press a surfacing nerve. And you can do likewise just above your eyebrows, in the supraorbital notch.

He looked over his shoulder. The young woman opened her purse, and rummaged through it.

"Did it give you pleasure to expose your face to the sun?"

"Well, yes," she said. "Why ask?"

"It makes sense to me—the facial nerves are capable of delivering more pain than nearly any other nerves in the body (just think of teeth), and so they should be able to convey pleasure, but who reports getting pleasure from his teeth? Or, for that matter, face?"

"I think you have forgotten about kissing. Lips are face, and there's no pleasure more delightful than the kiss."

"I totally forgot about it."

Ivan went on to report on the three points of pain.

"Could I take a look at your books?"

Ivan handed her the books.

"How can you read this? Don't you fall asleep after a page?"

"You always find something interesting in a footnote, like the pain points. Would you like me to show them to you?"

"Go ahead. What should I do?"

"Well, let's stand up and face each other and I'll gently press the points with the tip of my little finger."

"All right." They faced each other, and she trustingly closed her eyes, and flung her head backward, letting her hair hang loose, and her face shone again. Her lips curved into a smile of subtle expectation.

Ivan gently felt around her chin and once he found the slight indent, he pressed into it with measure, neither hard nor softly.

"Ouch! That hurts."

"Well, didn't I tell you it would?"

"Yes, but I didn't believe you."

"What did you expect? That I would lie?"

"I thought you would kiss me."

That startled Ivan. She had invited him to kiss her, did he hear that right? He blushed. She laughed and touched his hand with her fingers.

"If you really want to show me the other points, go ahead, but don't press so hard."

She closed her eyes again. Ivan took her face into his palms and brought down his lips onto hers, and they kissed, slowly. She opened her eyes. The softness of her lips tingled his lips.

Suddenly she pulled back. "Wait, I don't even know your name."

"Do you need to?"

"Yes, silly, if we are going to kiss."

"Ivan." He looked at her lips. They were redder than before. So, it wasn't lipstick but good blood circulation that made them so red.

"Mine is Silvia."

They walked to a snack bar, had burek (cottage cheese wrapped in thin sheets of oily sourdough), and when it grew dark, they were back in the park. "I like doctors," she said. "I visited my doctor for a checkup just yesterday, and he told me that I have a beautiful body."

"I am sure you do."

"Would you like to see it?" She stood up and undressed swiftly right in front of him. The full moon was out, so he could see the outline of her body very well. She turned around, displaying her supple waist and small, pointed breasts. It was charming how proud she was of her body, and it was amazingly shapely. He stroked her inner thighs as delicately as he could with the tips of his fingers. She breathed heavily, which he took as a confirmation of his theory. He had a sensation of being in control over the tempestuous sea of the senses, for the first time ever.

They didn't make love, but their hands, it could be said, did.

Back in the dorm, Ivan told Aldo how his evening went.

"I don't believe you. OK, let me smell your hand, and I'll know whether you are telling the truth. Yes, you are. That's excellent. Why didn't you bring her here?"

When he proudly retold Selma his adventure, she replied that he had behaved immorally, manipulating Silvia's emotions, that he had no right to do anything like that unless he loved her.

"I wasn't manipulating her emotions but her sensations and, for that matter, my sensations. It was a neurological encounter."

"How would you know where the line between sensation and emotion is?"

"They are two totally different phenomena."

"You don't sound like a doctor at all. Don't we believe in the unity of body and spirit?"

"I don't know what we believe—I know that everybody is having sex, even you and the Montenegrin are doing it, so why shouldn't I?"

"That's different. We are in love," she said.

"Love justifies everything?"

"It does," she said.

"So does the lack of love," he retorted.

She didn't say anything to that, and, after that, she would be cold to him for many months.

7

Ivan leaves his fingerprints on
a dead man's brain

In the middle of the winter, Ivan preferred to stay in his room rather than hike to the dining hall two miles away. He no longer went to church. He lived on eggs, milk, and bread. Not that he enjoyed living in the men's dorm, but he liked freezing in the northern winds (*kosava*) even less. He detested going to the dorm restroom. Most showers had no curtains, but the toilets often had doors. After a rough day, a door could be shattered and thrown in pieces through the window, or simply left unhinged in the corridor. Only between seven and seven-thirty was there warm water. Hordes of lads, some dressed in business suits, others naked, charged the showers, pushing, shouting, whistling, singing. Some people stood there just to be nice, indicating they were forfeiting their turns. Others were suspicious of such niceties in a room full of naked people.

In the first circle of hell, the anteroom with wet cement floors, you would leave your clothes. In the second, you'd step into a shower, if you dared. The third circle—a long sink with tap water where students gargled and spat out toothpaste foam and occasionally blood and teeth—led into the fourth circle, the greening pissoir, which led to the ninth, the doorless toilets. During the week, the janitors kept the toilet clean, but on weekends . . .

They were stand-up toilets. One stood as if one were skiing, and read papers, novels, or textbooks. Sometimes you were forced to comment—especially when there was no toilet paper—and lower the perused papers into the hole. Some students, unskilled in skiing, lost balance and regained it by catching the string for flushing (high above, along the wall), breaking it. That meant short guys couldn't flush. The pile of green, brown, yellow, red papers—enough colors to make many national flags—blocked the sewage. Muslim students walked to the bathroom with bottles. Parallel lines, each a finger thick, ran down the walls in semicircles, in groups of three or four. Some drunk students, if they ran out of water too soon, used the wall—though, with the lack of toilet paper and abundance of drunkenness, others, regardless of creed, resorted to the wall as well. Among these brown Byzantine fresco marks, Western-style graffiti filled the spaces, like musical scores. Flies buzzed and walked on the wall in the middle of the winter. In the doorless toilets, where everything froze, you often heard some student screaming out the vowels of his folk songs, echoing through the maze of corridors and ethnic groups. Ivan sometimes walked to a Hungarian restaurant just to use a clean toilet.

The dorm was not shy in announcing its presence. Within a two-hundred-yard radius of the dorm, you heard screams, laughter, Muslim prayers, Montenegrin mountain songs, partisan marches, classical violin exercises, quarrels, laughter. Lousy mono record-players, cranked up, distorted all shades of music. Cracked vinyl records flew out the windows alongside newspapers, soft-porn magazines, old textbooks, shoes without soles, beer bottles, yogurt containers. The closer you walked to the dorm, the thicker the junk in your way. You knew you were approaching a den of intellectuals; poor students—it cost only 16 German marks a month to stay there—stayed as prisoners, having no bail money.

Papers flew up in draughts. Nearsighted students watched through the windows, trying to make out where their notes would land. In the meantime, since the region was flat and the Danube was several hundred yards away, the wind blew and, by the time the student came downstairs, had carried off his precious notes on which passing the exam—his whole future in engineering—depended.

Almost twice as many people as there were beds stayed in the dorm. Some rooms with three beds accommodated eight students—three regulars and five illegals. Next door to Ivan, in a room with three beds, lived six students—mostly psychology majors. They had a Bohemian attitude—threw garbage into one corner and ignored it. The garbage behind the study tables grew, occupied half the room, and pushed the roommates against the door, and then they tossed most of it out the window.

Before the May Day, government hygiene experts examined the dorm, and workers in blue picked up the garbage. There was talk of closing down the dorm. Most students hoped to move to the fancy, glassy dorms of Liman—the new part of the university— with single and double rooms, where many pretty women lived. The students there were better dressed, more serious, and self-respecting; proper, intelligent, studious—at least they appeared that way because of the young women's presence. Ivan concluded that culture is nothing but courtship.

Jovo and Ivan pulled an all-nighter before their final anatomy exam. In the cold morning, they walked into the exam room, their teeth chattering. Since it was the first day of the thirty-day exam period, almost fifty people sat in the small amphitheater to find out what awaited them. A woman who was exhausted from studying day and night went first. She was so terrified by the examiner's cold and exacting manner that she fainted after she got stuck at the first, simple, warmup question: she only needed to list all the branches of the aorta. She was carried out and people splashed water over her, while the professor commented, "It's better that she fails than that many people die under her thumb. With nerves like that, one must not become a doctor."

Jovo was next. After passing the practical part in the lab,

now he answered his questions quickly, but mispronounced some Latin words, and Radulovic stopped him. "Wait, you can't do this by storm. Repeat slowly." And now Jovo lost his rhythm and stammered.

"Haven't you had Latin at grammar school?"

"Four years of it."

"Why haven't you learned it? What were you doing at school?"

In question after question, Radulovic undermined Jovo's confidence.

"I see you don't think. You learn by heart. What will you do with all this information?" And Radulovic described a shoulder dislocation. "If a patient comes to you with such a shoulder, what will you do?"

Jovo thought for a second, and said, "Console him."

"I'd like to flunk you now, even though I did swear that whoever passes all the colloquia would pass. But you are not worth transgressing my word, so, you creep through. D. Now get out of my sight!"

Radulovic wrote in the grade book, signed, and threw the book through the door. It slid on the floor nearly half the length of the corridor, and Jovo ran after it, kneeled, and picked it up.

Next was Ivan's turn. Without all the colloquial exams, Ivan had no guarantee. In addition, it was possible Professor Radulovic might dislike him because he spoke Croatian.

In the practicum, among several supine corpses, one with his legs stripped of muscle, another with his skin peeled, a third one with a cracked skull, Radulovic led him to a brain on an aluminum platter, fresh, smelling like an overripe apple, and said, "Pick it up."

Ivan didn't want him to see that his hand was trembling from stage fright, and, wishing to appear tough, he grabbed the brain. It was cool, like clay, and, like clay, it gave way to his fingers.

"Easy does it! You must be gentle."

Ivan was surprised: the rough giant admonished him to be gentle.

"Look what you have done! Your fingerprints are on the surface, look at it!"

Ivan bowed, and saw two fingertip prints. Not an auspicious start. Nevertheless, whatever the professor asked, Ivan answered, slowly, hesitantly, and accurately. For the theoretical part, Radulovic asked Ivan to outline the blood vessels of the liver and the path of the *nervus ischiadicus*. If the brain was crosscut vertically in line with the ear opening, what would you see? Ivan prepared his answers for ten minutes, in his head, and gave them, slowly, struggling through the mists of his memory, looking through the window at the rain. The rain tranquilized him; he grew calmer and calmer, and he realized Radulovic had made no undermining comments.

"Do you want a bonus point, or would you like to settle for a B?" Radulovic asked.

"What if I don't handle the bonus point well?"

"You'll get a C."

Ivan thought a little more, and said, "All right, let me have the bonus question."

"This is what my professor of anatomy asked me, twenty-five years ago: describe the anatomy of the inner ear in as much detail as you can."

Ivan thought this bode well: the professor reminisced about his own beginnings in medicine. Ivan dragged on with the answer, making sure to make no false steps.

"That's very good, you've got a doctor's temperament."

When Ivan finished with the ear, Radulovic asked him, "Although you haven't had pathology and physiology yet, where would you locate the patient's tumor if you encounter these symptoms: the patient whispers, has no motor functions in his right arm, but his sensory functions are fine."

Ivan asked for a time-out. The larynx was pretty high, so the nerves must be damaged higher—in the brain?—or in the larynx or near it. He traced the nerves for the larynx and for the arm. The damage cannot be in the spinal cord, because the sensations of the arm work. So it must be somewhere close to the surface. Where do the pathways coincide? "The tumor would be in the upper neck." Ivan pointed to the area on his neck, on the side of the affected arm.

"Beautiful. You'll make an excellent doctor." Radulovic walked around the table and gave Ivan a bone-cracking hug. "Next year, if you need some extra money, I will arrange for you to work as a teaching assistant in anatomy. Usually only people with MD's qualify, but I'll make sure we make an exception for you."

Clearly, nationality didn't matter.

The audience applauded. Ivan thought he hadn't done anything special, but the tension was such that after one student fainted and another took abuse, an A produced relief.

Ivan strode out of the school jauntily. I will be an assistant to the new students next year, to all the haughty young women who will be scared of corpses, and they will lean on me lest they faint. He felt that everything was possible. He could become a brain surgeon. He could assimilate in Serbia, and he could leave Novi Sad. He could join the KGB, the CIA, both. And he could become an alcoholic. He was absolutely free.

On the way toward the train station, when he smelled the coal from a steam-powered train, he felt melancholy, as though he had already departed, leaving behind the city, Selma, and his friends. He ran into a huge crowd of people lining the street. For a second, out of vanity, he imagined that the crowd was waiting for him. Aldo tapped him on the shoulder and invited him home, to a room in the attic he had rented for the summer some two hundred yards away from the train station. Aldo drew out two rifles. "Let's assassinate him. It would be easy." He showed Ivan holes among the tiles in the roof. "Put the gun in the hole."

"Assassinate whom?"

"Tito. Once again I haven't got Tito's Scholarship. I couldn't get through to him in person or on the phone. I froze waiting for him for three hours during his last visit, so, he's not my god anymore."

"What if the police see us?"

"They won't see us. They are idiots." Aldo put his gun barrel in the hole. "Let's make history. All it takes is a little finger control."

"You are demented!"

"I hate him."

Ivan winced. He didn't think he was particularly fond of Tito anymore, but to declare hatred like that sounded sacrilegious. "I don't hate him."

"How would you know? You just don't dare to think freely."

Fifteen minutes later Ivan and Aldo stood in the crowd. "My God, I forgot my gun," Aldo said. Two policemen looked at him and put their hands on their pistols.

"See what fun this is?" Aldo said.

Tito's long black Mercedes with tinted windows crept by. Children shrieked on the side of the road, and threw flowers and paper flags in front of the car.

"Look, his roof is open, like Kennedy's in Dallas," said Aldo. "What are we waiting for?"

Tito's waxed face glided by, without any reaction to all the love and adoration the people shrieked out. And as Aldo put his hand in his pocket, four policemen grabbed Aldo and Ivan, handcuffed them, and drove them to the police station.

Since Aldo and Ivan had no weapons, they were almost let go, with a reprimand, but just then a policeman who had searched Aldo's apartment showed up with the rifles.

"This proves nothing," Aldo said. "All it means is that as good Yugoslavs, we love guns. If an enemy attempts to invade, we are ready."

"Those aren't my guns," Ivan said. "In fact, I don't even know how to load them."

"Hey brother, you want me to go through this alone?" Aldo said.

"Absolutely. It's your stupidity that got us here."

"Quiet, both of you, nobody asked you anything," said one thin, mustachioed policeman.

"Yes," said the other policeman. "Your having rifles doesn't prove that you wanted to assassinate Comrade Tito. But you talked about assassinating him, your fresh fingerprints are on the rifles, and you imagined that you were shooting at our comrade, don't deny it!"

Ivan stared at the man's groomed mustache—he looked like Friedrich Nietzsche. Although Ivan was terrified, he couldn't suppress a laugh.

"So, Ivan Dolinar, you are a medi-cynical, er, medical student?" asked Nietzsche. "You know how much your education costs our people? While our workers bleed in the factories so you could study for free, you go around spreading your dreams of assassination."

"I am not spreading anything, it was just . . ."

"Don't tell me that you aren't the brains behind this! We know his grades, his background."

"I didn't know I had a background," Aldo protested.

"Soon you'll have plenty of it. We'll send you to the Naked Island."

"Where's the judge?" Ivan asked.

"In cases of state security, there's no need for a judge. We'll quarantine you."

"But we were only joking," Aldo said.

"If you had been serious, we would have shot you on the spot, and if not then, pretty soon afterward."

8

Ivan learns from the very best the proper technique for smoking a cigar

Ivan and Aldo were sentenced to four years in the labor camp on Naked Island (*Goli Otok*), a bare island in the Adriatic. Dante inverted the old image of hell from fire to ice; and Yugoslavia inverted the image of Siberian penal-colony climate from ice to fire—the island was scorchingly hot in the summer.

Ivan spent most of his waking hours digging into rocks with a pickax. Baked in the sun, he didn't know what was worse, to work with his salty shirt on, sweating, or without the shirt, with his skin burning, peeling off, and getting infected. Only occasionally could he get a moment in the shade of a rock.

His supervisors kicked him, spat on him, and broke his nose twice. He grew even thinner and more nervous than before. Sometimes the prisoners ate salty sardines for a whole week. The salt made Ivan terribly thirsty, and he never got enough water during the work hours. He suffered headaches, and several times, when he passed out from heat strokes, the image of Selma's shiny lips flashed through his mind.

They ate hot cereal made out of whole wheat that was literally whole and slightly boiled. You'd need to have teeth like a horse to mill all the grains in your mouth. Ivan didn't have all his molars. He had got so tired of slow root canals, which took multiple visits, that he had two molars pulled out of his lower jaw. Hardly any prisoners had all their teeth. If they had had them, the police may have knocked out a few during interrogations. In Siberia, prisoners were sometimes given cereal made out of whole grains of wheat and then asked to ax the ice that formed out of their excrement into chunks that would be cooked again for the next meal. The camp director had read what the Soviets did and imitated the procedure, taking it for a good sense of humor. Ivan's crew once had to wash their excrement in salt water and sift it with a sieve. What remained was cooked again. Ivan thought it was peculiar that Soviet tricks would be imitated here, when the prison colony was organized primarily to torture pro-Soviet activists.

This kind of environment is not where you would expect to run into celebrities, yet one day, when Ivan lifted his gaze from the rocks, there stood Tito with Indira Gandhi and several guards with machine guns. Through an interpreter, Tito was explaining to Indira Gandhi the virtues of reeducating some of his disobedient citizens.

"I guarantee that this man will be a beautiful citizen after spending a few years fighting the rocks. He will have wonderful work habits."

"He looks terribly hot if you don't mind my saying so," said Gandhi.

"That's the idea."

"I feel sorry for him. Do you mind if I give him my fan?"

"Not at all," said the marshal.

Soon a guard brought the fan to Ivan, and Ivan was ordered to start flapping it. He, of course, did so, lest he be shot on the spot. It actually worked, and it worked so well that his teeth chattered—well, that was due more to his fear than to the fan, but it looked good.

"Good device, I must say," said Tito. "He looks chilly right away. Maybe you'll let me have one, too?"

"Certainly, my friend. That's easier than giving you elephants, and giving them to you gave me a great deal of pleasure."

Tito turned to the guards, and said, "Make sure that nobody touches his fan, you understand that? And when he leaves the camp—when, in ten years or so?—let him take the fan along. Nobody is allowed to take it away from him."

"Would you like a puff from a Cuban cigar?" Tito said. "A little present from our friend Fidel Castro."

Ivan assumed that he was addressing Gandhi.

"Well, comrade, have you made up your mind?" Tito addressed him.

"I would love it, sir . . . comrade," said Ivan, who hated smoking cigarettes. In fact, cigars were the only thing he detested more in his mouth, other than gruel made out of grains from excrement.

A guard brought a cigar to Ivan, cut off the tip with a Swiss knife, and proffered it.

"Comrade Tito, I would love to keep the cigar as a souvenir. It would be a shame to let it burn away. I could always remember . . ."

"Just smoke it and enjoy it, my friend. You never know how long you'll live, souvenirs are not to be relied on."

Ivan turned pale.

Tito laughed. "My citizens are sometimes so sweet. I just love them," he addressed Gandhi, and, turning to Ivan, said, "Smoke away!"

The guard lit the cigar, and Ivan sucked on it. The flame was not catching on, and Ivan sucked harder until the guard deemed that the cigar was well lit. Now Tito puffed from his cigar, and Ivan puffed from his, and for a few moments they looked at each other, like Indians exchanging smoke signals, except Ivan had no idea what the hell this whole thing meant. Ivan noticed that Tito's skin was all pink and it had splotches of brown and even black marks. It looked like skin cancer—perhaps from smoking too much? He wondered what his eyes were like, but his glasses were so heavily tinted, he saw no eyes, only the blue sky reflected, with white clouds flitting across them.

Ivan inhaled deep, and actually liked the biting touch on his tongue. The smoke hit his lungs. He inhaled again, even harder.

"Won't you free the man?" asked Gandhi. "Look how gaunt and tormented he looks."

"You know, I was thinking I would, but he sucks too hard. Just look how he draws his breath, way too eagerly for my taste. I never trust men who can't pace their cigars."

"Sir, you have interesting standards. I will remember that one."

"Do. Never fails. Give the man a break, as long as it takes him to smoke the whole cigar—which should be about three hours," he said to a local guard. "And let nobody take it away from him."

"And just a little advice, my friend," he addressed Ivan. "Don't inhale all that smoke or you'll faint in a few minutes. The trick is to fake it. Pretend that you are smoking, and only here and there inhale just a little. Cigar is a nose sport, not a lung disease."

"Thank you, Comrade President," said Ivan.

"Let me show you something. Draw the smoke into your mouth, don't inhale it, blow it out twice."

Ivan did.

"Now blow again as hard as you can and watch what comes out."

Ivan did and he still saw smoke coming out of him.

"See, even if you blow it out, it will get into you unless you watch out. It takes work not to get the poison into your system. Always blow out three times before inhaling."

Tito made another puff. The ash on his cigar had grown long. The ash tip on Ivan's was longer, and Ivan shook it off.

"Wrong," said Tito. "When you are outside, let the ashes fall on their own. The longer they stay, the more aroma they give you."

"Thank you, Comrade President, for the tip."

"What kind of accent is that?" asked Tito. "Slovak? Moravian?"

"No, sir . . . comrade. Western Slavonian."

"And what brings you here, to our sunny parts?"

"I am not quite sure."

"You are not quite sure. Guard, can you find out why he's sentenced?"

But the camp director, who was there, behind them all, smoking his cigarettes and spitting politely, said, "I happen to know it, Comrade Tito, but I am uncomfortable saying it."

"Some obscene sex crime?"

"No, comrade. An assassination attempt on your life, I am afraid."

"See, I told you, you can't trust a strong cigar sucker!" Tito turned to Ms. Gandhi. "I could tell right away that he had suicidal tendencies."

"Suicidal? He was trying to kill you."

"Managing something like that with my agents, that's only a remote possibility, so it amounts to suicide."

"True, true," she said. "I make it impossible for them to get to me as well."

"There are attempts all the time, and I hardly ever hear about them. I like to hear—it's a form of flattery, a sure proof that people believe I'm in power."

"But, comrade, I didn't . . ." said Ivan.

"I like assassins. They have a natural revolutionary impulse—our nation has gone far thanks to it. I know there are many things wrong with our country and I would start another revolution if I were young. There are still a few people who need to be assassinated. Of course, I don't like the idea of *my* own assassination."

"So, what will you do with him?" asked the leader of nearly a billion people.

"I have several options. Execution—no more trouble from him. Freeing him—he would love me forever and could even work for me. Doing nothing. And one more piece of advice, my friend, go easy with that pickax. Pace yourself. Pretend to be working. When you get out of here, you don't want to have arthritis."

"Personally, I detest assassins," said Mrs. Gandhi. "I like to have them executed."

"Comrade Tito, let me explain. I was not really trying to . . . er . . . assassinate. I was only joking, and the police . . ."

"I don't approve of that kind of humor, however. You know, Indira, I spent years in prison camps, too. It's the best thing for a man to go through—you steel your will. How many more years do you have, comrade?"

Tito sounded friendly, puffing in a light fashion quite gracefully. Of course, it takes fifty years of practice to attain that kind of ease, and Ivan gazed at the holy smoke around the dictator. He recalled how the anatomy professor had reminisced about his experiences, when Ivan's answers reminded him of his own past. That was a prelude to a wonderful grade and a friendship which was so rudely curtailed by a joke, and now Tito behaved just like that brain surgeon. Maybe he is going to pardon me? All these thoughts merged with the smoke and Ivan's dizziness from the nicotine. Still, he remembered to reply to Tito's question. "Two, I believe."

"We'll make it four. And when you get out, I'll invite you to the Brioni Islands, and we'll drink Sofia Loren's wine. Maybe Sofia will be there, maybe Indira will be back. Anyhow, make sure to collect anecdotes and jokes—I enjoy prison humor. Understood? And now, sit on a rock of your choice, and enjoy the smoke. You are free as long as the smoke lasts—no supervisor is allowed to distract you until it's over. *Zdravo!*"

Tito and Gandhi climbed into a Land Rover, and his guards followed in two others. Ivan sat on a rock and watched the horizon, smoking slowly, till sunset. The Adriatic waters glared like molten silver beneath the purple sky.

9

Ivan practices philosophical
qualities of bachelorhood

Ivan was freed from the prison colony a year later, three years before his newly scheduled release. Perhaps Tito had merely threatened to increase the sentence; perhaps he had forgotten; perhaps the camp director had forgotten. Maybe Tito had actually decreased his sentence. Or it was possible that a general liberalization, which had taken hold of the country, had something to do with that. The chief of the secret service, Rankovic, was fired for installing bugging devices in Tito's residences. In general, as a consequence of the workers' self-management system (an innovation in Yugoslav Socialism), power was decentralized (theoretically, each workers' collective, such as a factory, would run its own affairs independently from Belgrade or any other center of power). Now political crimes were judged more rationally than before, and many cases of political imprisonment, such as Ivan's, were reviewed leniently. It was the Croatian Spring—each republic had the constitutional right to self-determination, and Croatian politicians, taking that right literally, gave speeches about how all the hard currency made from Croatian tourism ended up in Belgrade, and how Croatia should secede from the federation. Croatian intellectuals were trying to restore Croatian to its previous, pre-Yugoslav form, but what that form was, and which region's dialect it should represent, nobody could agree. People freely lined up outside the American consulate to apply for visas.

Despite his distinctive grades, Ivan couldn't gain readmission to the medical school in Novi Sad, nor could he transfer his credits to the Zagreb medical school; apparently, he still had a political record. He wrote a letter to Tito but got no reply.

He was admitted to the philosophy department in Zagreb, where at the time a bad political record did not mean anything detrimental—on the contrary, it was a matter of prestige to have been imprisoned.

The Croatian Spring ended quickly. When students marched in Zagreb demanding all sorts of freedoms, Tito sent in his special forces. The police, riding on parade horses, attacked the demonstrators and clubbed them, fracturing skulls and clavicles. Ivan watched it from the sidewalks. He had little sympathy for the nationalists—how could you be a nationalist? A nation is a huge group of people, and each group of people has a lot of jerks in it, so if you identify yourself with the group, you partake of the jerkdom. But the sight of bloodshed still made him cringe. The secessionist Croatian government was imprisoned, and a new one, made up of former secret agents completely loyal to Tito and Yugoslavia, was set up.

Ivan was happy with philosophy. If he couldn't do whatever he wanted, he could think whatever he wanted—who could prevent him? For Ivan this was a renaissance of sorts. He became a vegetarian and lived primarily on spinach stews and dark breads, and he remained very thin, as though he were still on Naked Island. He was lonely but claimed that he would not get married, because marriage was bad for philosophy. Plato, Aristotle, Descartes, Hume, Kant, Wittgenstein—none of the great philosophers, as far as he could tell, had married, and Ivan, as an original philosopher, wouldn't, either.

After lectures, Ivan joined his fellow students for discussions in a beer hall. Hegel had been fond of beer, and a good continental philosopher must enjoy combining two intoxicants—ideas and alcohol. The Greeks held their symposia over wine mixed with water in such a ratio that it basically contained the same percentage of alcohol that German beer does. The beer hall was so noisy that the only person whose ideas Ivan heard and understood was himself.

Although Ivan couldn't get any financial aid for his studies from the government, he managed to cover the basic living expenses thanks to his brother, Bruno, who had meanwhile become an electrical engineer. He worked in Germany, for Volkswagen, and made a fair amount of money; for him it was not a problem to send Ivan five hundred marks four times a year.

Ivan didn't suffer from nostalgia, but nevertheless visited his native Nizograd in the middle of the summer after his first year of studies when there were open nationalist tensions between Croats and Serbs.

Ivan attended an assembly, where Marko the tombstone maker interrupted a pompous speech by the mayor: "Comrades, enough bullshit. Our leaders are hypocrites. God created us equal. In front of Him we are all blades of grass. So, why all this nonsense? Why do some of you shout, I am a Croat, and others, I am a Serb? What the hell is the difference? Who cares? Let me tell you, God doesn't." He proceeded to preach in the middle of the atheist, Communist assembly, and nobody could stop him. Religion and proselytizing were strictly confined by law to the churches. Religion was considered a disease, a crutch for those who had no courage to face the finality of life. When he sat down, there was silence, marred by throats clearing phlegm. Thick blue smoke hovered like a large wreath above the assembly.

As a Calvinist, Ivan had seen many religious people of considerable courage remain silent in public gatherings. And here an old-time Communist, who would be expected to be an atheist, had spoken out. To Ivan, Marko's religiosity was not surprising; he remembered their conversations when Marko claimed to be serving Adam's sentence—a life of labor. But the audience looked stunned. Ivan felt proud of his and Marko's shared faith in God, for somehow, despite all the analytical philosophy, he still believed, at least that week. Shivers ran down his body into his shoes.

After the assembly, Ivan saw Marko in the shade of a kiosk,

amidst fireworks and crowds of people, for the Fourth of July, the Yugoslav Day of Independence. Marko crossed his arms, stood up straight, and in his grayness struck Ivan as Jonah awaiting the destruction of Nineveh.

In lieu of greeting Ivan, Marko exclaimed, "Sodom and Gomorrah! All these girls running around half-naked, and the boys don't even notice. What's it come to? You can just lift the flimsy piece of cloth and stick it in! What immorality, godlessness!" Marko's comments surprised Ivan. Marko had made a sculpture of a naked woman; Ivan had seen it in his cellar years before.

However, Marko did have a puritanical streak; when his daughter was in her teens he used to lock her up to keep her away from the town "dogs." She eloped, and her boyfriend left her pregnant after six months of free love. Marko, who had anticipated it, moralized, which made it no easier on his daughter, despite his material help. His daughter's promiscuity hurt his pride. After all, he was a bitter old man. He never laughed; like a medieval portrait, he displayed sorrow. He grieved for what had become of the country and the family.

When the fireworks crackled and shed light in many colors, Ivan saw the lines on his face, expressive like the lines he had drawn on Ivan's trees to make them come alive. Although the sunken change in Marko's appearance was striking, the old Marko, who was vividly present in Ivan's mind, seemed stronger. By what force did the weaker Marko suppress the stronger one? Time chiseled into his face so steadily that Ivan should have been able to tell, just by looking into his face, how many years had passed. In the impression of Marko's face there was a little less, a little less of what? A little less flesh, but not exactly; even if he had gained weight, there would still have been a little less something, a little less Marko. His flesh had lost vigor, but the vigor had moved into his eyes. But even his eyes seemed to have shrunk; they were a little grayer—a cataract?—as though he had begun to turn into a stone of his own making.

Ivan marveled and thought, Time is black magic. Time

drains a bit of the tissues from under the skin down the lymphoid channels out of the body until only skin and bones remain. But time does not stop; it thins the skin, empties the bones of their marrow. Only the broken skeleton remains under the tombstone. Marko had struck Ivan as permanent as the tombstones he was making, and now Ivan was afraid to look into his decaying face.

When the fireworks and his prophetic anger were over, Marko masticated as he used to, his jaw muscles popping up, and said, "For God's sake, where the hell have you been?"

"I'm studying philosophy in Zagreb."

"Philosophy in Zagreb? They can't teach you nothing. Visit me in my workshop, and I'll show you what philosophy is!" He spoke in his sharp, take-the-whole-world-by-the-throat voice. "I'll tell you some things that I have understood, something nobody understands. If you listen to what I say, you'll be able to demolish all the philosophers over there by the force of your arguments. You'll sink them!" He spoke calmly, spreading his right arm forward and moving it level with the horizon, with a distant look in his eyes, as if he were razing a city.

Three months later Ivan walked through the park to the periphery of the town, toward Marko's house. Instead of piles of rust, there was a garden, and in the garden sat his daughter, reading a book, and a child was swinging on a swing hung from the branch of a large oak. Ivan walked in and asked for Marko. The swing stopped, and the child ran into the house. Bumblebees buzzed, bending stalks of flowers. The daughter closed her book and told him Marko had died several weeks earlier.

As unbelievable as it sounded, Marko had sunk into the ground before his sixtieth birthday. In the war, in the mountain forests, sleeping in torn tents in snow, sleet, rain, and mud, eating wild mushrooms and drinking from puddles, he had destroyed his kidneys. So, while appearing to be a man of steel, he had been a man of iron, rusted inside, though standing firm.

Jehovah's Witnesses wanted to bury Marko Kovachevic in their way, Serbian Orthodox priests in theirs, and the Communists in theirs. Kovachevic had left a spoken will with a friend of his who had also earned a couple of medals as a Communist partisan but had lost faith in the Party. If somebody wanted credit for having a medal, Marko's friend would reply, "So? Even my German bitch has a medal." In the streets you could occasionally see his German shepherd with a medal around her neck and a shopping bag in her teeth, proudly carrying groceries home. The friend and Mrs. Kovachevic warded off all the groups that fought for the right to bury Marko Kovachevic. Now that Marko was dead, it was easy for the townspeople to claim he'd been one of them. Kovachevic was buried according to his spoken will, without a star, without a cross, without angels, and without food—as is the Serbian custom—on his tomb.

Atop his grave was placed one of his own products, a cubic tombstone from his own machine, formed by his own chisel, with an inscription cut by his own hand. His stone arose among many stones, sticking out of the ground like a tooth among the many sparse teeth on the lower jaw of Mother Earth—a molar crown among canines.

The fact that someone apparently so strong died so easily filled Ivan with fright. Despite all the philosophy and religion, there was no rising above nor crawling beneath death.

Once Ivan was almost done with his studies five years later—he merely had to finish his thesis—he tried to find a job as a philosopher, but nobody needed him. Only a few old Marxists were employed by the government who, every five years or so, devised the rhetoric of a 'new' variant of the old communist ideology to give the appearance of progress.

Ivan landed a temp job teaching basic sciences in the Nizograd Elementary, because there was a shortage of science teachers. He had taken enough chemistry and physics in his preparation for medical studies, and so he imagined that he was competent to teach the sciences.

Ivan had to explain various phenomena in simple and understandable terms. In some instances he managed to explain the miracles of the universe just so; in others he resorted to a hopelessly high rhetoric acquired from reading too much philosophy, so that the poor children only gazed at him with terror: yet another generation of children was alienated from the sciences and would end up seeking careers in economics and law, or, more likely, in bartending, gun handling, and truck driving, but certainly not in physics, chemistry, or engineering.

Sometimes, as he paced around the classroom and chattered about subatomic particles, he forgot where he was—such is the power of rhetoric—and fancied himself lecturing at the Sorbonne; consequently, he Latinized and Hellenized his terms with the swiftness of a juggler, in constant fear that some of these terms might fall flat on the ground. And just as he was reaching for the understanding of the substance itself, with his eyes closed, his arms and long hair waving around, either a rotten apple would strike him on the forehead, flung from the hands of some freedom-loving child, or the bell would ring, marking the end of the class.

He gave bad grades to his pupils, which contributed nothing to their learning but only solidified their hatred of the natural sciences from a liquid haze into a solid ice cube lodged somewhere in their left cerebral hemispheres, which nothing would manage to melt, not even soft-spoken promises of large salaries.

In his free time, he occasionally felt so sociable that he organized soccer games with his school colleagues. True, his moods quickly swung to the other extreme, so that after organizing a game he'd be the one not to show up.

■

In order to supplement his pitifully low income, Ivan worked on translations in his spare time. He had picked up some German, to read Hegel in the original. However, his German was miserable, but that did not prevent him from translating German into Croatian. He translated for several Protestant churches a couple of books on the subjects of marriage and theology, where indeed one could not err much—Ivan's failure to grasp the meaning of the source language did not interfere with the text sounding quite fine in the target language. The moral arguments and lines of reasoning were all highly predictable—sanctity of marriage, no sex before marriage, wonderful duties of child-rearing. He could easily improvise a whole paragraph upon reading the first sentence.

He chuckled at the fact that in some ways he was the perfect Christian bachelor—he hadn't had sex yet. His petting with Silvia in Novi Sad didn't amount to consummation. Now at twenty-nine, he was still a virgin, and, day by day, he perceived that the gap between women and him appeared greater and greater. Ideologically and philosophically he didn't mind that, but all the reading and talk about the purity of virginity and making love for the first time had the reverse effect on him. Sometimes in the middle of the page he'd yield to his daydreams and go out to watch some Italian soft porn (at that time, these were popular in Yugoslavia just as Yugoslav war movies were in China) with Laura Antonelli as a maid seducing teenage boys. He gazed at her curvy body, and the combination of lust and beauty and unattainability made him long for a paradisiacally free youth, such as he'd never had; it would have been perfect to have made love only once with an amazingly beautiful woman, even if one ended up, like Nietzsche, with syphilis. Nietzsche—according to the gossipy history Ivan read—had made love only once and that was enough to turn him into a syphilitic madman.

Ivan was scrupulous. He looked up nearly every word in the dictionaries; he labored over each sentence, shuffling appositives, participles, and adverbial clauses into elegant sequences; he inserted extra periods into the long-winded, gymnastic German syntax in order to gain a breather. He stared out the window for at least a dozen minutes out of thirteen, at doves—that is, pigeons—on the roofs, letting his intuition work for him, so that the text would be translated holistically.

The ministers were pleased with his work and paid him handsomely, in German marks and Canadian dollars, in reward for bringing the gospel to the heathen Slavs. Ivan could now afford fine clothing, daily beer, and imported shampoos, so that, with his long hair shiny, his mood tranquilized, and his black blazer and polished black Italian shoes, he began to look like an eligible bachelor.

10

A chapter containing not much more than one extended metaphor: the state as an organism with many organs

Ivan liked to think of himself as a solitary man in need of no one; nevertheless, he looked for company in that international establishment, the tavern, which, wherever it be planted, even in a large city, soon acquires the local, provincial color, and, if it stays in operation long enough, becomes the last refuge of living folklore; dead folklore, of course, reposes in airless museums. Usually he drank wheat beer, but to discuss big issues—Communist Imperialism versus Capitalist Imperialism—he drank vodka. He enjoyed picturing himself as someone thoughtful, who gladly discussed politics and philosophy, but whenever he entered a discussion, he grew agitated. He was rarely pleased with his contributions to the discussions, and was even less pleased with what others said. Whenever somebody spoke more than he, he refused to listen. The more eloquent his fellow drunks grew, the more he drank and sulked, attempting now and then to impose a new topic. When asked a question, he listened for as long as it would take him to come up with a counterquestion, to which, if he got any answer, he would add another one, and yet another one, wishing to lead his comrades into contradictions by the Socratic method, albeit in a quest not for the truth but for dominance, power.

Now and then he did manage to point out to his comrades that they had contradicted themselves—an observation so innocuous to them that they laughed in his face for being pedantic. For what is a contradiction in a Marxist bar? As long as the negative dialectics work, contradiction is a sign of health, a sign that the process of thinking is going on; it is when things are too harmonious that one is in trouble and one's thought is stagnant, bourgeois, one-sided, dead.

And what hurt his highbrow vanity most was that whenever there was talk about soccer (something highly lowbrow), he grew lively and relaxed. In soccer, there is hardly any regularity (except that the team with more money usually wins, and that Croats root for Croatian teams and Serbs for Serbian) and therefore nobody could be beaten in arguments.

Still, Ivan persevered in attempting to have intellectual conversations—especially after the second shot of vodka. And one evening he shone, or at least he thought he did. He raised invectives against Marx, Lenin, Stalin, and Tito—explicitly against the first three, and obliquely against the last one—and with other vanguard members of the working class, he praised capitalism.

"In Holland, if you are fired, you get paid unemployment for seven solid years, nearly the full amount of your pay. And in our rotten Socialism, if you get fired, you are finished! And they call it the dictatorship of the proletariat!"

When somebody mentioned inflation, Ivan shouted: "Inflation, of course we have inflation, what else. Nobody works, everybody eats; the bosses steal money and send it to Swiss banks." Ivan forgot that he, too, stole whatever he could lay his hands on at the school and at the local foundry, where he led the technical education practicum for high-school students: he stole neon lamps, gasoline, pencils, wrenches, welding sticks. Actually, Ivan got carried away in the discussion, and expressed his views quite freely. "You know, a government should be a good thing. The Anglo-Saxons and the Germans rejoice in the phenomenon of government. They think that the recipe for human happiness is that you should make your desires and actions concordant with those of the government. So a German and an American will try to make the government work for him, protect him, and he will be more than happy to murder to preserve that wonderful symbiosis. And if he has some money to invest, he will invest it in the government, buying government bonds. He does this regardless of whether his government happens to be trillions of dollars in debt—that is, practically bankrupt. Despite his rhetoric of private enterprise, a Westerner will invest in his government. And we, Eastern and Central Europeans, and particularly Slavs, we all consider our governments to be absolutely the worst in the world. We are ashamed of our governments, and, as a rule, our government is ashamed of us, trying to improve us statistically, to say that we work more and drink less than we do. We think that there's no greater obstacle to human happiness than the government. So even if we have an institution pregnant with democratic potential, such as workers' self-management, we never even bother to attend a meeting unless absolutely forced. And as for voting, we circle any name without looking at whose it is, out of spite. To a Slav, there is nothing more disgusting than voting. We have an aversion to investing trust in any human being. So how could we single out someone we haven't met, but whom we know a priori to be a social upstart and climber? So we spend these workers' self-management meetings, where democracy could be practiced, in daydreams of sex and violence.

"The only use we put our government to is to blame it for our personal failures. And the government reciprocally lays the blame on the people and now and then attempts to reform us—through policing and jailing us. So we get the paradox that as freedom-loving people we're stuck without freedom.

"Too bad we don't know how to work with a government, because a government that works is a beautiful organism. The parliament works like a brain, the blue-collar workers like red blood cells. And, of course, the government diplomats employed in the foreign service could be compared to a penis, and the various foreign-service secretaries who welcome foreign diplomats—to a vagina. Anyway, the army works like white blood cells—ready to push out any foreign bodies that attempt to invade. The subset of this immune system is the police, whose function is that of an organism gone awry, so that instead of attacking a foreign invader, they attack their host: so you get something like leukemia and lupus—a police state, and that's, of course, what we have."

The topic of organized power had a mesmerizing effect on Ivan. To see what effect his rhetoric produced, he paused and took a big gulp of warm beer. What a beautiful moment, he thought. I've got the momentum, I'm even, if I may put it in such crass terms, happy.

"Our country is a sort of hermaphroditical organism, even though we call it 'she.' This is perhaps because we perceive our nationality and country as a sort of womb that we don't have to leave—we can warmly stay within and let the mother country make all the decisions for us."

The people around the table smiled and grinned. And then a colleague wearing dirty glasses contributed, a little out of sequence—but then, after a monologue, nothing seems out of sequence. "Did you hear that? I mean, this is ridiculous. Some geologists discovered huge deposits of bauxite near Split. So, what else should we do but build a huge aluminum factory? But naturally, we don't trust our own people to do the job, so the Soviets did it. After the factory was finished, the deposits ran out in less than a month! And now, since the politicians don't want to admit that the whole thing is a failure, we import baux-ite from the Soviet Union and make aluminum at huge losses. And to make the whole thing perfect, the government block-heads have signed a contract with West Germany, obliging us to export aluminum for five years at two-thirds of the world mar-ket price. And so, we produce aluminum at double the world market price and throw it away! No wonder our inflation is two hundred percent—it should be more!"

"Shitheads!" Ivan and some of his other colleagues exclaimed, while the man wearing dirty glasses scrutinized everybody seated at the table (and most especially Ivan), took out a notebook, and began to write down something—perhaps a memo to himself about what he should buy in a hardware store. But Ivan and whoever else exclaimed "Shitheads!" quickly left the tavern, suspecting that whatever they had said that evening would be reported to the police.

He imagined his dossier at the police station was thick; it was probably a veritable novel written with a lot of imagination, featuring him not as the protagonist but the antagonist—it was a novel without a protagonist. All of these spies, they should have been writers, but there was no literary scene for them to belong to. Given an outlet, they could dream like absentminded children and write fiction so passengers on trains, stranded in the snow, would not die of boredom. No matter how inane and idiotic that dossier must be, he knew it threatened his well-being. He wished he could sneak into the police station to get hold of the folder and burn it. The folder was full of antibodies, aimed at him, and he was treated as a foreign organism, a bacterium.

When he got home, he had another beer, and was actually proud of his thinking. The quality of a thought could be judged by how long you could sustain it, and he sustained one metaphor for quite a while, and he was sure he could go on with it, so he sat on the sofa petting his shaggy, blue-fur cat, and kept thinking of the relationship between various bodies, political and personal. As for a body being a metaphor for the country, he thought it could work the other way around, that Yugoslavia was a metaphor for his own state of being, various republics not getting along, like a variety of his organs not getting along. He burped, and said, *"La Yougoslavie, c'est moi."* Hearing that pronouncement, or smelling the beer, the cat growled and shook her fluffed-up tail.

11

Ivan attempts to become unique

Ivan could have been satisfied with his lifestyle had he not been obsessed with becoming distinguished. If he could not be powerful, at least he could be unique. Anyway, everything should have been fine; Ivan had a fairly good education, a fair job, good bars, and what more should a man want?

To become a master—at least a chess master.

Ivan visited the chess club, where he played high-school dropouts, government lawyers, teachers, cops—in other words, people of leisure. Most club members played the clock. These five-minute games were short enough to eliminate the discomforting process of thinking, long enough to arouse intuition, memory, and anticipation. The elongated room had greasy beech floors, flying ducks painted on the high, blue ceiling and two brass chandeliers with small, candlelike lamps. It resounded with men's palms slapping chess clocks. Loosely stacked coins, resembling crumbling towers of Babel, trembled on the tables.

In the coal-heated room coated with a blue haze of tobacco smoke, coughing, sneezing, and blowing of red noses contributed to an alarming atmosphere. Quarrels arose mainly because a player slapped the clock before making a move. The party with his right hand closer to the clock won at least 51 percent of the time, because he wasted slightly less time than the other party slapping the clock.

Ivan, who considered time to be his personal enemy, detested the clock; in fear of making the wrong move, nevertheless, he needed time's assistance to examine positions, and his opponents found it irritating to wait. He combined his paranoid way of thinking with aggression. Peter, his childhood friend, was his most frequent opponent. Their games took a long time; after fondling about half of their pieces, they'd finally move one and bang it against the hollow board abruptly, to startle the opponent, or they'd rotate the piece on the target square firmly and silently as if turning a screw. While screwing a piece into the chosen square, the screwer would look at his opponent coldly. They talked before making the moves:

"Now just a quiet move." (When making a major threat.)

"We'll teach you some humility, clearly your parents failed to."

"Let's see whether your king has any balls."

"Your queen is a little too horny, how about rubbing her behind with a little pawn?"

"Not even Karpov could save you now."

"I didn't know your IQ wasn't below average."

One evening Peter swept off a whole battlefield with a right backhand so that the pieces flew all over the room. He spat at Ivan, shouting, "You take too much time!"

Ivan smiled superciliously.

However, a smug math teacher continually gave Ivan sound beatings and further humiliated him by reading Serbian political papers in Cyrillic while Ivan racked his brains for the best line of defense. The teacher would never have grown tired of the low chess quality, because he enjoyed victories, so Ivan gave up the chess club. Instead he visited Peter in the tavern named Cellar. Peter's father had quit this world in a traditional fashion, by cardiac arrest, leaving the tavern entirely to Peter.

Years before, Peter had tried to become a professional soccer player, and though he was clearly a genius at the sport, he never made it, not even to the reserve bench of *Dinamo*. It turned out that in order to be considered, you had to bribe the management, and Peter's father never had enough money for that. A few people made it on talent alone, but Peter wasn't one of them. He had aspired then to become a poet, and spent his early twenties diligently vomiting in various Zagreb taverns with other poets and pianists (while nominally majoring in sociology). After an education like that, he was most comfortable in the bar.

Peter and Ivan reminisced about their childhood, and their favorite memory was the flag fiasco. "Look at how I decorate!" said Peter, and pointed at a large Yugoslav flag on the wall.

"I don't mean it as a joke. I love Yugoslavia."

"What's there to love?" Ivan thought Peter was cynical. While Ivan believed he had much in common with Yugoslavia metaphorically, he resented the country.

"The older I grow the more I like our homeland," said Peter. "Just last month I spent a week in Germany visiting your brother. I rode in those soft trains, waited for red lights to turn green even when there were no cars around, and looked at their watery women. Bruno worked from eight in the morning till five in the afternoon, and by the time he got home it was dark and rainy. He actually *worked,* and all he could do was stare at the TV until falling asleep. He told me that's how they all live. And look at us here, it's a continuous party! How wouldn't I love it? Another shot? On the house?"

"If you insist. But still, why should you put a flag on the wall? That's very Canadian of you—I've read they put their flags all over the place, homes, bars, churches, and buttocks."

"Look how beautiful it is—the way the red and the blue run together."

"These are the two most inimical colors, the hottest and the coldest, symbolizing strife and hatred when put together. Revolting!"

"Here you go again!" Peter said jovially.

Ivan studied Peter's face. Now that they didn't play chess, he could look at him in a friendly way. Peter wore a rich, black beard, his hair was streaked with white, and his dark eyes shone with alertness behind his gold-rimmed granny glasses.

"And how's my brother?" Ivan asked. "He doesn't write to me."

"Well, do you write to him? Why don't you visit him?"

"I still can't get a passport. This country won't issue me one because of my *political* record."

"Don't you know anybody in the county offices?"

"Sure, but that only detracts from my chances."

"Bribe them."

"I am not that skillful. Plus, you know, I don't need to travel. Kant never left his Koenigsberg and that didn't prevent him from becoming a great thinker. I don't need to travel."

"Who'd want to be a great thinker? Thinking isn't good for you—it gives you migraines and ulcers."

"Of course, if you aren't used to it. Anything you aren't used to as an exercise, hurts; if I lifted weights now, I'd probably dislocate my shoulder. Anyway, how's Bruno?"

"His wife is pregnant, as you know, and he's a little panicked about that."

"Pregnant? Bruno didn't tell me she was pregnant!"

At that, Ivan grew quiet, while Peter served a few customers, who wanted a round of beer. Ivan thought that after a certain age, that is, twenty-eight, if you are a bachelor, you remain a bachelor, but here, his brother was married at twenty-nine and right away making babies, what a quagmire. His life would soon be over at that rate—he might as well start filling out his death certificate. Who needs families? What use was there to families except to show you what you are not? And Ivan's showed him that he wasn't a family man.

Peter and Ivan started making music, Ivan on the violin, Peter on the piano. (Ivan used to play the violin in the church orchestra and now he built on his basic skills.) Ivan, in this respect, by no means unique, reverted to preadolescent behavior, playing with the other "boys." This type of lifestyle is very common in small towns—among married men and bachelors alike—and deserves, if not to be pitied, at least to be studied. No one, however, should say that it is not a charming sort of life, perhaps better than figuring out mortgages all day long, which is considered the mature way.

One evening Ivan and Peter played the Hungarian czardas

for the patrons of the Cellar. Swarms of Yugoslav federal soldiers crowded the small bar and drank one another under the table. Ivan played like a master of passions, winking at both men and women. But most often he winked at a buxom woman whose shirt kept sliding off her shoulders. She argued with her uncle, who said, "Please, Mara, don't drink anymore, you know it's not good for you."

"Of course it's good for me. You just don't want women to have fun, that's all."

"Don't, you might do something stupid!"

"Like what?" Mara leaned against the table, her copious breasts sprawling. Soldiers nudged each other. "What are you afraid of? That I'm gonna have fun with some of those boys over there. I'll tell you what: not a bad idea!"

"But you are married."

"Phew, married! It never prevents a man from running after whores, does it? So why shouldn't I have some fun with young sluts while I still can. Just look at them, fresh like pumpkins!"

The music was reaching for a wistful sound. The violin whined for pleasurable sorrow, and the bass—they were a trio now—massaged something deep in the brain and in the thighs.

Mara stood up to go to the toilet, and a soldier walked after her, his face as green as his uniform. Ivan remembered a passage from the Bible: "He goeth after her straightway, as an ox goeth to the slaughter, or as a fool to the correction of the stocks; till a dart strike through his liver; as a bird hasteth to the snare . . ." Two minutes later, the soldier strode out.

Another soldier crawled on his elbows. Mara ripped her shirt open and warmly nurtured the poor boy on her bosom and they disappeared behind the bar. When the music suddenly stopped, everybody heard gasps and cries of orgasmic panic—pleasure expressed as pain in a natural lie. If people lie even in the supposedly most spontaneous moment, orgasm, dissembling pleasure as pain, or pain as pleasure, where could they be truthful? If Ivan had more discipline, he could write a philosophical tract on the topic, *World as a Lie,* paraphrasing

Schopenhauer's *World as Will and Idea*. Behind nearly every human motive seemed to lurk an irrepressible impulse to distort everything into its opposite, so that at the root of hate could be love stifled by lies, and at the root of love hate stifled by lies, and at the root of philosophy, instead of the love of wisdom, the hatred of wisdom. Myso-sophy, not philo-sophy, was the root of thought. Nearly everybody twisted facts into their opposites, and the only truth was people's twistedness, the perversion, the process of wiggling away from the truth, like a snake under Adam's foot. The World as Malaise and Perversion.

Occasions to philosophize can be peculiar, Ivan reflected self-consciously. Another orgasmic cry reminded him of the root of his quest for "wisdom": judging by his erection, he felt like joining in the libidinal mayhem. He yearned for more elegant surroundings, where in privacy (that is, dissembling) he could sleep with a pretty woman. Then the beauty, partaking in the perfection of Platonic forms, would spiritualize and elevate the crass bodily commerce, which was so bloodcurdlingly disgusting in the beer- and vomit-besotted tavern.

a) Almost every southern Slav wants a fortified house with a fallout shelter

Ivan's ailing mother moved to the coast, to a large brick house, which Bruno built according to the latest German suburban fashion. Visiting Ivan, he described the glories of the coast while they strolled through Nizograd. "We are above Opatija, and on a clear day we can see the islands of Cres and Losinj. When the winds blow from the south, you smell cypress and the sea, and from the North, spruce and fir."

"What's the difference between spruce and fir?"

"And sometimes you get all the aromas at once, the Alpine air and the Mediterranean air mixing. You stand on the terrace, look over red roofs down at the heavenly blue ocean . . . and breathe deep. You should move in with us. I plan to spend all my free time there."

"But it's too sunny! You can get skin cancer through the ozone hole."

"Not if you are as dark-haired and dark-eyed as you are."

"Thank you if you perceive my gray hair as black."

"The main thing is that it used to be black when you were a kid—that means you have the pigments. And then, you can swim and sunbathe on topless beaches."

But the image of a beach, with pebbles and rocks, made Ivan shudder with memories of the Naked Island, and his skin felt like it was burning, peeling, and boiling.

"Just the idea of lying on a towel and frying in the sun and going blind from all the glaring light makes me ill. And add to that getting horny unnecessarily, and you are in an awkward situation indeed. No, thank you."

"You'd feel differently if you lived in cloudy Germany."

"Well, why do you? Just look at the horizon."

They had walked up the hill above the town cemetery, and both of them panted. The sun was setting, and darkness had already filled up the town valley—only the castle and the church steeples still received licks of golden light. Below the brothers, a multitude of candles flickered, more and more brightly, and orange light trembled over a silver inscription, *Milan Dolinar,* on a glossy black stone.

Bruno sniffled.

"You have an allergy attack? See, our vegetation is vigorous."

"Eh, Ivan, I've never met my father. The whole thing is doubly sad when you live abroad, far from home—for me, this is still my homeland, *rodna gruda.* And that's all that will remain here, Father's bones."

"Hardly worth sticking around for, now, is it?"

"My point—why don't you join us at the coast, so we have something like an extended family. We just have to sell Mother's house."

"Houses here are worthless. Lend me a few thousand marks, and I'll buy it. I'll give her the money and I'll be indebted to you—that is, if you feel like trusting me."

They walked through the town park to a restaurant called the Terrace, and sat down for a meal—the Balkan platter: grilled pork, veal, lamb, with onions and a pepper sauce, *ajvar.* Bruno's eyes watered again. "The onions are strong," he apologized. He had already downed half of the meal, and his mustache bubbled with the foamy local beer. He was rotund, and with a goatee and cleanly shaven cheeks (the upper layer of his skin was scraped away by a sharp blade, leaving a reddish hue) and his black leather jacket, he looked like a German, and, more precisely, a Bavarian. Although he was a couple of inches shorter than Ivan, he must have weighed twice as much. Ivan chewed a little and found the meat stringy and oversalted. He grabbed a toothpick and grappled with a string, perhaps a nerve from the lamb, which got stuck between his first and second molar. He grew agitated when he couldn't get the animal nerve out of his mouth, and he pricked his gums; he found the pain enjoyable, so he pricked himself again.

"What happened to your appetite?" asked Bruno. "As a kid you used to sneak into the larder to eat the smoked ham."

"True. I used to eat when I needed to—now, it seems to me, the growing process is finished, and all you can grow by eating is cancers, tumors, and clogged arteries. I'm not that rational about it, but decades of eating the same crap kind of knocked the hunger out of me."

"You look a little depressed here, and the town looks depressed. You need to live somewhere dynamic. Why don't you come to Germany?"

"There's no such thing as depression here—that's a foreign word. Gloomy would do."

"You do look melancholy. May we call it melancholia?" Bruno asked.

"That's a Greek word, Balkan. Black bile. I won't resist that one. Well, speaking of black bile, how about a chocolate cake?"

"You look bored. Why don't you get married?"

"I'm sure I won't know what boredom is *unless* I get married."

"The first step on the road to building a family is home ownership. We'll get you there yet!"

At the end of the evening Ivan was a home owner thanks to his younger brother's pity. Ivan didn't mind that—he thought he deserved to be pitied.

Ivan rejoiced at having a house—his own private world—and he decided to make it as solid as possible. Permanently moist crusts of mortar covered thick brick walls. Ivan did some renovating, primarily solidifying the foundation. Somewhat ironically yet sincerely, Ivan thought that for a Yugoslav there was nothing more important than owning a solid house. The house had to possess thick concrete walls—unlike most American family homes (often seen in natural-disaster news on TV), which were built out of glue and sawdust, and which, even if priced at a million dollars each, any strong wind or flood would blow away—particle boards floating down swelling rivers, together with teddy bears, smiling wedding pictures, and red diet pills. For an optimistic American, it was all right to live like that. But a mistrustful, Socialist Yugoslav—whether Serb, Muslim, or Croat—needed a private fallout shelter. In case of war, the cellar would be a bunker, warm in winter and cool in summer—ideal for storing potatoes, wheat, and salt.

Behind Ivan's house warbled an orchard: large walnut trees, apricots, pears, apples, peaches, cherries . . . This slice of Eden was fenced off from other fragments of Eden, belonging to his neighbors. Although the neighbors barely nodded to one another in the streets, one evening they convened for an emergency session at the baker's house, where Ivan had been an apprentice for a month before it was clear that he could gain admission to a university.

The baker offered the guests his homemade pear brandy, *viljamovka*. "This may be the last brew I ever make! The vermin want to build a four-lane highway through our orchards."

"You can't find a swinish scheme like this in any other country," said the butcher. "Why don't they bypass the town?"

The baker pulled out a piece of paper with pale blue official stamps and uneven typewriter print—some letters higher than others, some close to the neighboring letters, some far apart. "I will get only a hundred thousand dinars—five percent of the real value of my orchard!"

"We mustn't allow the Communist bandits to confiscate our property!" The butcher raised his heavy hand to strike against the table; the coffee cups trembled as if in anticipation of the blow, but the blow never came, since the butcher was used to self-restraint.

"We must sign a petition of protest," Ivan said.

"A petition? Phew!" the butcher said. "You young people are so naive—what do they care for a bunch of signatures?"

The Catholic priest wheezed, asleep, his stringy hands clutching each other. He ran a sort of convent. Three toothless women dressed in black never walked outside the perimeter of his house and garden; it was rumored that the women were not nuns but concubines who exhausted the Father with relentless fellatio.

Ivan submitted a written appeal to the county officials, but a law-abiding clerk tore it up in front of him. Ivan traveled to Zagreb, to the Supreme Court of the Republic. His application was placed in a large drawer, where it stayed. Ivan wanted to address the president himself, but the president was on a long tour, drinking two-century-old wines, hunting for extinct tigers, shaking hands with the king of Sweden—in short, advancing the interests of the world's working class.

One late summer day, an army of tattooed laborers—their skins covered with expanding and contracting Cupid's arrows, snakes, and demons in scuba-diving outfits—bulldozed the orchards.

Looking through the windows, Ivan spat, like a citizen of Prague observing Soviet tanks invading. Until then Ivan had felt nothing of the famous Slavic attachment to the soil, but now he muttered, "There is nothing more sacred to us Slavs than a bit of our own land: Our soil, our soul."

Ivan's walls shook, windows buzzed, utensils clanked, tables traveled, and ceiling mortar crumbled onto the floor, its sand smoking. Every so often a mouse would squeal and run out of its hole, darting across the living room, but Ivan's Russian blue-fur let it pass without pouncing. She kept moving her ears and whiskers back and forth. Her pupils contracted into exclamation points, her tail coiled into a question mark; clearly she could make no head or tail out of it; her hair stood straight up.

When the road was finished a couple of years later, many drunk drivers sped through the intersection. Czech Skodas and East German Trabants, made of soft metals and plastic, crumpled like a newspaper in a fist. Hearing explosive collisions, Ivan leaned through the window and with horror, sorrow, and even glee (against the local government) watched the bloody bodies being cut out of the cars. After dozens of people fell in the undeclared war against northern tourists, four traffic lights arose at the intersection. Now, at night, red, yellow, and green alternately shone through Ivan's curtains.

Ivan developed insomnia without delay. And during his insomnia, he read books, such as Tolstoy's *War and Peace*. Well, there is only one *War and Peace*. Ivan admired how insufferably boring it could be for a hundred pages at a time—the fact that the book was considered such a grand classic had to do with another highly probable fact: hardly anybody made it to the end. In the middle, many people were dying beautifully in graphic detail. The descriptions appeared to Ivan so detailed and lyrical that they became the erotica of death (even pornography of death), or thanatography.

b) A surprisingly touching death

On the bland morning of May 4, 1980, Ivan took a bus to Zagreb to buy copper pipes for his house, but all the shops were closed. The president, who had been ill for a long time, died at the age of eighty-eight. Ivan had joked about Tito's gangrene— *Tito's left leg was amputated; soon afterward a cablegram from hell read: "The leg arrived all right, please send the rest, urgently."* Ivan had joked quietly, because his humor could have landed him in the Naked Island prison colony for the second time. He was standing outside of a shop that imported technical goods when he heard the news on a loud radio—with the sounds of the second movement from Rachmaninoff's Second Piano Concerto in the background—and his head swam through the large waves of music and emotion. Or the city streets and stalled trams swam through his wet head; his lachrymal glands gushed tears, his nose and sinuses drowned in a brilliant and hot ocean.

Ivan staggered to the train station to see Tito's blue train carry the coffin from Ljubljana. Crowds of people thronged, weeping, lamenting, with goose bumps on their forearms. The father of their nation was dead.

Ivan stood close to the tracks, elbowing an old man with medals and a woman smelling of garlic, with silver teeth and silvery eyes; everything looked silvery to Ivan through his tears. He surprised himself; he had understood himself so little. He had thought he couldn't care less about Tito, and now this—awe, reverence, grief, a solemn sense of tragedy.

Most shops were closed, but in the center of Zagreb, Trg Republike, he found an open kiosk and bought a cigar. It was a cheap Macedonian product, but, nevertheless, Ivan lit it, sucked eagerly, and waited for the familiar bite on the tongue and the vile hit to the lungs. He blew out so much smoke that he saw a cloud, and in the cloud he had the impression that the marshal himself was standing and puffing as well, and so, silently, in sympathy, they smoked, and he kept smoking for a whole hour. And when the cigar was over, he realized that his cheeks were wet from tears, for there was no Tito and there never would be again. It was the end of an era, the end of Ivan's young manhood as well. Now he was on his own, and the country was on her own. Woe to the country!

Several days later, Ivan resented his grief. As he piled bricks into a wall for an addition to his home, he wondered why he had shed tears for the president who had caused so much pain to him. He blushed as red as a brick, and, among so many bricks, he looked faceless. His figure looked like blue clothes filled with air, floating next to the bricks, beneath a blue cap. Ivan should have felt joyful, but he was afraid to feel joy at the end of the "cult of personality" era, as though Tito had supernatural powers and his bugging system could access minds, register thoughts, report them to the police, and as though Tito himself would arrange for his tortures here and beyond.

Besides, who would replace Tito? Under the slogan "After Tito, Tito," the representatives of all the republics and autonomous regions would be temporary presidents, each only for a year, lest the image of Tito have any competition.

Would the Party display Tito in a mausoleum, as evidence that Tito was dead? No, they would hide his body, so his death would never be absolutely certain. Tito would haunt Ivan and other citizens at night, in sleep, and during the day, in the cobwebby state apparatus, with the invisible sticky threads and threats all around. What madness, this totalitarian socialist psychology!

Ivan wanted a stiff one, and strayed into the Cellar, only to find out that Peter was gone. Ivan hadn't seen him in a few months because of the construction craze. Not only was Peter gone to serve in the army, but his Cellar had changed hands. The new owner was Nenad, who had flunked out of the school for veterinary medicine in Belgrade after studying for ten years. The Cellar was reorganized like a disco bar, with glass tables, fake-leather couches, and speakers suspended from the ceiling.

13

A rondo sucks in everybody's mind and body

One late Saturday afternoon, several years after he'd nearly finished reading *War and Peace* (he had only twenty pages to go), Ivan went to a village tavern in the hills half a dozen miles outside of Nizograd. It had become a local fashion—and, for that matter, a national craze—to go to village taverns to enjoy the peasant style of partying, and although Ivan resisted the fashion, he came out on this occasion because it had been a humid—outright moist—day, which sapped his energy and made the town appear even more tedious than usual. A couple of trout seemingly sprang out of the blue paint on the advertising board of Trout Haven. In the foamy rapids behind the inn, leaping trout glittered as if to tease the innkeeper to catch them so they would continue playing sprightly games on the palates of the tavern guests.

Ivan ordered grilled trout with garlic. He ate slowly, savoring the tender white flesh that dissolved on his tongue, while the fish heads, with their mouths open, stared at him as if accusing him of condoning the food chain. The flesh slid off the thin bones, and he rummaged through it, studying the tiny pink arteries self-consciously, as though the fish eyes were alive. The more he looked at the heads and their eyes, the more uncomfortable he grew, and he wrapped them in paper napkins, walked outside, and threw them into the bush, where a mother cat and two little tabbies reposed.

So, for a meal, he had a liter of beer. Darkness gathered outside, and mist drifted low through the valley, and a crowd assembled, slamming doors of their smoky cars. Ivan watched as a dance formed. An accordion began a fast Serbian *kolo* (a rondo), a bass jibed in, oiling the fire of instincts, and a circle took shape out of the commotion. Although Ivan resented the fact that in no taverns in the Croatian region could Croatian songs be sung without the singers being jailed, the dance fascinated him.

Cheap tobacco smoke drifted and stung his eyes. He occasionally smoked fine imported cigarettes, but for domestic smoke he had only contempt and Indira Gandhi's fan. He took out the fan and flapped it, chasing the smoke away. A propos of Indira Gandhi, so he wouldn't have to look at the crowd too much, he read *Vecernji List,* the Zagreb daily, and, on the front page, he saw the announcement that Indira Gandhi was assassinated by her Sikh guards. This startled him. No wonder she didn't like assassins. He kept flapping the fan slowly, and its golden and crimson hues flashed. Tears spilled out of his nose. What the hell is going on? he wondered. Do I feel so close to all the world leaders? He smoked one filterless Chesterton, which dried his nose.

The balance of centripetal and centrifugal forces—and hooked elbows—held the dancers together. The circle became a centipede, running after its own tail, catching it. The legs kicked up, red skirts flew wide, and as the bass sped up and deepened, the centipede whirled faster, so that the legs turned into a hazy rainbow, whirling a couple of feet above the floor. The broad red bands prevailed in the fiery mouth of the tornado sucking in everybody's body and soul. When the music slowed down, Ivan made out the colors of particular dresses—red embroidery on white and black. Among them was a blue suit—a cop's uniform. The cop looked backward, seeking eye contact with a young woman, Svjetlana, who followed him in the chain. Her face was pale yet flushed, as if she had passed through a snowstorm.

During the break, people stood in disarray, turning to all sides in search of free tables. The policeman and Svjetlana went to a cliché: a dark corner.

Suddenly a door flew open. A young man was carried in, like a coffin, on the shoulders of several people. A golden tooth shot beams of light from his euphorically red face. Ivan was pleasantly surprised: it seemed to be Peter—a little gaunter and grayer than before; well, that was not the pleasant part, that Peter had aged so much, but that he would talk to a friend was a delightful prospect, for Ivan didn't talk to many people. Generally, people of his generation seemed to avoid one another; if they waited in the same line at the post office, which was rare, since they didn't like to write to anybody, but let's say if they were paying bills, they would chat most formally and inanely, to make sure that nothing personal would be said. Peter waved a bottle of slivovitz in his hand like a saber. The men who carried him shouted, "Saint Peter, drink another liter!" He responded hoarsely, "When the liter is done, the saint's begun!" After several exchanges of rhyme, Peter threw his head backward and poured plum brandy into his mouth from a foot away. The diamond-colored liquid splashed, some into his mouth, some over his chin and down his neck onto his white shirt, so you couldn't tell whether it was wet from drink or sweat. "Hurrah for Peter! Damn Saint Peter, where's your meter? Spurt another feeter, you ugly wife-beater!"

Ivan admired how popular Peter was among the peasants, but then, every bartender is a celebrity in small towns and the surrounding areas. An accordion started to wail again, a bass jibed in, soothing the pain, and another *kolo* was formed, and it soon became another whirlwind. Peter didn't join; without the support of the other dancers, he staggered. Ivan waved to him and Peter stumbled to Ivan's table and sat down, nearly missing the chair. Ivan hadn't seen him in two years; Peter could no longer defer his military service by pretending to be a student, a method that had worked for him for eight years.

The boiled oak of the table resonated with the bass, shaking Ivan's bones pleasantly. Ivan knocked a Chesterton out of his pack with his middle finger. Peter snatched the cigarette, licked its tip, and put it between his lips. Ivan lit a match. Peter's hands grasped his wrist and tremblingly kept the flame at the cigarette.

The reddish glow of the match lit Peter's face from beneath; light in his nostrils glowed like Halloween candles in a pumpkin, with the edges of his eyelids translucent and his forehead dark. He leaned back in his chair and drew a lusty suck out of the cigarette so that its tip glowed like a stop signal. He broke into a cough and exclaimed, "Fuck the sun!" and other folk swearwords, having to do with the planets and other cosmological units; the saints were not neglected. Calming down, he asked Ivan to box the cough out of his back. Ivan hit him hard.

"Harder!" said Peter. "Some stubborn son of a devil sits right there in my windpipes. Get him the hell out of there!"

Ivan hit as hard as he could, nearly injuring his wrist.

"Better!" Peter said. "And how the hell are you? I haven't seen you since we were infants."

"How about our playing music together a couple of years ago? You don't count that?"

"I mean that—now it feels so long ago, just like babyhood." Peter's breath carried the smell of anchovies and stomach acids. "I caught a cold in the damned train—the windows were open. I sang with the wind, and suddenly my guts almost exploded. I thought they'd come out of my mouth, and when the pink stink came out, I thought it was my guts. I vomited through the window and all over the compartment and moved into another. I snored for I don't know how long. Instead of getting off in Duke's Hollow, I overslept, and woke up at the Austrian border, some two hundred miles later! Hahahahah." He coughed again, and Ivan beat out his cough, so the narrative could continue.

"And there I was, eager to go home to see my brothers, sisters, friends, parents—snoring my way to the West! When a cop shook me and asked me for a passport, I was ready to obey him. I searched my pockets for a passport, forgetting I never had one. I thought he might be an MP who'd put me in jail for deserting—I didn't understand that I wasn't a soldier anymore. He led me off the train; splashes of my vomit had painted its sides, all ten coaches. I was proud of that. He interrogated me. I tried to be coherent and thought that the secret of coherence is long sentences that include everything you have in mind and everything they might have in mind. A clerk typed it all down, with his two fingers, like two woodpeckers. You couldn't even see the fingers, unless I paused at a loss for a word; then the fingers hung over the keys, pointing down like they wanted to say, 'That's where it's at.' It took self-control not to go over there to see what was on the page; he might have gone a little ahead of me and given me a clue as to what to say next. His nose pointed toward the keys, too.

"It felt good to be saying whatever nonsense came into my head and to know that the clerk would have to type it all. It took me a long time to say that I got wasted. On the train going back I fell asleep. When I woke up I heard a buzzing in my ears—it sounded like a beehive. My eyes ached. And then, my friend," he sat up straight, slowing down his words, and enunciating. "I fell asleep again after Zagreb, and . . . I overslept the Duke's Hollow." He puffed out several rings of smoke.

He waited for Ivan's reaction and would not say another word until he got one. He left his mouth open, so that the curve of his lips began a metamorphosis into a large ear in the middle of his face. Like Saint Peter, who distinguished himself in the Gospels by his ear fetish—cutting the Pharisee's ear—Peter insisted on winning an ear.

Ivan gulped his beer, losing interest in his friend's report. A peasant named Bozho stood up with a glass and threw it at the wall, aiming at the sign EACH BROKEN GLASS: 5,000 DINARS. He shouted, "That's not much, five thousand. So much fun for so little. I better buy the fun today, inflation's gonna eat it away tomorrow!" He threw another glass at the wall. The policeman paid no attention to him, but wistfully gazed at Svjetlana, who acted too proud to look at anybody.

"To hell with glasses. They are useless. You don't need them, not even for drinking!" Bozho flung another glass. It crashed beneath the semi-profile portrait of the stern, sleek president Tito, who didn't blink when the glass fell apart into smithereens and sand. "Bravo! Hurrah!" people goaded him on. A waiter tried to intervene, but his boss shouted, "Leave him alone! He'll quit soon enough!" and kept careful count of the number of shattered glasses.

Somebody pushed a whole table with empty glasses and bottles toward Bozho. He grabbed a bottle and poured the dregs of brandy down his mouth. The empty bottle exploded against the wall. The deceased president's portrait shook a little, but didn't blink. The president continued to look at some unidentified horizon past the peasants, probably the future. A white handkerchief stuck neatly out of his upper left pocket where you'd ordinarily see medals, as if he were the chief waiter of a multistar hotel—and the future he had in mind for the southern Slavs and Albanians was a gigantic tavern, where all the nations would toast him, the superwaiter. And now that future had come. Tito was gazing from beyond at them in this suspension of alcohol.

Bozho flung another glass and struck the sign EACH BROKEN GLASS: 5,000 DINARS. "How about each broken sign?" He looked at the heap of shattered glass on the floor, at his soiled rubber boots, his worn coat with threadbare sleeves. He seemed to be realizing that he was too poor to afford the glass-throwing sport. He shook himself and threw a new glass against the sign, and another one, faster and faster, in the rhythm of the *kolo*, which went on without any dancers, faster and deeper and deeper. The crashes of the glass blended into the music as emphatic drumming. Bozho cursed the stars, and then pigs, donkeys, and members of the government.

A peasant grabbed him and dragged him back to the table. "Enough, you've done enough!" Bozho staggered into a corner, where he wept, and fell asleep at the table, his forehead on his crossed forearms and his nose in an orange ashtray.

The *kolo*, a creature of many lives, circled in a slow, warm-up rhythm. The smoke was dense, blue. It arose from the tables toward the ceiling, forming a sterile cloud, out of which no rain could fall. The cloud twisted around the room gently, like a long, blue, silk scarf on a breeze, or like an abstracted wave that lost its water but retained the form—a ghostlike wave. The pub was an aquarium with people as fish, reflections of the trout from the brook behind the inn.

Peter fetched two glasses of slivovitz. Ivan's head nodded sleepily. Peter tapped him on the shoulder, and toasted, *"Na zdravlye!"* They looked each other straight in the eye, as the custom demanded; not looking in the eye during the knocking of glasses could be taken as an insult deserving bloodshed—at least in a Serb bar. Not that the two of them would resort to violence, but that was as powerful a custom as, for example, closing your eyes during a prayer or standing up during the playing of a national anthem. Ivan's eyelids drooped with exhaustion.

Peter joined the shuffle of the dance and ended up with Svjetlana, who danced with the limberness of a belly-dancer, facing him challengingly. The displaced cop quit dancing and brooded in his corner. Svjetlana abruptly left Peter to join the cop.

Peter was back at the table. "Oh, yes, where was I? Hm, fuck the sun, where was I? Oh, yes, that's the point! I did not know where I was. I'd overslept my stop, and when I woke up, I intentionally remained on the train at the next station, and I enjoyed every mile afterward—the pleasure of deliberate negligence, of fucking up. I don't know how it is for you, but for me, these are the moments of greatest freedom."

As if to illustrate his point, Peter puffed out a sharp ring of smoke. "Ha, see that! Halos—first they are small and sharp, then they grow bigger and bigger and lose their sharpness; just like in life! You grow, get bigger, accumulate property, and fizzle out! Can you blow smoke rings?"

"No, never could. I don't smoke."

"You don't smoke? But you've already smoked half a pack of cigarettes right here!"

"Oh, yes, tonight's an exception. I do it on special occasions, usually when someone dies."

"Every night's an exception. You should smoke, just for the pleasure of blowing smoke rings! Look, it's simple . . ."

"I know, not for me."

Peter slowly rounded his lips, his tongue peeped out of his mouth, like a curious head through a window, and receded back into the mouth. A ring of smoke traveled straight into Ivan's eyes, and he rubbed them. Ivan took out his Gandhi's fan and flapped the smoke away.

"Man, it looks like something you'd expect a harlot in an exotic film to handle. Are you now gay or something? Come to think of it, I haven't seen you with women that much."

"Indira Gandhi gave me the fan."

"You're crazy."

"I told you about that before. Do you know she's dead?"

"Who cares?"

"A billion Indians and me."

"When I was in good shape, I could string the Olympic Games emblem!" Peter puffed several more rings that merged into the long, silky streaks of smoke that adorned the nakedness of the room. The smoke scarf moved toward the dancers and was sucked into the whirlpool of the rondo.

"Oh, right, I was on the train," Peter went on, "and I got off at Brod. The train conductor said I needed a new ticket. I couldn't deny that I'd already made the trip. I told him to let me ride, that I deserved it, that it was not my fault that I got drunk but the army's. We quarreled, I fell asleep, overslept again, and jumped off the train right after my station, and then I walked home."

"All twenty miles?"

"Why not? I was delaying my homecoming. Home had seemed freedom compared to the army. And now, just look around! Stupid drinking and dancing, just like the world will end tomorrow. And I don't know what I am doing here. I should go home and finish my studies. You must know the feeling."

Peter waved, and, when the waiter lowered his shiny head,

Ivan could tell the thickness and the spacing of his comb teeth by the parallel streaks of his hair.

"Get two double slivovitzes," Peter ordered.

A blue uniform stuck out in the new *kolo*. "They still come here," Ivan said. "I'm not even sure they are on duty. They keep their uniforms on for girls who like uniforms. After we are all wasted, they come here fresh, and listen to what we shout, probably write it down in their notebooks . . . and then swoop down on the girls, like scavengers."

"Many people love uniforms."

"Many," Ivan agreed. "Every year Weeping Willow and other Serbian villages lose several young men who hang themselves on walnut trees or blow their brains out with a great-grandfather's powder gun when they are rejected by the army."

"Powder guns? Are you kidding? They all have the latest AK's and Uzis, some of them have cannons in their barns. You are right, though. Croatian lads go home singing if they are rejected. I would have been singing, too. I tried everything to get out of the army. I faked high blood pressure. My pressure was two hundred over one hundred. I was put into a military hospital, where nurses woke me up in the middle of the night and tied cold rubber around my biceps. After five nights the pressure went down to normal."

Svjetlana walked to the dance floor, perfectly poised as if she were carrying a water jug on her head. Peter's facial muscles twitched as his bloodshot eyes' focus followed her. Before her the wobbly crowd parted.

Peter didn't lose the thread of his monologue: "I was put in a solitary cell for malingering. And then they stuck me on the Albanian border. Whenever there was a snowstorm, I had to stand guard overnight. And all the cops and the military officers were Serbian. That irritated me—don't get me wrong, I'm not a nationalist, but that's why I can't stand nationalism. To have a Serbian army in an Albanian province is offensive. The officers made me clean bathrooms because I spoke Croatian. And look at Nizograd. Croats are the majority and yet all the police are Serbs. Shit. Who cares, anyway. We are all mixed here. Nation is like religion, you've got to believe in it . . . I don't."

"Yugoslavia was always Serboslavia, so what? You've had enough time to get used to it. Why are you complaining? Become a Serb, if you like. Anyway, if you don't like Serbian officers, why, you could have gone into a military school or a police academy, become an officer, and risen in power to compete with them. After all, look at the top general, Kadijevic, he is mostly Croatian."

Peter stared at the dance and plucked his nose with his thumb.

"If you hate the cops and the army, how can you allow a cop to dance in front of you with a pretty girl?" Ivan said—he resented the sight but had no intention of interfering.

Peter swallowed a big gulp and stared at Svjetlana whirling around with the cop. It was no longer *kolo,* but some sort of a couple dance.

"What does she have to do with him?" Peter asked.

"They are engaged!" Ivan said.

Peter heaved his chest and blew massive smoke out of his mouth. When there was a pause in the music, he rushed to the dance floor. He cut in between the cop and the young woman and took Svjetlana's hands into his; she blushed, looked apologetically toward the cop, who stood on the side awkwardly, checking the buttons on his shirt over his beer paunch.

Peter turned Svjetlana around on an invisible axis. He lifted her up, and whirled her like a Sufi dancer; the two of them became a burning cloud. When she jumped down, her skirt opened like a parachute and collected itself on the floor. During a break between songs, Svjetlana and Peter laughed, emanating merriment. She did not glance at the cop at all.

The cop darted toward the dancers, and on the run hit Peter's neck with his fist. Peter bounced off and punched the cop's nose. They exchanged several blows, and the cop jumped in the air to hit Peter, using some Eastern technique, for which he was too slow. Peter moved aside, and treated the cop's leg as if it were his partner's arm after a whirl-around in a dance; he pushed the leg up and the cop fell, his head thudding on the planks of the maple floor.

"Legs, ha? Here, damned beer barrel!" Peter kicked the cop's stomach. "If I dig a hole through your lard, we'll have a beer fountain!"

The cop writhed on the floor. Peter grabbed him by his ears and dragged him. The blue uniform was smeared from the oily floor and torn from a couple of nail heads. Peter rolled him down the steps of the Trout Haven.

Reentering the Trout Haven, Peter corrected his shirt, sliding it back into his trousers, and shouted, "Music, I want more music, with a singer! A drink for everybody!"

"That was pretty impressive," Ivan said.

"Oh, no big deal." Peter paused to catch his breath. "After running a bar of my own, I developed bouncer skills. I could never afford to pay anybody to be a bouncer. Anyway, I don't think there's a bar in Nizograd with a bouncer—for that you have to go to Zagreb. See you later."

The music did go on, reluctantly, as if rehearsing, with the players watching the door. Peter and Svjetlana were the only dancers; at first she was pale, but her cheeks became flushed. The two danced as if nothing had happened, since, after all, fights were an ordinary thing, and it might happen that the evening would end with the cop and Peter singing together in an embrace—at least such things used to happen.

On the stage a singer wailed. She wore heavy makeup, and her eyelashes were glued into several streaks, like the top rays of a star. Her breasts, exposed almost to the nipples, swayed sideways in her slow rhythm; her bloated belly seemed about to tear her skirt. Through the layers of her persona some primal force exuded, permeating her languorous chesty voice:

Ah, please, all the taverns close, so my sorry soul can repose.

*My life's already, alas, half over, and I don't have a
    Land Rover.
Please, close all the inns, for the sake of my cousins.
Shut down the whiskey bars, and let us leave this Mars.
Ah, the taverns, all, please close, so my roving soul can
    repose!*

The singer's eyes closed; people screamed, men in high
pitch like girls; many wept and closed their eyes; others threw
glasses so wearily that some didn't even break.

The door opened slowly, the cop staggered in, his face
bruised, his eye swollen, his nose bleeding. In this closed-eye
community, nobody seemed to notice him. Peter danced with
the woman in an embrace, the two of them like two lead pieces
melting on a flame. A gunshot exploded from the cop's hands.
A bullet hit Peter in the lower back, from the shank, and he
shook and unclasped his arms from around Svjetlana's waist.
The music stopped. Blood flowed out in gushes from Peter, to
the rhythm of his heart.

He grinned as if he were enjoying himself. The cop hesitated, looked around, and fired at the lamp above his head. The
floor darkened. From the corner, a bottle flew and struck the
policeman on the head. The policeman fell, unconscious, and,
several minutes later, without getting up, snored. From Peter's
body arose steam that resembled the steam rising from the back
of a horse in a cold rain.

Ivan stood and watched. He was fascinated by the evil that
glared obscenely in the murder. Would other people start shooting? Should he join in with chairs? Several policemen dragged
their colleague, placed him on a table, and poured water to
wake him up.

Ivan was so stunned that he gasped and wheezed, and he
walked out into the wind, and shivered. Did I goad him on? He
was despondent, filled with sorrow for his friend. An ambulance
pulled up. With Bozho and two other men, he carried Peter;
they each held him by one limb, Ivan by the left leg, which was

still loose. They laid him down on a stretcher, while the doctor, the driver, and a nurse, shared the flame of one match, huddling together, to get their cigarettes going. Only after they'd smoked their cigarettes all the way to their fingers, did the crew get into the ambulance and drive off—slowly, without the blue light and the sirens.

14

After a soccer war, Croatia
becomes a banana republic

Incidents like Peter's murder had become commonplace. Soccer matches between Serb and Croat teams sometimes erupted in physical fights between different segments of the audience, and the police often intervened to protect the Serb fans in Croatia, enthusiastically clubbing Croatian fans. In one match between Dinamo, Zagreb, and Red Star, Belgrade, even the players joined in. Zvonimir Boban, the Dinamo captain, attacked a policeman, who had been beating a Dinamo fan.

With the Yugoslav army firmly on the side of Milosevic and the Greater Serbian aims, and the Serb police ready to shoot in the other republics of Yugoslavia, Ivan felt threatened. If Serbs came to his home, they might cut his throat—to them, he would be a Croat even if he didn't feel Croatian. So, on the essential level of survival, the threat simplified him into a Croatian. He voted for the Croatian Democratic Union—which promised strong self-defense—despite his theories about the Slavic predilection for abstaining from voting. He didn't join the CDU, however; to vote without belonging to parties was his assertion of individuality.

Just as Croatia was about to organize its own police, he was drafted into the Yugoslav Federal Army. An officer with dirty, thick glasses, whom Ivan recognized as the note-taker from the Cellar, came to his house with a couple of other soldiers, and, like a prisoner, Ivan walked with them to a shaky green truck, where he sat with thirty sullen youths (although Ivan himself was far from his youth by now), inhaling oily diesel exhausts.

In the army, Ivan was waking up much earlier than he would have liked, and eating far too many portions of beans and bacon. Every day he had to march for ten miles, and with each step, his backache intensified.

In the meanwhile, Croatia and Slovenia declared their independence and statehoods. Soon the war in Croatia broke out, and Ivan was sent into Croatia to fight against the new Croatian army.

Outside of Vukovar, which was under Croatian control, in the barracks, Ivan and Nenad, the bartender from Nizograd, who happened to serve in the same unit, sat up on their beds, the two of them alone. Prolonged cries of cricket wings came astride frogs' voices on damp winds from a distant pond and drowned in the grease of Ivan's ear, scratched the eardrum, bounced around in the cochlea, and entered through the Eustachian tube into his throat, where the cries were hard to swallow, thick with the blood of the prisoners slain in the marshes the night before. The fact that the Yugoslav Federal Army protected Chetnik terrorist bands, such as the one run by the international criminal Arkan, sickened him. As he paced around the barracks, his sweat glued his shirt and socks to his skin; he shivered now and then despite the heat as though he could shake off the clothes, the sweat, and even his skin, and emerge into the cleansed world of his imagination, except that he could not imagine anything clean and cool.

"Nenad!" Ivan startled his fellow soldier. "It's going to rain." He laughed, although it was hard to laugh through the heavy phlegm of his throat. "Your nerves are raw! Don't worry, so are mine."

Nenad lit a cigarette.

"Put it out," Ivan said. "You mustn't smoke at night."

"This is my last cigarette. That guy last night gave it to me."

"I wouldn't take anything from him. Man, he boasted of smashing the heads of . . ."

Ivan snatched the cigarette out of Nenad's lips and squashed it under his boot into the screeching sandy cement.

"Jerk!" Nenad said. "If I wasn't so sleepy, I'd trash the crap out of you for this!"

"I doubt it. You have no courage. If you had any, and if I had any, would we stay on in this ridiculous army?"

Blue lightning silently spread through the humid air.

"Where would we go? They shoot deserters."

Far away, a steam-engine train whistled its cry, sounding like an owl without a mate. Then, a succession of explosions came so strongly that pots in the storage room rattled.

In the morning, loud rain knocked many yellow leaves off beeches and oaks. Drops hit the mud, splashing it. The wetness carried the smells of poisonous mushrooms and old leaves, not only of the leaves that had just zig-zagged to the ground but also of the leaves from the last year, and from thousands of years ago, with mossy, musty whiffs of old lives in the soil, and new lives that slid out of the cloudy water and soiled eggs: snails, frogs, earthworms. When the rain let up, the leaves sagged, and a cold wind swayed them, and water continued sliding down in large, slithering drops, which hung, growing luminous, glittering, before falling onto the men below, into their shirts, down their hairy necks. Most men sat beneath green tents, and some, including Ivan, sat beneath oaks. Water darkened the bark. Ivan wondered why the oak bark was cracked—beech bark stretched like rubber, but the oak bark burst open, shaggy and jagged.

Ivan tried to light his wet cigarette. The sulfurous red tip tore trails in the wet matchbox and fell into a large boot imprint filled with water. The match tip shushed, and a little frog leaped out, young, brown, and merry. Ivan spat into the puddle, pursing his lips, thumbed his nose, knuckled his eyes (set beneath his high-arching brows), but he could not get a sensation of alertness.

Most nights the Yugoslav Federal soldiers fired from mortars, tanks, and canons, into Vukovar. They aimed wherever the Croat soldiers could hide, and they also fired randomly, at the civilian houses.

"Don't pay any attention to where you hit," said the captain. "They are just Croats, *ustasha* children, *ustasha* parents, *ustasha* grandparents. They will always be the same, and they would love to be doing the same thing to you. If you don't wipe them out, they'll wipe you out." As he talked, the captain's disheveled silvery hair shook, and his eyes beneath thick black eyebrows blinked quickly.

Half of the canons did not work, because they were rusty and soldiers forgot to oil them. When they did not fire, the soldiers played cards and watched American porn movies on VCRs hooked to tank batteries. And they sang:

> *Oh my first love, are you a bushy Slav?*
> *Whoever you rub and mate, don't forget your gun to*
> *   lubricate.*
> *Oh my first hate, how could I tolerate?*

They sang many other lyrics that Ivan despised. He wondered why so many songs dealt with first love, lost love, why all this nostalgia? His first love was only a childhood thing. On the other hand, childhood was perhaps the only genuine time of his life, to which all the other experience was grafted, like apples onto a plum tree, where apples grow stunted.

In his childhood, he had a crush on a girl, Maria. In the early, blue, winter afternoon, before going to a New Year's dance, he had put his shoes on the stove to warm them, and he went to the bathroom to shave, though he had no need of shaving yet. The rubber soles of his shoes melted, but he didn't have any other shoes, so he went to the dance in them. Waiting to meet Maria atop a stairway, Ivan dug the nails of his forefingers into the flesh on the edge of his thumbnails, so that several drops of blood dripped out of his thumbs on the ochre tiles of the floor.

He had followed Maria to the gym where the dance had begun. Her hair smelled like chamomile. He stepped on her feet, and, to avoid that, he stood away from her. Her friends whispered. It seemed to him that his melted soles made them giggle. He slipped out of the room, with his cheeks burning.

Several days later, Maria and he talked in front of her house. He walked around her, desiring to touch and kiss her, though he knew that he could not do that. His tongue probed several cavities from which the fillings had fallen. He cursed the people's-clinic dentists.

Thinking back, he still felt ashamed. He drank more *rakia*. In the beginning of the campaign, they had fine slivovitz, golden-colored, throat-scorching, and now only this rotten, pale *rakia* from double-brewed grapes. There was no coffee. The captain had thrown a sack of coffee into the river, saying, "No more stinky Muslim customs and Turkish coffee dung here, is that clear?"

"But coffee comes originally from Ethiopia," Ivan said as he watched brown fish come up and open their yellow mouths and swallow the black beads, which looked like unstrung and spilled rosaries of unanswered prayers for wakefulness.

"That's Muslim," the captain said.

"Didn't use to be, and it's Coptic, too—that's very similar to Orthodox," Ivan said.

"That doesn't matter. We don't have any filters, and if you don't filter the coffee, it's Turkish. It's all right for them to drink the mud, and to wipe their asses with fingers, but not for us."

"You could filter it through newspapers," Ivan said.

"You'll get lead poisoning."

"You will anyway," Ivan mumbled quietly—thinking of bullets—so the captain, who was edgy, wouldn't hear him.

"Anyway, Soldier Ivan, what is your occupation?"

"Baker," Ivan said. He was sure that if he said he was a philosopher, he'd be ridiculed, so this sounded better.

"Why not a smith, or something more vigorous?"

"I wanted to become a doctor, but unfortunately I had to drop out. My relatives convinced me that being a barber would be almost like being a doctor. So, at first, before becoming a baker, I was a barber's apprentice. It was all right—until one day my neighbor Ishtvan came along for a shave. I set him up in the chair, placed a white apron around his neck, sharpened the switchblade on leather, and lathered him up. Foam touched Ishtvan's hairs, which stuck half an inch out of his nose, and he sneezed.

"'Do you want your nose hairs cut or plucked?' I asked. He did not answer but sneezed again, blowing the foam all over the shop.

"'Gesundheit!' I said."

"Hey, no German allowed here!" said the captain.

"Ishtvan sneezed again, for the third time, and I said, 'To your health, neighbor Ishtvan! May you outlive many wives!' But Ishtvan did not say 'Thank you!' though he was a famously polite man. Instead he kept his hand in front of his nose. He waited for the sneeze to come up and out. After he hadn't sneezed a minute later, I said, 'Should I hit your back?' As I raised my hand, his hand dropped into his lap. His head nodded to one side. I took a look at him and shook him, until I realized that he was dead. I fetched his wife. She ran in and said, 'He's going to get rid of his mustache? Is that what the fuss is about?'

"'Just look at him,' I said. 'Don't you see? He's dead!'

"The woman gasped, and shouted 'Oh my God! *Wie schrecklich!*'"

"I warned you!" interjected the captain.

"So, I asked the lady, 'What should we do? Should we carry him back?'

"'Tell you what, why don't you finish the shave?'

"'But what good will that do?'

"'A lot of good,' she said. 'He'll need a clean shave for his wake.'

"She liked the shave so much that she made me promise that during the wake I'd give him two-three more shaves, because the hairs of the dead grow fast. As soon as we carried him back home, I closed the shop and ran off. Not that I was horrified—actually, I was so surprised by how calmly I took it that a man died while I worked on him that I thought I should become a doctor. On my way home, I saw a sign at the baker's, APPRENTICES WANTED, and I became a baker!"

"Hm," the capain mused, "in other words, you deserted. A very bad sign."

In the evening the air was dry and clear, and the mood was festive. A masterless herd of pigs ran down a low slope, as mad as the pigs possessed by demons that ran into the Sea of Galilee and drowned. The soldiers shot several pigs. They found it hard to start a fire, because all the wood was wet. Nenad came up with the idea to strip the fat off the pigs, because the fat would burn like gasoline. So, after they put pig fat among the branches, the fire caught on and sent up a cloud of smoke and steam so that the pigs were both burned and steamed. The soldiers ate heavily, soaking up bread in the grease that dripped into pots, and drank slivovitz. A soldier noticed streaks of melted gold and silver dripping from inside a roasting pig. In the pig stomachs, they found human fingers with wedding rings, necklaces with crucifixes, golden bridges. The starving pigs had eaten their slain masters. There was so much grease dripping that the drunken soldiers polished their shoes and oiled their guns with it. They feasted for four days.

One morning Ivan sat on a rock in the sun and read the New Testament, which he had stolen in a deserted village on the way toward Vukovar; after all his doubts, he reverted to religion, as was his wont in times of fear. The captain snatched the New Testament. "Why were you so stingy? We could have started the fire with your book! My, what silky pages!" The captain fingered a page between his forefinger and thumb. "Fine English paper, isn't it? Good, I'll use it to roll my cigarettes." And he tore a hundred leaves, and tossed the rest into the glowing coals beneath a piglet. The paper burned blue, and, as the fat dripped over it, changed to red, hissing. Ivan gripped a stone in his fist. When the New Testament had burned, the ashes retained its shape; Ivan could see between the fine pages into the pink middle. A slight breeze shifted the ashen pages of the book open to the right angle, almost turning them, as though it wanted to open to the right page to find its golden verse, the guide for the day, which would tell the breeze where and how to blow next. And then one large drop of fat fell on the silhouette of the New Testament, piercing a hole in the middle. The ghost of the book collapsed into flimsy ashes. Above the camp, the absolutely fine, transparent, gray paper hovered and floated, with millennial letters falling apart midair.

Just as the biblical words had all scattered around the camp and fallen softly on the trampled ground, the party came to a close. Croats had blown up a dozen tanks in a single day. Forty Yugoslav army soldiers were left dead in the fields.

Many soldiers deserted—whole companies from Serbia, from Nis and Sabac, had left—but Ivan's company was solid. The army was the safest place for him. Despite temporary setbacks, with twenty thousand well-armed soldiers surrounding a city with two thousand soldiers, there was nothing to fear. They ought to be able to take the city in a day. He did not understand what they were waiting for, launching thousands of bombs every night. What would be the point of taking a devastated city, a mound of shattered bricks? But when the tanks went forward, heat-seeking missiles blew up many of them.

In the middle of November, the Serb ring around Vukovar seemed impenetrable. Vukovar had not gotten any supplies from Zagreb in weeks. The Serb guards did not allow the UN ambulances through for fear of smuggled weapons. Croats had run out of food and out of their heat-seeking missiles. The tanks and the infantry progressed steadily and took a suburb of Vukovar. The regular Yugoslav Federal Army advanced, with Croat, Albanian, and Muslim soldiers in front, at gunpoint from behind, so the Croat gunners from Vukovar would kill their own and run out of ammunition. Then followed the various reservist units of the Federal Army, including Ivan's, and then the Chetnik units, with picturesque black caps with skulls and bones painted white over them. Ivan's company moved from house to house, block to block, smoking people out of their cellars with bombs and tear gas, and dragging them out. Some people had lived in the city's sewer system. No water flowed through the pipes, and most of the system was empty, and the people lived like rats, together with rats, who waited for them to die, to eat them.

The Serb soldiers killed men between boyhood and old age, and they killed many old men as well as young boys. The captain said, "Just shoot them. If you don't, someone else will, so what's the difference?—as long as there are no journalists around, and if you see a journalist alone, shoot him, too." Ivan went into a moldy cellar, feeling vulnerable despite his bullet-proof vest. He stumbled in the dark as he leaned against the dank sandy wall, sliding forward. The captain shouted from above, "What are you waiting for? Keep going. There's nobody there." Ivan stumbled down an unsteady stone stair. He saw a man's silhouette against the light of a window. The light fell into the cellar in shifting streaks, which hurt his eyes. The man was silently crawling out the window. "Stop, or I'll shoot," Ivan said. The man slid from the window, the sand shushing. Ivan faced a tall bony man with a widow's peak and deep creases around his thin mouth. Ivan felt neither hatred nor love. He certainly did not want to shoot him. Could he save the man if he wanted to? He could not run away from the army himself. Still, he said, "Do you have any German marks? Give them all to me and I'll get you out of here."

"I have nothing. I spent the money on food."

"That's too bad."

"If you know God, don't shoot," the man said. "You have kids?"

"Maybe."

"I have two kids."

"You'd better come up with better reasons for me not to pull the trigger."

"I'm too tired to do better. I'm not a poet."

"I can't keep jabbering. Let's get out of here, with your hands up."

They walked up the stairs, into the late fall light, which

slashed at a low angle into their eyes. Ivan's captain said, "What's taking you so long? Shoot him."

Ivan raised his rifle unsteadily.

"You haven't shot anything in your life, have you?" the captain said.

"A bunch of rabbits and birds, that's all."

"You must start somewhere. What kind of soldier are you if you're squeamish?"

Ivan said nothing.

"You can't be in a war and not kill, it's like working in a brothel and remaining a virgin."

And Ivan was curious, not so much about how men died but how they killed, about whether he could kill. If he couldn't, he'd still have to be a soldier. Maybe it would be better to go along with the tide, as part of the machine, the army, without a will of his own; maybe that would be better than to go against the grain, terrified of blood. Some of the bombs he had handed on to the cannon man may have killed, probably had. But he had not seen it. Maybe killing an unarmed man was wrong, of course it was wrong, what else would it be, but he thought he needed to pass the test, to be able to kill.

Ivan still could not shoot. He imagined this man's grandchildren, and how much misery his death could mean to the people close to the man. If the roles were reversed, would anybody miss Ivan?

"Do you want a cigarette?" Ivan asked.

"What, you are playing the last-wish bullshit?" the captain said. "If you don't shoot the bum, I'm going to shoot both of you." He lifted his pistol. "If you want to be a good poet, you've got to be able to pull the trigger."

So the captain had listened in on their conversation in the cellar, Ivan thought.

"Maybe if you want to be a novelist," the captain continued, "you keep him around, find out everything about him, fuck him, and save him. But we don't have the time for that."

Several other soldiers gathered to see this initiation rite.

Ivan abhorred this public performance. He tried to conceal the trembling of his hand. He used to get stage fright whenever he addressed audiences, and his right hand, holding a glass of water, would tremble. This was partly a result of a painful memory of it shaking during a particular high school oral exam. He was scared in front of groups. In that sense, he and the man had more in common than any of the soldiers; they both faced the group. The man could do nothing about it; for him, this was fate. Ivan, on the other hand, could pull the trigger, or not. Objectively, not to pull the trigger would be the right choice. But in front of the deranged group, it would be the wrong choice. No matter what he did (or did not do), it would be wrong and would work against him. Maybe he should not have the illusion of choice. He was weak and had no choice, essentially. He breathed hard, as though he was about to have an asthma attack.

Can the man see through me? Ivan thought that everybody saw through him, through his thin guts. The man's knees shook. His green pants sagged. There was a streak of urine on his pants, growing bigger and bigger. That reminded Ivan of the childhood incident—when, in terror of a horse, he'd shat himself in front of an army garrison. Crap, solid and dark red, shaped like cattails, had slid down onto the cobbles and smoked.

Ivan pulled the trigger three times.

The man fell. His hazel eyes stayed open while blood gushed from his neck onto the brick-laid yard, the narrow yard between two three-story buildings, with the dank dusty smell blowing out of the cellars, as though the Danube water had softened the clay beneath the cracks of the cellar cement; as though the drying river fish breathed out the river mud and caviar yolk. On the red bricks, uneven over the melted soil, the blood did not leave much of a mark; the bricks darkened only a little more than they had from the rain.

Ivan coughed. So that's it. It did not feel like anything, as long as you watched the details. He watched red earthworms sliding straight, unable to coil, in the cracks between the bricks. Ivan was jolted. The captain pinched his buttocks. "Good job. I was worried that you were a sensitive, Croat-loving homosexual. You passed the test." The captain pushed his finger into Ivan's buttocks.

Ivan jumped. "Stay away from me!"

"See, you passed the test."

Accordion music, a bass, and shrill voices came from around the corner, from a tavern with a burned-out red-tile roof. Ivan waited for a long while and walked in. Water leaked through, and beads of precipitated steam slid down the walls, like sweat on a harvester's back. Disheveled, bearded soldiers danced *Uzicko kolo,* more slowly than the accordion rhythm called for, in their muddy boots. They yodeled derisively and fired their guns into the ceiling. Mortar was falling, thudding onto the wooden floor. They tilted gasoline-colored bottles of slivovitz and amber half-liter bottles of beer into their mouths, imprecisely, so that some of the liquids poured down their chins, beards, shirts.

Ivan heard a scream in the pantry. He kicked the door in with his boot, and saw the hairy buttocks of a man above the pale flesh of a woman. Ivan's lips went dry with a strange excitement, which he did not know how to interpret. Was he appalled? Yes, he was. Was he lustfully curious? Yes, he was. He grabbed a bottle of pale brandy from the shelf and gulped, feeling no taste except a burning in his cracked lips, but inside he felt nothing of the liquid. The woman's face was contorted in pain, but even so, the face struck him with a familiar beauty, pale skin with black eyebrows, under streaks of wet brown hair falling across high cheekbones. He did not know where the familiarity came from; for a moment he thought it was Maria from his childhood, but then he recognized that it was Selma from Novi Sad. He had never thought that the two were similar, but they must have been. And he recognized the man, the captain, who turned to him and said, "After I'm done, you go ahead, too, dip your little dick and enjoy. Hahaha. You'll have a complete education today. You know, Stalin recommended rape as a way of motivating soldiers and keeping up the aggressive impulses."

"Don't worry about my aggressive impulses," Ivan said. He lifted the rifle and, with its wooden end, struck the captain's head. The captain's head collided with the woman's, driving hers onto the brick steps. Ivan kicked his head away from hers, and, as his rifle struck the captain's skull again, the bones crunched. The man bled from his mouth onto the woman's belly. She had fainted. Ivan dragged him away from her, covered his head with an empty coffee bag. What to do with her? How to protect her from the bar? His heart beat at a frantic pace, and his windpipe wheezed. He felt beside himself, like a cornered beast, and like a cornered beast, he felt an amazing power coursing through him. He could do anything.

He gazed at Selma's parted scarlet lips, which were opened a little, with thin lines crossing the shiny skin vertically. The swollen lips were shapely, twin peaks of a long wave, a wave of blood, whipped by internal winds, from the heart, and netted in the thin lip-skin, which prevented it from splashing out, onto the shore, onto Ivan. Only the thin membrane, the lips, separated his rusty plasma from hers.

In the labor camp, he had continued to yearn for her. In a dream, he met her on a bald mountaintop, and she said, It's too late, I'm married now. Ivan walked away, with headphones, over which Stravinsky's *Rite of Spring* was piped into his ears, with deep bass shaking him, making his skull buzz at the seams, like a window when military planes fly low . . . and he ran through evergreen forests, and, no matter how far he ran, the cord of the headphones continued, and the music kept jabbing his brain.

He suspected that his longing had been unrequited because of his cowardice. He had not had the courage to explain himself. In a dangerous world, wouldn't a woman be attracted to courage? Later, he heard that she had dropped out of the med-

ical school, gone to Zagreb, graduated from the school of architecture, and married a doctor, who died in a car accident.

Ivan now stared at Selma with a sorrowful glee as she lay at
his feet, her skirt and bra ripped open, her breasts hanging sideways, spreading over her blood-smeared ribs; her thighs, ample,
curvaceous, defenseless, loosely stretched before him.

Ivan carried Selma outside and gave her water to drink from his
aluminum flask. She looked at him disdainfully and asked: "Do
I have to thank you? You saved me or something?"

"You could thank me. I don't know whether anybody saved
anybody, but you could thank me. It could have been worse."

"And what are you doing in this army? That is you, old
anatomist?"

"I don't know, believe me."

As he escorted her to a bus with Croat women and children, she stumbled alongside him but refused his support. He
wondered whether the rusty bus with bullet holes would make
it, or whether, at some drunken sadist's whim, a sulfurous bomb
would strike the bus on the road and burn all the passengers,
including her, and whether—the way things were going—he
would be the one firing.

In the bar, the soldiers danced another version of the *kolo*.
Ivan took a dead Croat soldier's uniform, dressed his captain in
it, bludgeoned his face so nobody would recognize him, carried
him out, and dumped him on a horse-drawn carriage, onto a
dozen corpses. Ivan shifted uncomfortably, because the blood
had soaked through his uniform and shirt, gluing the cotton to
his skin, warm, sticky. A dark orange horse, with strong, round
buttocks, stood, his head bent to the road covered with empty
gun shells. His hoof screeched over shards of glass. The shrill
sound mixed with the smell of grassy dung and steamy whiffs of
gangrene. The horse shook its ears, through which sun rays

streaked and reddened, while a thick vine of veins branched out. A round fly sat on the ear, with its green-and-purple belly, filling up on a vein. Ivan wondered why the horse hadn't been eaten. Ivan could not get rid of the jitters, as though he had fever, *delirium tremens*. Who knew what diseases lurked in this city, where less water flowed than blood, where cats were eaten, and rats frolicked in the walls; where cat and rat skeletons lay entwined together; where human corpses lay unburied for weeks, in the sewage tunnels and in burnt-out cars, where pink maggots formed shifting gray mounds over loose flesh detached from the bones. He did not dare to take a deep breath, for fear of inhaling a plague. Piles of bodies lay on almost every street corner, women's stockings torn, skirts muddied, men's blue buttocks slashed, purple faces gaping with yellow eyes hanging in the dust.

Soldiers, some grinding their teeth, others chattering and vomiting, poured gasoline over a pile of corpses and burnt them.

15

Hearts leap over the barren land

Several months later, southeast of Slavonski Brod, in northern Bosnia, a mixture of Yugoslav Federal Army soldiers and a band of Chetniks marched through the oak forest, cracking branches and sliding over last year's leaves that had rotted but hadn't yet turned to soil. After they spotted a Croat bunker, the commander selected three soldiers—including Ivan—to creep up to the bunker and take the machine-gun nest. "Go up and prove yourself. We'll have our guns aimed at you so you better not try any tricks."

As low clouds drifted, and the forest steamed up under a fresh sun, the three soldiers crawled up the hill. Ivan was enraged that he should be given this horrendous task. If Ivan failed, the commander would continue to party, as though nothing had happened, while Ivan would be left dead, to rot like the last year's leaves. As they crawled up the slope, they caught glimpses of a machine-gun barrel sticking out, like a hollow finger of a sinister god above the clouds. The finger pointed far above them, to the horizon. When he was a hundred yards away from the bunker, the machine-gun barrel turned downward toward him. He fired at it. A series of bullets shot out from the bunker. Ivan rolled down, like a child on a meadow slope. A bullet struck him on the side, near his kidney and spleen. The sensation that he was losing it, that he was hit, comforted him. Bullets whistled down the slopes, swishing the brush, the tall grass, cracking stones, sinking into tree barks. A verse resounded in Ivan's head: *The earth is utterly broken down, the earth is clean dissolved . . . The earth shall reel to and fro like a drunkard.* One of Ivan's comrades rolled past him, red, missing his face. Ivan stood up and ran, and—feeling no ground—flew. He was running away from the bunker and the camp.

Being wounded gave him courage. If he went back, the commander would find a way to get him killed, sooner or later, anyway. Ivan stopped to examine his wet wound; the bullet had blasted away his skin, a layer of fat, and the muscles above his left hip. He tore a sleeve off his jacket and held it tight over the wound, but the jacket kept drinking his blood like an ink-blotter.

His gun had disappeared, though he did not remember dropping it. Should he run back to Nizograd? How? That was too far away. Besides, he would be convicted as a Serb war criminal despite being a Croat. Should he look for a Croatian army? No, they were too weak, it would be too dangerous to be in one. He was through with the armies. But could he make it alone? He wished he had his Bible, because it made him feel secure, like an amulet, and without it he felt absolutely desolate. But what good did religion do him? He wondered whether his religion had merely misled him in these dark woods, and just then he chanced upon a pine forest, a calm in the cool darkness. He stepped over the carpet of pine needles, half a foot deep, treading softly.

Beyond the woods, he staggered into a burnt-down village. He crawled into a house and collapsed in the ashes. He slept for days until a wet sensation on his forehead and eyebrows awakened him. A purring cat was licking him. He did not resist the raspy tongue, which now covered his eyelids and pushed them open. That seemed to please the cat, so she ceased to lick him and rolled up against the side of his face, warmly purring, instilling the rhythm of life into his neck. He tried to move, but a thick pain in his left-kidney area dissuaded him. He felt his side—a rough crust covered his wound. There was no wet blood there anymore, no great swelling, apparently no abscess. Being in a burnt-out house helped, because there weren't many germs around, and so there was no danger of gangrene, he thought. Was the cat dangerous for his wound? Did she lick it, too? Now the cat licked and tickled his ear, as if saying, You'll never know.

When he got up, the cat walked into the yard toward an

unusually large brick-oven, which the owners must have used to bake bread for most of the village. She walked proudly and significantly, lifting her tail straight up and letting the very tip of it wiggle out a code of satisfaction. She invited him to follow her, as though he were her kitten, to a nook where she must have been spending her days. He gathered hay in a meadow to make the small abode comfortable; that he did not have much space was good, because space was not to be trusted. Armies that might pass through would not bother to look in here.

In the woods Ivan gathered wild strawberries, mulberries, cherries, wild onions, and mushrooms of all kinds. In the bushes he found a nest of lark eggs and made a mushroom omelet with chanterelles.

His only preoccupation was food. From an old linden, he scraped fungi, which he burnt to smoke out a nest of wild bees from the hollow of an old mulberry. He chewed cool honey out of the oval balls of wax, honeycombs, with its acacia aroma pleasing his tongue and scratching his throat.

When his tabby vanished at night, he missed her purr. He woke up to a choir of nightingales, which had flooded the forest with a brilliant melody. His cat appeared after sunrise, dragging a young rabbit nearly her size over a brick pathway to the oven. Ordinarily, he'd think that the cat was boasting, laying her catch at his feet just for show, but now he understood it as salvation. He started a fire with two stones and hay and roasted the rabbit. He felt a little selfish doing it, until the cat caught a nightingale and ate it ostentatiously, as though to tell him that he should not worry about her going hungry. The following morning, the cat caught another rabbit for him, and then, to pay her back, Ivan sharpened several twigs and went down, below the village, to the creek, which was so quiet and slow that it formed a pond. The cat loved the carp he gave her.

He couldn't identify all the mushrooms, but knew what the Destroying Angel and the Death Cap looked like, and the rest he didn't fear, since they could cause only digestive problems or headaches. Besides, many mushrooms were medicinal, and they would give him strength in mysterious ways. He was sure that it would take medicine a hundred years to find out all sorts of restorative powers that many mushrooms—even the poisonous ones, when eaten in moderation—have. Penicillin was a micro-mushroom. So he ate nearly all the mushrooms he found, in small nibbles. He hallucinated, with the green leaves pulsing radiantly at him, but he wasn't sure whether to attribute that to the mushrooms or his strained nerves and injured spleen, if it had been injured. He boiled boletus—with their moist, brown heads that he eagerly pressed his fingers into, leaving fingerprints in the cap—with wild onions and nettles into a most delicious soup.

The summer, the blessed season when it was easy to hide, went quickly. Leaves began to turn red, and cold winds blew from Hungary. What chilled Ivan most was the image of the leafless and bare mountains. Food would escape his reach unless he figured out a way of storing it, like a squirrel.

He would perhaps have managed to spend the winter in the burnt-out village, had not the sounds of gun battles come close. Detonations, explosions, and machine-gun fire ignited the vegetation several miles away from him and drifted in dry, biting smoke toward him. From a crack in his oven, one day he saw Chetniks walking through the village, and a day later, Muslim soldiers, and a day later, Croats. Alone, he would be a sitting duck for all of the armies in the winter. But he still might have stayed if his cat hadn't vanished. He wondered whether soldiers had killed her, for food or for an exercise in cruelty.

Walking east, outside a village on the Bosnian-Croatian border, he found a Golgotha monument. The statues of Christ and the two robbers were torn off and thrown onto the thick heathers on the side of the road, and three corpses were pierced and hung on the crosses with large rusted nails. Two were circumcised Muslims, and the third, occupying the place of the talkative thief, was a Catholic, with a tattoo of the Virgin Mary on his forearm. Now and then their browned blood emitted a sparkle of ruby red in the sun. Every head had a hole in the pate—a Chetnik signature—with a thick trail of blood curling around the neck onto the chest. One Muslim looked familiar, and although he nearly vomited from the stench of putrid flesh, Ivan poked the head with a branch. He recognized Aldo, his roommate from Novi Sad. What horror! And what cynicism, to crucify a Muslim. He'd actually often cursed Aldo for the stupid assassination joke during Tito's parade. Without him, Ivan would most likely now be a doctor. On the other hand, he didn't really want to be a doctor, at least not now, nearly a couple of decades later. Although he had resented Aldo for the Naked Island imprisonment, he had often wondered what that old passionate and peculiar friend of his was up to. He had missed joking with him, and, occasionally, he thought with nostalgia of their stealing at the food fair in Novi Sad, of Aldo's unsuccessfully approaching women with silly lines, of eating Aldo's mother's bacon together, with Aldo giving him the meaty parts. Now he felt that crystalline bacon salt under his tongue, but when he spat, his spittle was bloody, and he realized that his gums were bleeding, perhaps from exhaustion, or from not having toothpaste in months, or from the shock of seeing his crucified friend. *Sic transit gloria mundi, sic transit miseria mundi.* The Latin line sounded in his head in a priest's voice, and paraphrased itself, and he looked around, but there was nobody talking. And he hadn't even eaten mushrooms.

After a stormy night, Ivan sat on the edge of a whitewashed village, on the smooth bark of a thick beech tree that had apparently fallen that night, not because the winds had been powerful but because the waters had loosened the ground so much that the tree fell like a tooth pushed by the tongue out of an old abscess. The rain had washed all the soil off the roots so that the blind naked limbs silently groped in the air, black against the translucent turquoise of the emptied sky. Ivan squeezed water out of his shirts and socks and lined them up on the bark. He gazed at old women in their black skirts and wooden shoes herding geese with sticks down the main—and only—road of the village. When the women saw him, they shrieked. Ivan still had his army uniform on. Soldiers were prone to pillage and rape.

Ivan said, "Calm down, I am not going to shoot you."

The women cried even louder. When he found out that there were no men in the village, Ivan went into the nearest house and picked up a Sunday-best suit; he left behind his military uniform and ran into the woods.

Ivan avoided people and stayed in haystacks, and when he couldn't find any haystacks, in ditches, even in late January when a terrible winter gripped the continent with an excessive ferocity as though God had tried to freeze out the destructive race for the sake of the rest of creation. He had tried fire, brimstone, and water before, and none had worked. And now, He tried ice—water with fire taken out of it—and Ivan, who shivered and plucked ice out of his beard, felt that this new cataclysm might work.

With bulging eyes, driven out of his mind by solitude, he shivered in a haystack. He recollected glimmers of his boyhood: every Sunday after church he would bicycle into a field, where a shepherdess waved him to sit by her and lean his cheek against her neck. She bared her breasts and let him squeeze them. With his tremulous hands upon the smooth, venous warmth of her skin, he admired the delicacy of her skin, the yielding flesh. He caressed the shepherdess's breasts every Sunday, for a summer and that was all, but now it came back to him as a modicum of warmth in the glacial universe.

That night he was caught by Croat soldiers. They wrapped him in a rough woolen blanket as though he were a corpse and drove him to their barracks in Sisak. They gave him hot tea with aspirin, which dissolved in his throat before he could swallow it, and there it spread its dusty bitterness of bleached charcoal, a mock Eucharist.

That winter pneumonia filled Ivan with fevers and nightmares, and he replied to no questions until he saw the rising sun in the spring and recovered. The Croats kept him in jail for three months, because he could not prove his identity, but they believed him that he was a Croat, because of his Croatian way of speaking. They transferred him to a small camp of combined Croat and Muslim forces near Sarajevo.

When three thousand Yugoslav-Serb soldiers surrounded the encampment, a commander gave Ivan a rifle to be a regular soldier once again, and Ivan could not decline. For days Serb howitzers and mortars fired upon the camp, setting cabins ablaze; many soldiers burnt to death. The Muslims and Croats had only rifles and machine guns and a couple of mortar launchers. So when his regiment surrendered because of a promised amnesty, Ivan became a captive of the Yugoslav army he had so recently served.

At gunpoint, he climbed into a cargo train with two hundred other soldiers. But as the POWs exited from the trains into a field, a dozen machine guns strafed them down. When it was Ivan's turn to step out, the machine-gun fires quit, and Ivan's detachment was held at bayonet point. Chetniks pushed bayonets into the captives' ribs and said, "You want to go home? Fine, we'll show you your home, pigs." A soldier pumped a machine-gun round into the group of captives, as if to punctuate the speech, but nobody fell to the ground, because the captives were so squashed that those who were killed or bleeding to death remained standing in the crowd.

"The rules are simple." The main speaker went on, with a megaphone. "If you make it on foot to Drvar, you are free, if not, you are dead. You aren't going to get any breaks, food or water."

They marched for a hundred miles over mountainous terrain. Whoever among the captives leaned on a fence along the way was bayoneted and left massacred in a ditch, his eyes spooned out or ears cut off as trophies.

The second day was scorchingly hot, as though God had changed His mind and turned away from ice; He again contemplated burning the sons of men off the crust of the earth. Ivan stumbled, his feet blistery and bloody, and wistfully gazed at spindle wells in the village yards. At dusk, a soldier poked his bayonet gently into Ivan's kidney area, on the healed side. "Long time no see!" Jovo, his old roommate from Novi Sad, laughed. "How in the hell did you get stuck here? I thought you were dead and gone. I bet you wish you were! Jeez, you are a legend in Novi Sad, you and Dracula!"

Ivan did not say anything. Jovo had a gulp of slivovitz; he passed the open bottle under Ivan's nostrils, asking whether he'd like a sip. This style of torment was usual—a cheerful soldier tantalizing the POW of his choice—and nobody paid any attention to Jovo's pushing, jostling, and nudging Ivan; not even Ivan, until Jovo slid a flask of water into Ivan's pocket. When clouds covered the moon, Ivan gulped all the water and tossed the flask during a thunderclap.

The clouds grumbled, cleared their throats, but did not spit out a drop of rain. They gathered low, furrowed, like Stalin's eyebrows, trapping heat and moisture, making the air musty. In the morning Ivan sweated profusely, salt from his forehead sliding into his eyes and biting them as though they were open wounds, and that they were, with dust specks, gnats, sand, grating them almost as much as did the sight of his colleagues collapsing, with Chetniks crushing their heads with the wood of rifles, brains flowing out like borscht.

By noon of the following day his lips were cracked-dry and swollen. Even the Serb villages they passed seemed peopleless, for if there were survivors, they hid, as though witnessing the horrendous procession would be an awful burden to carry into peace—and beyond.

One night, as the Chetniks got more and more drunk on plum brandy, some POWs managed to sneak out of this march—patterned after a similar but much larger forced march in WWII—though most were stabbed as soon as they jumped into the ditches on the side of the road. Ivan did not try. He trudged, stumbling over stones. Ivan was sure that he would have collapsed had it not been for Jovo's giving him that flask of water, but now Jovo was gone. Ivan wished he could sit down with him somewhere, to reminisce. The insides of Ivan's thighs bled from the constant friction and sweat, but that may not be right, for by now there was no sweat because he was too dehydrated. He could barely swallow whatever was in his throat, but it was not spittle, it was dust. Once he tried to spit, but nothing came out of his mouth, and his throat itched.

At night, he tried to urinate, stealthily taking out his penis. Nothing came out, except scorching pains, burning from his kidneys down his penis, into his fingers. He put his penis back and remembered how when he was a young boy, six years old, he loved to piss in public, even in the churchyard, until his mother taught him how to be modest. He had just pulled out his weenie, proudly, when she said: "Put it right back. A cat will snatch it and eat it like a fish." That memory made him smile, and his smile widened the cracks in his lips so that blood oozed down his stubbly chin.

The captives made it to another village, where they were allowed a pot of beans. The Chetniks waited for a two-day storm—a tremendous outpouring—to end, and then they pursued their captives, for many miles more, to a detention camp.

Past a burnt-out and gutted steel mill, the decimated regiment of Muslims and Croats stumbled through a field of bomb craters. Water filled the craters, out of which rough-skinned gray frogs leaped like beating hearts that had deserted the bodies of warring men and now roamed the doomed landscape. Ivan found the sudden leaps of so many hearts out of the gray earth unsettling. He could not see any of them until they were in the air, so it seemed to him that the earth was spitting up useless hearts and swallowing them back into the mud.

16

Ivan tries family happiness

Three months later, on a cobbled street in Osijek, Selma walked past the scaffolded redbrick cathedral. Workers plastered it, filling the holes in the bricks. Wet cement kept falling, thudding like hail. She walked toward the Drava River, wondering whether to kill herself. Since she had survived horrors in Vukovar, to end her life when the Serbs hadn't struck her as absurd. She had a good job, in reconstructive architecture—figuring out how to rebuild collapsed hospital wings, factory roofs, bridges, cathedrals. But while she could repair buildings, she was not sure she could repair her life.

"Hey, how is it going?" a familiar voice spoke from behind her. She turned around and saw Ivan. He was bony, and white streaked his oiled dark hair. Still, his face was unmistakable, with a tall and broad forehead, eyes set deep and wide apart under the brows, and large ears that stuck out. He looked like a boy, had the expectant, big-eyed look of desire, hunger, envy, even love, perhaps.

"What are you doing here?" she asked.

"I'm looking for a job."

"That's brave of you, after what you've done."

"What have I done?"

"Don't pretend. You bombed, burnt, pillaged . . ."

"That may be true, but I did not want to. Anyway, I was in the Croatian army, too, and was captured by Serbs again, and it's a miracle I survived. I was wounded, and exchanged from a prisoner camp in a swapping of soldiers."

"So you think that's a touching story."

"Truth is always touching."

"So now you want to live as though nothing happened. You want us to forget."

"What else?"

"It might be easy for you, not for me. I am pregnant—must have conceived in Vukovar."

"Really? I thought I had killed him before he could do it."

"Can you imagine, I couldn't have a baby before, and now . . ."

"Let's get married. I'll take care of you and the baby."

"That's generous of you. But what can you do now? I'd be supporting you."

"No, I can do all sorts of things."

"You are persistent."

"Yes, for a change. I wish I'd been like that when we were students."

"Weren't you? You were a pest."

"Is that how you saw it? I had a big crush on you, for years."

"I don't know about crushes, but I knew that you were there, behind street corners, near my windows, outside the school door, in the church, everywhere."

"So why did you talk to me so much?"

"You seemed pathetic and needy; I detest needy people and yet I want to help them. I mean, your attention did flatter me, but it also threatened me."

Here they looked into each other's eyes, calmly, and listened to the ice in the river cracking. They walked on the cemented embankment of the river and watched floes piling atop one another, breaking, sinking, rising, colliding, exploding—sharp, white, jagged, glaring in the sun like gigantic glassy swords clashing with slabs of marble. It seemed that the ground they stood on floated like an iceberg, north, while the river stayed in place.

"You think the ice comes from Austria?" Ivan asked. "And it's flowing down to Serbia, where waters from Bosnia flow too."

"So?"

"These damned countries are united by water. Blood shouldn't divide them. The pope made a big point out of that. Anyway, I'm not arguing in any unitaristic way, you know, but at least you and I should get along."

"That's all he's made, a point. Points can't be big. Don't you know the geometric definition of a point? Points can't add up to substance."

The wind that blew chilled them, and they walked past a kiosk with blue postcards, white cigarettes, and a gray saleswoman. The wind pushed Selma and Ivan from behind, and they walked effortlessly, with their chilled ears red and translucent against the sunshine that had broken down into thick rays through black branches of leafless acacias. They pulled up their collars and stepped into the tobacco cloud of a tavern, listened to the czardas, drank red wine. At dusk, in sleet, they walked out, with lips purple from the dried wine, and they huddled against the weather, against each other, making one standing mound, a man and a woman against each other.

The rents in Osijek became too high for the new couple. Selma got a job offer in the Nizograd town-planning department, and they moved to Nizograd. Her pregnancy grew big, and when the water broke, Ivan took her to the hospital in a cab. Selma moaned for two days, but the baby wouldn't come out, as though she knew the world out there was a threat. The obstetrician insisted that a C-section was absolutely necessary. Ivan watched with horror Selma's lower abdomen cut open; the quick pool of scarlet blood formed in the resulting opening. The obstetrician's chubby gloved hands pulled out a little, red-aquamarine creature out of the pool, with the umbilical cord trailing after it like a snake. After the cord was cut, and the creature washed, Ivan could see it was a human baby. He trembled with anxiety and anticipation, and when a nurse let him hold the baby, who began to cry, he was overjoyed. He held the baby in his hands—she fit in two palms—and admired her tiny features: she already had black eyebrows, plenty of black hair, and her minuscule fingers reached out and grabbed his beard. Her legs kicked, so one of her knees got him on the side of his cheek. The kick tickled warmly. She will be a tough one, he thought. She opened her hazy eyes and stared at him and grew quiet. So, mine is the first face she ever saw, he thought. Will she imprint on me? I will have a friend for life.

Selma's abdomen was stitched up, and when she regained her senses, she continued to moan. Ivan held her hand, horrified by all the pain she'd gone through, and decided he'd be a faithful family man. As soon as she saw the baby, she quit moaning, and her face lit up. They named the lively baby Tanya.

Ivan loved to listen to his baby breathe at night, slurp milk from Selma's breasts, and giggle in her sleep. What could an infant dream of? A clean butt, aired pee-pee, nipple in the naked gums? Or perhaps a baby is solving math puzzles and grasping the difference between infinity and nothingness?

At first the marriage was quite spontaneous, physically— they could all move through the house naked, and Selma and he slipped into love-making at most unexpected moments. Tanya, who was months old, wouldn't remember it anyway later on, so there was no point in being shy in front of her. But the novelty of happiness wore off fairly swiftly. Tanya slept between the couple in the marital bed, and now that she was pronouncing her first words and becoming more conscious, Ivan and Selma didn't make love so often. Gradually, Ivan felt displaced by the infant—the infant climbed all over Selma, while he waited for his turn, which often didn't come. Selma fell asleep, tired from work. She was in sync with Tanya—so while she hummed the baby to sleep, she fell asleep nearly at the same time as the baby, and Ivan stayed up, listening to the sonata for little lungs and big lungs, the two females breathing together.

He tried to change the cloth diapers, but his awkwardness disgusted him and made him uncomfortable with his baby's body. He liked to watch her and to play with her once she was clean. Selma took care of the baby after work, swiftly and dexterously.

Selma's mother moved into the neighborhood and attended to the baby during the day. She sang songs off-key for the baby; she tickled her, made faces for her, soaped her in bathtubs, powdered her little ass, washed her diapers, prepared hot cereal for her, and even shouted at her when she thought it necessary for the baby's growth.

Ivan had walled off a small study to study philosophy further, in the hopes of finally completing his thesis for the faculty of philosophy. In fact, he read sports papers, solved crossword puzzles, and chess problems. And he played his old violin.

With his eyes closed, he dreamed of playing Tchaikovsky's Violin Concerto in a concert hall, driving the audience into a swoon. At the end of the concert, there's a momentary silence, awe, and then the audience, including eighty-year-old invalids— even the paralytics in wheelchairs—leap and clap their hands, making the sounds of an ocean smashing against cliffs. Ivan bows, a merciful expression on his face; he is Poseidon who enrages the ocean.

But more often, trying to visualize a comforting scene of that sort, Ivan imagined an audience made of retired, bloated officers; wheezing judges; gay architects; old, bald German war criminals; and wiry old women, survivors of three or four wars. The people laugh shrilly, shriek, and throw their dentures, hearing aids, artificial eyes, liquid spermicide, rotten turkey eggs, and used condoms. These daydreams made Ivan melancholy.

At home, a matriarchy spread: a wife, a mother-in-law, a rug rat. He loved the rug rat, but was at the same time jealous that she got all the attention in the family, and he none. If the baby cried, the women were by her side instantly, and Ivan could shriek for his cup of coffee, but nobody would hear him. Both women were absorbed in tending to the child—powdering her ass to prevent diaper rash, and preparing chamomile tea with honey.

Coming home from work, Selma's first question wasn't "How's my hubby?" Instead, she leaned over her baby, tickled her nose, and uttered incomprehensible sounds of motherly affection and attention, which retard a child's learning of the language in particular, but advance its learning of emotional life immensely, which are indispensable for understanding the role of language in general—the meaning of language is in the tone and modality rather than in diction, and so it must soothe and comfort the child.

From his study Ivan watched the scene, happy that he had such a lovely family and upset that he was the least necessary part of it, a mere drone. To protect the honey, two bees drag a drone by his wings, tossing him out of the hive, and the drone falls on the ground, freezes, and ants pull off his wings, tear him to pieces, and carry him into their establishments to store for the winter.

Late at night, completely exhausted from work, Selma rarely felt amorous. She rebuffed Ivan's manual attempts at affection, saying, "Darling, please let me sleep! Tomorrow I have to wake up at six."

And one morning, Selma said, "You know what? You snore horribly. You've kept me up most of the night. It's not good for Tanya, either. You should sleep by yourself."

Now Ivan moved to the annex, which he'd made with his own hands after Tito's death, and slept on a mattress on the floor. Sometimes he started the night in the family bed but always ended up on the floor. He had good enough reasons to feel jealous now—Tanya had more Selma than he did, and Selma had more Tanya, and, although he had finally become a real family man, he felt more forlorn than ever.

At night Ivan had nightmares—of being shot, of killing old people with a knife, of tanks driving over him—and he couldn't sleep. Medical examinations yielded something terrifying: arrhythmia. He was warned that he might suffer a stroke. Now Ivan would wake up at night, dreaming that he was dead. He felt for his pulse on the carotid artery of his neck; it was irregular— three quick beats, and then none for several seconds to follow, which seemed like half a minute. Sometimes, while his daughter played with tinkling balls, his heart would start leaping against his rib cage.

Believing the cause of Ivan's illness to be psychological, a doctor gave him placebos and said that the pills were a kind of lipostatin (the most potent drug for clearing arteries), the newest development in Swiss pharmacology.

Ivan's skin turned olive-green. As his metabolic rate increased, hyperthyroidism was added to his list of accomplishments. No matter how much he ate, he stayed thin and anxious.

He got used to doctors and nurses sticking needles into his veins, and enjoyed seeing his crimson blood squirt into bottles. He was used to doctors hooking him up to EKG machines, tying tickling, cool metal receptors to his skin, used to fingers in gloves being stuck up his anus and warmly feeling his prostate, used to urinating and defecating into containers of various sizes. He could not, however, bear thin tubes sliding through his penis toward his kidneys. The medical exams turned into what they were initially supposed to be: martyrdom.

He did derive a certain dose of satisfaction from medicine. He was now undeniably a complex and special being—if he could not become powerful, at least he could become complex: a being no doctor could fathom. The physicians knew very well that hypochondria was an oversimplification and a diagnostic cop-out, though, of course, in addition to everything else, he was afflicted with hypochondria. The test results were never satisfactory, there was always something amiss with them: too much albumin in the urine, too few white blood cells, pH in the stomach too high. Fortunately, his wife's job's medical insurance covered his medical and pharmaceutical gluttony.

Ivan could no longer have a single meal without choking on at least five pills—in a variety of colors, for the greater customer satisfaction.

17

Family resemblances aren't always reassuring

One evening there was a family gathering in Selma's mother's house. Everybody remarked how similar to Ivan their two-year-old daughter looked. Tanya had the same kind of drop-off between the forehead and the rest of the face, and her large hazel eyes peered hungrily from beneath the brows. Selma's plump mother smiled benevolently as she observed the child's features. Selma's father was not there—he had disappeared in the war.

Later in the evening, when Ivan and Selma were back home, kicking their way through piles of plastic cars, trucks, and animals donated by UNICEF, Caritas, and German Protestant churches, Selma asked, "She does look like you. How come?"

"Isn't it obvious?"

"I can't believe it."

"Let me explain."

"You bloody bastard!"

"Shush, you'll wake up the child."

"I ought to cut your balls off."

"Listen, let me tell you how it went. You know, that commander was raping you. I killed him for you. Several hours before, he'd forced me to kill a man. Throughout the war, I was forced to bomb, I was pushed around, I was psychologically raped. My soul was raped. And once I freed myself, killed your rapist and my rapist, I felt free, for the first time ever. But I didn't know that I could have children. I mean, obviously I do have a daughter—a wonderful one—but I never believed that she was really mine. I believed my sperm count to be low—I don't know why, I just did. I never had much biological self-confidence. So I didn't think it made any sense to tell you that I may have . . . you know; I thought it was either the commander's seed, or who knows, there may have been people before him."

"So you killed the rapist, to rape me, and you'd never tell me!"

"No, that's not it. I was by that time unconscious, drunk, and there you were, my soul mate. I just lay with you. I did not force anything. And it seemed to me that you were sort of awake, that you knew what was going on, had come to, did not want to acknowledge that, ever, out of pride. Anyway, I felt entitled, after being in love with you for years, and I did it lovingly, in some kind of grace period, away from normal civilian life, in a moment of fate, where I was free from everything, even from the past."

"But I was unconscious!"

"So?"

"That's rape."

"Rape is when it is against your will. This did not concern your will, you were unconscious. And if you were conscious, you didn't object."

"Still, it's a violation, a rape."

"Come on. I saved your life. I put you on the bus. If I hadn't, the whole bar would've done it."

She wept, and tore her gold necklace with a crescent moon hugging a star, and twisted the moon in her fingers. Her canines bit the insides of her cheeks, until her mouth became salty, and she felt no pain. "If it weren't for the child, I'd kill you. But, she needs us. I can't help it, I love the child. Do you promise you'll always love the child?"

"Of course, does it look any different?"

She wept on. He came close to her and put his arm on her shoulder.

She shuddered. "Don't touch me!"

He sat on the crimson sofa, dejected.

"I can only hope that culture, nurture, will have the most important influence on how the child turns out, and not genes, your nature," she said. "I hope she grows up to be different."

"I'm sorry, what can I do? I love the child, and we could be a happy family if you could forgive me. But considering the circumstances, the times, the drunkenness, I don't see what wrong I've done anyway."

"I'd like to forgive you because of Tanya. Maybe it will take months. We can try. If I can't, I'll kill you." She looked at him earnestly, her face contorted with anguish, hatred, worry.

"Come on, don't talk nonsense. Good thing Tanya's not listening to this." He frowned, and put his head in his hands, moaned, and tore his hair.

"So, you do feel guilty?" Selma asked.

He was pacing the room. Lightning filled the room with flashes of blue light, followed by total darkness, and Selma saw him like a series of snapshots. Selma did not say anything, but listened to his steps, to his stumbling into chairs, stepping over toys, crushing them.

"Somewhere in me was buried the lad who was in love with you," said Ivan, "and he came out, possessed me, and he made love to you, not I. It's the past that did it."

"Don't philosophize. You've never been good at it. And you call rape making love?"

"It was so gentle it couldn't have been rape. Maybe it's not me philosophizing now. We all have multiple personalities; and one of us is the past, and another the future, and there's no present me. We are vacant right now, spaces in which the past and the future disagree."

"Philosophy is an excuse. You have no excuse," Selma said. Although there hadn't been a lightning flash in a while, thunder grumbled and rattled the loose silverware on the table. Tanya cried in the bedroom, and Selma went to her. Although two years old, Tanya sucked eagerly, kneading a breast with her little fists, sinking her untrimmed nails into the opulent flesh. Selma did not mind the slight pain from the scratchy nails, the little loving kitten's claws, nor did she mind her raspy tongue. Tanya let one of her hands roam and catch the other venous breast, and she smiled when she could get it to squirt.

Ivan undressed and went to bed. The baby, as though sensing the commotion and tension in the room, kept sucking for an hour. Selma said, "It's empty, they are both empty, can't you stop? Do you want some salami?"

"No. Milk, I want milk."

"Time to go to sleep," Selma said, and turned off the light.

"Light. Read book!"

Selma switched the light on, and read a book about happy bears and happy eagles eating happy fish.

The lightning storm continued, and the thunder roared. "Lions are fighting," Tanya said.

Loud raindrops hit the windowpanes. "They are crying, too," Selma said. "They are up there in the clouds, unhappy that they can't visit us. They are knocking for us to let them in."

"Lions, come in," Tanya said.

When Tanya was asleep, Ivan began to snore on the living-room sofa, his loud, arrhythmic snore, and out of his mouth came a stench of sprouting onions. Selma wished he'd die in his sleep, but as he was not about to, she went to the kitchen and fetched a knife. She should hate him for what he had done, no matter what he had said about being a victim too. It was her duty to avenge herself. She would feel better if she righted this wrong. She plunged the knife into his abdomen. She thought maybe it would be better to cut his neck, easier, safer in the sense that it would be more likely that she could kill him quickly. Or she should cut off his testicles, but then again, she didn't want to see his testicles. She shoved the knife into his abdomen again and pulled it sideways, against the vertical muscles, surprised at how hard it was to cut through, and pushed, leaning on the knife until the stainless steel ground against a rib.

He stood up and staggered, bleeding, and collapsed. Tanya woke up and screamed. "Mama, I'm afraid. Lions are biting. Where's Dada?"

Now Selma panicked, too, with the blue lightning showing the spooky aspect of her deed, a man torn open in a black puddle. She called an ambulance, and went to the hospital in it, alongside Ivan, with Tanya sucking her breasts. She did not know what her husband's blood group was; finding out took extra time. The hospital had no more blood of his type. She did not know what her type was, and asked to be tested, and her type was O. She gave a couple of pints of blood. It was enough to exhaust her, and enough to save his life. Now her blood would stream through him.

Tanya wanted to suck, but nothing came out. "Milk," cried Tanya, and sucked hard. Selma's breast hurt, and her eyes hurt, and ears buzzed.

"Milk," Tanya cried.

"No, no more milk," Selma said. "Maybe blood, if you'd like. Keep sucking, it will come. There's some left."

18

No unhappy marriage is unique

After Ivan's recovery, the marriage went on. At first Selma and Ivan eyed each other warily, but after considering all the options, they decided it might be best to stay together and raise a healthy child. Much could be blamed on the war, and now that the Dayton Peace Accord had been signed, it was time to rebuild the country and the family. Because of Ivan's revelations, he lost stature in his family. In that respect, he simply followed the pattern of most families in the region.

In a small town, it is common for the wife to head the family (she pays the bills, raises the children, calls the plumber) and for the husband to shirk (he gambles the money away and commits major pedagogic errors by suddenly slapping his children). At least he had nothing to hide anymore, and he didn't have to keep up any high standards, so he could relax and subsist. He was even joyful to be alive—he'd been so close to death once again. He decided to be a good man, as good as possible, and as such he would contribute to his family's happiness, and he went to the library to borrow books on family psychology, and they turned out to be nearly all American. He leafed through the books, and admired the straight white teeth shining. He didn't mind America, and though it looked a bit cheesy, judging by the soap operas it produced, it was a powerful country without which nothing could take place in Europe. Several wars were started in Europe in the twentieth century, and each one could end only after Americans thoroughly bombed the entire troubled regions.

Ivan bought several American books on how to raise happy, positive-thinking children with healthy teeth. He accepted the idea that one should never beat the child, but should manipulate the child through assigning "quiet time," with the child having to stay alone in a corner. The reward for good behavior should be expressions of love rather than unrestrained giving of candy (regardless of how much the American Dental Association benefited from that kind of love); and the silent punishment for misbehavior should be the omission of the expression of love, but certainly not an outbreak of violence and hatred. One should express love gently and reasonably—in calm moments, when the child is not pulling down tablecloths with china on them or playing with a cigarette lighter in the closet.

Ivan was nervous about declaring love to Tanya, especially in calm moments. It would make much more sense to wait till the emotional intensity of the household was raised by whatever means, even by beating, and then, while tears flowed, to declare love. But while the child put together jigsaws, to blurt out something about love would only puzzle her. He paced up and down the room until Selma begged him, in the name of family sanity, to go someplace else.

The right opportunities did arise; Tanya tripped over a root in the park and fell on the gravel, tearing the skin off her knees. While she cried, Ivan put her on his knee and told her (in the third person) that Daddy loved her. She cried even louder, and Ivan was not sure that the association of the impressions— bleeding knees and Daddy's love—was what he'd aimed for. And Tanya was, as far as Ivan was concerned, too young to be bothered with any verbal expressions of love.

Selma was enthusiastic about raising children like little Americans. That certainly was a novel approach in the neighborhood. From blocks away, as cooking steamed up the ceiling, you could hear loud shrieks of children being instructed in the art of proper conduct; parents wrote down the lessons in their children's soft skins with belts and willow branches, and sometimes with simple and unadorned fist blows. Selma bought a whole set of toothbrushes, and Tanya now brushed her teeth thrice a day, each time for two minutes, with all kinds of fancy strokes, up and down, circular, backhand, forehand—American tooth-brushing seemed to be even more intricate than the Czech style of tennis, and much more so than the Croatian style of tennis (exemplified by Ivanisevic: powerful serve, smash to follow, either hit or miss, no long points and no need for thinking).

The enlightened upbringing made Tanya uninhibited, or, to put it more bluntly—the way the neighbors did—she turned into a spoiled little brat. However, she did smile, sometimes quite unprovoked, because, unlike most Croatian children, she didn't suffer from chronic toothaches.

Ivan envied his child; how freely she shouted! What spontaneity. Among adults as a child, Ivan had been allowed to open his eyes and ears, but not his mouth, unless in quiet amazement. When a grown-up stranger visited the Dolinars, Tanya would in no time start tugging at Mom's skirt or Dad's beard, climbing over his crotch, screaming into Dad's ear experimentally and asking whether it hurt.

Ivan wanted to improve his marriage. He read another bunch of American how-to books, how to make your wife happy. It took the American and British air forces to placate Serbia and Kosovo, and just so it could take American science and psychology to placate and gratify a Balkan couple. After the second American display of power in the Balkans, Ivan definitely turned highly pro-American, an attitude which naturally wasn't common among Serbs and somehow even among Croats, who resented that Americans had let Serbian forces ravage Croatia, imposing the arms embargo that made it hard for Croatia to defend itself. Most Croats currently resented the fact that the Croatian generals, who had liberated and ethnically cleansed the Serb-occupied territories of Croatia, were wanted in The Hague as war criminals, and that, although Croatia had won the war, not a single officer or soldier was allowed to be declared a war hero. Ivan had loved the reports of sorties, explosions, and even the American rocketing of the Chinese embassy struck him as wonderfully precise. At any rate, now he read a bunch of American books on sexuality, such as *The Joy of Sex II*; the American engineering talent would make him a good lover yet. He didn't particularly like the chapter in which there were stereotypical descriptions of different national proclivities in sex. Simulation of rape was asserted to be the folkloric Serbian style of sex. Considering the war in Bosnia and the rape camps there, he had no objection to that absurd assertion. *Hrvatski jeb*—the Croatian style of sex—was described as a simulation of male crucifixion. The man would be laid out, and the woman would do with him as she pleased. Who gave them that notion that Croatian men were passive? Anyhow, maybe there was something to that, too, and although he found these passages irritating, he continued reading the book and others, because now he had a mission of becoming a good husband.

The books asserted that peak experiences are the key to harmony, and recommended that the husband reciprocate sexually, so if the wife performs fellatio, he should respond with cunnilingus, and that in fact he should be the first to initiate oral sex; that the husband should buy candles rather than to imagine that the wife should, and he should discreetly place them all around the bedroom (to Ivan it seemed a morbid idea, reminiscent of a wake).

Ivan laughed at the pragmatic approach to conjugal bliss, which, to his mind, got the details right but missed the point of marriage. Maybe it was akin to American wars: they got the details right with a lot of precision bombing, but they missed the point or even forgot why they fought the war in the first place. Ivan was not quite sure what the point of marriage was, but it did seem that it required precision.

Selma had decided she did not need to pay attention to her appearance; she did not need to win a husband—she had one; not a great one, but a husband nevertheless. She preferred to spend extra money on Western-style diapers—and, later, Barbie dolls—rather than on skirts for herself. Giving birth to Tanya and taking tetracycline damaged her teeth, so that Ivan no longer liked to kiss her, and she liked it even less.

Selma, too, attempted to improve the amorous aspects of

marriage, presenting the *Kama Sutra* to her husband for their fourth anniversary, which had slipped Ivan's mind. Ivan opened the tinfoil paper: two bodies supplely intertwined around the axis of a huge phallus. He took the gift as an insult.

When they did have sex, Ivan was so little used to it, and so much excited by it, that he ejaculated prematurely. Ivan had never been used to affection. Physical touch in his youth took place in the form of blows, choking, whipping. His mother used to punish him not when he had expected it—because then he would have simply jumped through the window and run away—but when he hadn't; usually just as he was passing by, she would slap him on the neck, or kick him. A math teacher used to tickle Ivan under the chin to raise his jaw to the optimal angle to slap. So Ivan had assumed a circumspect manner in his childhood (he often turned his head to see whether there was any threat behind him), and though fully aware that it was exaggerated, he could not change in his adulthood. And bullets and knives later on did not help. At the lightest touch, he'd be startled.

The gentler the touch was, the more it irritated Ivan, sometimes sending his abdominal muscles into convulsions. Ivan often pinned his wife's arms onto the pillows, avoiding her skin, delegating all the responsibilities of communication to his penis. When, in the libidinal excitement, she touched him with her feet, he ejaculated at once, grinding his teeth and growling like a desert dog.

He had no proof that Selma still despised him, but he imagined that she did. He knew that his imagination could be the product of his paranoia—or his paranoia the product of his imagination—but that did not console him. He was afraid that he was going out of his mind. And in the town there was no "family therapist"—that usually divorced professional—and as for psychiatry, though Nizograd had been a part of Austria for centuries, psychiatry was only applied to the mentally ill.

—

After the war, Ivan could not find another teaching position. He used to imagine that once Croatians ran their own country, the economy would prosper and there would be jobs. Croatia would become a southern Norway, with a coastline full of fjords and efficient factories with an excellent workforce; Croats would come back from Germany and Australia and with their wonderful working skills turn Croatia into the promised land. However, the economy was now nearly nonexistent. He and many other Slavonian Croats blamed the Herzegovina Croatian newcomers for taking over all the worthwhile jobs. Tudjman and his Herzegovinian team had embezzled everything that could be embezzled. The national factories were privatized behind the scenes, and the factory equipment immediately sold to Turkey and a few other countries. Factories stopped functioning. So, people became nostalgic for the old Yugoslavia and almost longed for Serbs to come back.

Miraculously, the metal factory in Nizograd still functioned, perhaps for no other reason than to fill the valley with poisonous gases and noxious, heavy-metal dust. Ivan managed to get a job at the factory, and so for a while he joined the labor force, inhaling exhaust, listening to the crackling hiss of electricity spark from his welding machine. Actually, the factory did produce something—bombs and cannons for potential wars against Serbia, Slovenia, Hungary, and all the other neighbors Croatia had at the time; for some reason, Croatia couldn't get along with any neighbors. During breaks he talked to nobody and sternly read philosophy, plucking at his beard brutally yet contemplatively, or thumbed the mucus in his crooked nose. If the philosophical arguments were particularly twisted, he ground his teeth and plucked his nasal hair so abruptly and mercilessly that blood dripped from his nose. Forgetting the cause of the bleeding, he thought of checking his hemoglobin. Workers laughed at him. Each day they invited him to drink beer with them at a tavern during morning coffee breaks, and thought him strange for turning down the invitations.

Ivan was transferred from his welding job because of lung

problems; he had coughed constantly and spots showed up on his X-rays. As soon as he began to work in the factory's administrative office, his spots disappeared. He began to develop other symptoms: a variety of digestive problems and the crowning end of the digestive troubles, hemorrhoids.

He was on very good terms with the physicians: they got to know him, despise him, and like him. As soon as Ivan showed up at the door, one physician—without examining Ivan's anus, mouth, and chest—shouted out a diagnosis, and his secretary filled out a couple of forms, releasing Ivan from another week of work.

Selma completely lost interest in sex, and Ivan suspected she did so not because it was bad at home but because it was good elsewhere.

He followed Selma in the streets when she went shopping and saw her talk only with women. It's not natural for a woman with a university diploma not to talk to men. Unless she's a feminist, and his wife was no feminist. Her behavior must conceal . . .

He contrived excuses to visit her in her office—Tanya's sneezing once in the morning would do. He inspected nooks and crannies in the county architecture department to see whether sex could be executed there. He sized the male architects up and down, and all of them appeared to him handsome, though a little too refined, effeminate, perhaps gay. This slim one, look how he avoids looking at me, he must be the one! No, that one in the tinted glasses!

He knew that his jealousy was not of the healthy sort that could spice up a marriage with flirtatious cheer, but rather of a harmful, morbid sort. But morbidity had always appealed to Ivan. Morbidity could be likened to subversion, to the collapse of functioning, and, on a larger scale, to an anarchist insurrection. And there's always something more impressive in the destruction of a building than in the construction: a greater and more ecstatic release of power.

"Yes, yes, let's get this whole thing over with!" he muttered now and then, daydreaming about the collapse of the government. He detested the nationalist government of Tudjman. And he daydreamed about divorce.

His life became odious to him, and the sunshine that warmed his skin gave him no joy; he preferred cold rain and, even more, thunderstorms. He felt cuckolded. Whether his wife really cuckolded him was almost immaterial; he thought like a cuckold—not an unwitting but a fully conscious one.

Even if she hadn't committed adultery, preemptively he should. Then he would not be a cuckold, but rather he would enjoy a modern, open marriage. As he contemplated cosmopolitanizing his marriage so simply, he smiled, and while slurping soup, he kept looking warmly at Selma's clavicles—how tall, thin, and gentle they looped below her neck—so that she asked him what was wrong.

"Nothing—there are moments when a man feels happy— and why shouldn't I be happy with a wife like you!"

His wife looked at him as though he had displayed the symptoms of acute hepatitis, and actually he suspected that he had. Another reason to visit the doctor.

19

Ivan discovers the thrills of adultery

Where could he find some extramarital sex? It was easy for a single man to meet women, but for a married man, in a small town, to approach a woman? That simply wouldn't do. If you didn't know people, they knew you by sight and gossip. Of course, you knew most people likewise, but the number of people you acknowledged as acquaintances was small. The art of introduction did not exist in Nizograd. If you sat at a table with people you knew and people you didn't, nobody would introduce you. You should have something intriguing to say to catch a stranger's attention, and, even so, she might not acknowledge you next time she saw you in the street. And, by greeting her first, you'd effectively say, "I would like us to be acquaintances." As that was usually too much to admit all at once, few people acknowledged each other.

Ivan knew several secretaries at work, but there would be nothing cosmopolitan about sleeping with them. How to meet a lady?

He racked his brains for weeks. He ate a dozen egg yolks a day, because he had read that the yolk contained lecithin, a memory enhancer. But he had nothing to remember, other than perhaps Aldo's—Allah bless his soul—lowlife tricks for picking up lonely women in the streets of Novi Sad. And that, in turn, made him shudder with horror at the memory of seeing Aldo crucified in Bosnia. A wave of terror seized him, and he trembled and rushed to the bathroom with an upset stomach. And soon, rather than feel sorry for Aldo, he worried about himself; wasn't this the posttraumatic stress syndrome? He had certainly earned one. But could he trust a psychiatrist trained in Socialism to diagnose and straitjacket politically undesirable "elements" as schizophrenics? Of course not, so the hell with war syndromes. About the war he had thought more than enough, with no satisfaction, and about adultery, not enough. At least adultery would be an activity, a way out, a form of not being a victim, but an actor, even if a misguided one. (And adultery was a form of biological warfare, far more sophisticated than the mechanical and chemical warfare, which was the usual fare. Suppose he picked up chlamydia and brought it home—that would be quite a subtle counterattack in the marriage.) It would be even more misguided to do nothing but merely sit and wait for the brooding to choke him.

He read short stories and novels to find out how to meet a lady. Usually, you have to go to a spa. If a lady has a lapdog, you first acquaint yourself with the dog—you throw him greasy ribs from your plate. When the dog sees you next, he cheerfully wags his tail, and now you can bend down and pet him and compliment him on his looks. And then you may quite spontaneously ask the lady how she manages to keep his pelt so shiny and elastic. Nizograd had a spa, but to play the game there would be too public, and it would be half a year before he could be sent to another spa on paid sick leave.

Most of the pretty ladies in the town were married to the county judge or the chief of police or a doctor or a colonel. He was fond of doctors; so, seducing a doctor's wife wouldn't make sense. However, he harbored resentment against all the rest. But how to meet these wives?

Well, the chief of police spent his evenings in the chess club. His wife was none other than Svjetlana, the bewitching dancer from Trout Haven. And he was none other than Peter's murderer. Before the war, Vukic was a Communist who subscribed to the political journals in Cyrillic, pretending to be a Serb, because that helped him advance in his post at the police station. And now he was a staunch Croatian nationalist. Ivan suspected that Vukic could adapt to anything—he was a man of a singular lack of self-consciousness and shame.

Although Ivan hated to face the cop, he played him. After Ivan defeated Vukic and the club closed, Vukic invited him home. They opened a chess set of ebony and ivory on a coffee table, and the host called his wife, Svjetlana, to serve chocolate pastries.

She came out in a pink nightgown, her eyes bloodshot from reading a horror novel. Without looking at Ivan, she brought out Turkish coffee and then shimmeringly disappeared into her room. Although it had been only twelve years since the Trout Haven rondo, her looks had somehow faded—breasts sagged, lip edges wrinkled, chin tripled, eyes dimmed—but she would do, thought Ivan. There was still a luscious vulnerability and softness about her. The plump texture of her freckled curves and the melancholia of her cheeks invited exquisite squeezes.

Ivan played confidently, patronizingly offering pawn sacrifices left and right for the advantages of development and space. The chief was enthusiastic. "Wonderful! I feel we are evenly matched! You play modern chess, open, Kasparov-style. I like that."

"Did you know that Kasparov spends his summers in Croatia? He's even a member of the Vukovar chess club, in solidarity with the victim city."

"Who do you think I am? Of course, I know. In fact, I was his bodyguard when he played in Dubrovnik last summer. But let me tell you, that guy is so penetrating, he needs no protection. His eyes could melt keys."

"Why isn't he a thief then?"

"He doesn't have to be. He gets what he wants—he just thinks hard and stares!"

"Maybe we should try the same method."

"Go ahead, but it won't work, I can guarantee you that."

But at that moment, Ivan was trying at least the staring part of the Kasparov method—penetratingly examining the self-assured sway of Svjetlana's hips as she walked to their table to serve them another round of frothing Turkish coffee and tortes of nuts and cream. She sat at their table and sighed: "If only I could play this game better. Ranko, why won't you play me?"

"Because it's no fun playing a beginner," Vukic, who did not stand well in the game, groaned.

"There're computers that play chess," Ivan said to Svjetlana. "You could practice with one."

"Phew!" Vukic said. "She's a woman—computers and chess aren't for women! Chess requires foresight and rationality."

"Women could play like men," Ivan said. "Chess isn't a part of their upbringing, that's all. There're no women playing at the chess club—if they played as much as we do, they'd play better than us because they aren't drunks."

"Prove it," said the chief to Ivan.

"How could I personally prove it? I am not a woman."

"I could make a joke."

"You'd be better off not to. I understand that your feelings are hurt a little after so many losses, but you needn't turn nasty."

"How come you champion women so much?"

"How about the Polgar Sisters from Budapest? There are three of them, and two are grandmasters, and now and then they whip old symbols of male rationality and stamina, such as Spassky."

"Spassky belongs in a museum."

"That's a sexist statement," Svjetlana said.

"Which one?"

"That women aren't drunks," Svjetlana said. "What else can we do in this little town but be drunks? You men do it in the bars, we do it at home. If we lived in a large town, I'd get private lessons, and then I'd show you. But here . . ." She drew a big breath, and her breasts filled and rose—the skin smoothing and illuminating a steep precipitous cleavage that halted Ivan's breathing.

"Well, I . . ." Turning to the chief, Ivan whispered, "How about a little penetration on the queen's side?"

"A waste of time."

"All right, we'll do the king then. That's more direct anyhow. Do you know that the word checkmate comes from Arabic, from sheik and maat, king and death, meaning dead king?"

"So what?"
"So, check."
"That's just a tickle."
"Mate!"
"Mother."

A week later, Ivan ran into Svjetlana near the old library, and while they stood in the stream of dank air coming from the dungeon-like library cellar, Ivan asked, "How's Mr. Vukic's health?"

"He's out of town for a week. Another conference."

"That's the good life. The Communist habits die hard, don't they? I think our government is bound to go bankrupt."

"It already is bankrupt. I am so frightfully bored. You know, you cannot read all the time."

"I could offer you chess lessons?"

"Oh, yes, that would be lovely!"

She walked on, and Ivan stood in the stream of dank air that carried the dust of crumbling fly wings and dried cobwebs into his nostrils, and he admired the swing of her broad hips and the tightness of her skirt on her undulating buttocks, which were grooved by her high panty-lines; and as the lines slid closer to each other, like the profile of a stork's wings rising higher and higher, he gasped with an asthmatic shortness of breath. He walked east, into a steamy cloud of fermenting hops that pistoned out of the brewery through a barbed-wire gate beneath the large Croatian emblem—iron red-and-white squares, resembling a chessboard—and the squares' redness diminished in the pastel shades of misty rust.

In the chess club, at a large table, tapping his feet on the floor (where black oil covered generations of dust and ash, melting them into a soft, asphalt-like grime), Ivan showed Vukic several games from a book, *500 Most Exquisite Mates.*

"Ah, old dog, so that's how you do it! No wonder you are beating me—you study from books!" Vukic said.

"Well," smiled Ivan, "I don't study, but I like to see a brilliant combination. Look at this." Ivan showed a mating combination by heart.

"I'll be damned. Could you run that one by me again?"

Vukic, who had drunk a quarter of his brain to death, stared blankly. "Gee, you are a born teacher! My wife says you're gonna teach her?"

Ivan blushed, but believed that the chief couldn't notice it in the dim lighting.

"Ivan, you are an intellectual. I am surprised that you don't have a teaching job. We'll see what we can do about that."

And when they stood up, Vukic kissed Ivan on his cheeks and embraced him and blew a mixture of white-wine vapors and stale cigar smoke past Ivan's nostrils into his ears.

Ivan burped.

Ranko Vukic, apparently not minding Ivan's spending time with his wife, watched the newsreel while Ivan tutored Svjetlana. Ivan might have been more perceptive had he not lost his respect for Vukic. How can you respect someone you easily outsmart on the board?

When Vukic went out of town for a soda-drinking conference—televised, so that people would see that their leadership was sober—Ivan called on Svjetlana. She welcomed him with a scent of carnations crushed into oils and with the damp touch of French skin lotions on her cool cheeks. These lotions came from whales, and Ivan thought of Jonah, because he identified himself with Jonah. Jonah had wanted to see the destruction of Nineveh, and Ivan had enjoyed seeing NATO bomb;

Jonah would no doubt love NATO if he were around, and he'd work for British intelligence or the CIA.

Ivan grew nervous and kept his head bent toward the chessboard, playing earnestly. While he showed her a fork combination, Svjetlana crossed and uncrossed her legs, flashing her glistening skin.

"Could you repeat that?" She touched him lightly, as though unintentionally, on the back of his hand and, as if catching herself in the act, she quickly withdrew her hand. Ivan was startled.

"Oh, I'm so sorry," she said. "I hope it didn't hurt."

"No, no, of course not. Actually, it was pleasant."

"You have strange notions of pleasure, to be scared of it!"

"I am not scared."

"And how can I get out of this pin?"

As Ivan showed how to wiggle out of the pin, she passed her fingertips above his hand as though caressing him, and said, "Wait! Couldn't the bishop . . ." Her fingertips were half an inch away from his knuckles. The static electricity of the rug discharged from her onto Ivan's skin in pink sparks, crackling. The waves of voltage sucked his blood into a seething erection. After a tremulous hesitation, Ivan pounced on her, knocking the chess pieces off the table. Thirstily she moistened her lips with his. He pressed his palms against her bosom, as though to defend himself from its motherly power, and peeled flesh-colored silk away from her nipples, and held up her delicate flesh, before he let it slip. His hands passed down her belly, and brushed her stray and unplucked pubic hairs, on the way to the mons veneris. Soon Ivan and Svjetlana engaged in the ancient activity, a prehistoric merger. They took a voyage down the evolutionary tree, becoming more and more supple, and more and more spineless, moister and moister, until they whirled down into a maelstrom, into the submarine world of cold eros.

Ivan did not know how to explain it, but somehow everything worked, and after making love vigorously, he fiddled gently, as if stroking the E string on the violin in a pianissimo passage of an adagio movement.

Svjetlana and Ivan took a ride in the chief's Audi as far as the road went into the mountainous woods. They hiked down a steep slope through the thick oak forest, until they hit upon a breath-giving meadow. The sunlight narrowed Ivan's pupils, and for a couple of seconds he saw nothing but a glare, as if the slope were covered with snow. The smell of thousands of teas—most strongly rose hip—floated. His eyes felt more through the sense of touch than vision—the stirring goodness of the meadow winds caressed his eyes.

A clan of winds chased one another and frolicked in the grass; one skimmed the slopes, another whirled by, like a dervish who had become the breath of playful demons. The winds lifted Svjetlana's dark red hair, and tumbled fallen oak leaves, and swept down the grass again, but stayed out of the forest, where ruddy pigs crunched acorns loudly.

The grass kept shimmering, changing into dark and light tints depending on the direction of the winds, which turned now the inside then the outside of the blades toward Svjetlana and Ivan; the blades alternately absorbed and reflected the sun.

Svjetlana and Ivan jumped into the grass as though into a lake covered with a film of algae. Meadow creatures scurried under them and pricked them. The pricks of wasps, ants, and spiders added to the lovers' sensual urgency in a maddeningly moist wind. When they climaxed, groaning, there was a sudden outpouring of rain, a relief from the clashing of laden winds. Svjetlana and Ivan stood up and faced a flock of sheep silently gazing at them; two shepherds smoked pipes contemplatively beneath a lone, rough-barked pear tree. When Ivan and Svjetlana had hopped into the meadow, they hadn't seen a single incarnated soul, and now hundreds of eyes rested on their reddened flesh, on which insect bites budded into dozens of milk-less nipples. Ivan and Svjetlana ran into the woods, away from the eyes, and jumped into a grimy creek, soothing their new nipples, and played in the mud, plastering it on each other, searching with their fingers for skin; and like that, like earth melting, they stuck to each other and gasped and moaned, slippery and gone. Then they washed themselves in the cold creek.

After taking a hot shower in Svjetlana's apartment, Ivan sodomized Svjetlana in the chief's bed—Ivan saw this as a triumph of humanity over the nationalist regime. (He also felt that he was a fashionable man now, for at Nenad's bar he had recently seen a porn tape from France, and it seemed this manner of sex had become the most sophisticated way of doing it.) He now felt so comfortable with the regime that he thought of joining the Croatian Democratic Party. He might even hang a picture of Tudjman—a plagiarism of a picture of Tito—on his wall. He thought of a joke. "Why does Tudjman so often put his right hand over his heart? So you wouldn't see *Tito* on his shirts." The immortal Tito lived on only in jokes. He squeezed Svjetlana's thighs again.

Ivan sang partisan songs on the way home. He soared above the rusting steeples in his imagination. Who knows? One day he might even become a concert violinist and a chess grand master. It was not too late for anything. He was barely fifty, and he felt as though he were twenty. (Although, when he was twenty, he had felt as though he were fifty.)

20

The joys of cuckolding

come to a sorry end

Tudjman had just died. The radio played the Dvorak Cello Concerto, the second movement all day long. This time Ivan didn't feel sad that the nation had lost its paternal figure. In fact, he felt elated, and wondered whether this meant that pretty soon Croatia would be prosperous, the quiet sanctions could be lifted, the West might like Croatia and lend it money, tourists would come to the coast, and so on.

To celebrate, Ivan visited Svjetlana.

The stereo exuded quasi-folk music, with accelerating rhythms and quickening warm bass notes. The chief of police had gone away because of heightened security. Svjetlana and Ivan kissed. Saliva tasting of toothpaste and chocolate dripped down their chins. Her creamed lips irritated him into lust. They slid off onto a new Turkish carpet with a variety of red and black dragons, flames, snakes, stars, moons, and thousands of intricacies, which only bored mountain peasants had the time and ingenuity to stitch. The carpet gave them no static shocks. He closed his eyes. The music sped up, the bass hit the lows, stirring something deep and low in Ivan, perhaps his prostate, and, with the slivovitz and the heat, Ivan had an impression he was flying on a magic carpet. They tore off their clothes and wrestled playfully. Their martial arts went on in her marital bed.

The wood of the large cupboard squeaked. A big man jumped out of it: Vukic. He leapt on Ivan. Smash! Boom! In a couple of seconds Ivan was covered with various organic colors for which he provided the materials, and more were coming. A wreath of red surrounded his eyes; soon it would blend in with blue, green, and other rainbow colors, as a sign of his glorious love conquest.

Chief Vukic shoved Ivan out through several doors, and kicked him out of the house, his boots grinding Ivan's *glutei maximi et minimi*. Electricity flooded Ivan's brain, triggering all sorts of lights, thoughts, sensations, and emotions—primarily of panic, shame, humiliation, and pain: everything that mortals can feel, Ivan felt, except perhaps gratitude.

After a somersault he landed on his posterior in the street. It was Thursday, the town market day. Throngs of people walked back from the marketplace with supplies of cool cheese, butter, celery, eggs, and shrieking chickens. When Ivan stood up naked, with his penis still half erect, and Comrade Vukic stamped his feet behind him, the crowds burst out into loud laughter.

Ivan wanted to run back into the building, to hide in the corridor, but Vukic stood in the door and proceeded to pull out a cigarette and light it. Ivan struggled through the crowd.

"Look at our Don Juan!"

"Casanova, could you teach me how to seduce married women? How much do you charge for thirty seconds?"

"What's that small thing in front of you that looks like a dick?"

Ivan broke through the crowd and ran home, his balls hopping, while children ran after him as if after a circus, hollering and throwing stones at him.

And so Ivan contracted a grave illness: chronic shame. In spite of wishing to quit thinking about his disgrace, he thought about it all the time.

At his office he had the impression that people avoided looking into his eyes. He thought, It's unpleasant for them to think how I would feel if they looked me straight in the eye. But that's not out of consideration, I know them!

That nobody seemed to look at his eyes convinced Ivan that

everybody watched him, laughing behind his back. Once, Paul, a colleague, suddenly burst into a peal of laughter—his abdominal muscles, that is, the abundant animal fat that covered them, shook in visible waves beneath his white shirt.

"What are you laughing about?" Ivan asked.

"I just remembered a joke," Paul replied.

The clerks and secretaries chuckled or laughed, although they looked straight at the papers and typewriters on their desks, as if minding their own business.

Ivan reddened. He did not believe that there was a joke. "Well, tell us the joke!"

"It may not be decent in front of the ladies," replied Paul.

"Oh, no, we want to hear the joke," they said. "We'd love a good one!—especially a dirty one!"

"All right, all right, if you really want me to, I will," said Paul, affecting resignation. "Two women are pulling out carrots in a garden. One suddenly stops, holds a carrot in her hands, stares at it with abandon, and says, 'My hubby has one just like this!'

" 'What, so big?' asks the other.

" 'No, so so . . . dirty.' "

Ivan did not laugh. He thought that the joke was aimed at him.

He had a sensation that people's stares followed him the way tails follow cats, and no matter how quickly he turned around, he could not catch their looks, just as a cat cannot catch its tail. Ivan made many mistakes in his work.

Ivan's health deteriorated. He had heart troubles, arrhythmia, and, on top of it, though spatially below it, an ulcer.

His wife hardly bothered to look at him, let alone talk to him, as though he were a slimy pig.

In his pent-up rage, Ivan ground his teeth, wishing to beat her. If he was an ass everywhere else, he could yet be king at home. But that would be too base: wife-beating was the standard solution of many a humiliated man, and for that reason it was not an option for Ivan, who, though sinking low in self-respect, still held a notion of himself as uniquely refined and exquisitely unlucky.

Tanya continued to scream at home as if nothing had happened. She ran through the house after their cat, and the two of them, like two little squirrels around a tree trunk, whirled around.

He brooded. I could die of a heart attack in this armchair while reading some tedious article about the last annual meeting of the Russian Parliament, and nobody would notice. It makes no difference to them whether I am alive or dead.

He smoked filterless cigarettes, so that his mouth and throat itched. He cast smoke out of his mouth, left and right, like a steam engine working its way up a steep incline.

At night he fidgeted in bed, each successive night more and more, until the most dramatic night of his life, or rather, death.

That night frogs sounded like remote pigs. Buzzing mosquitoes zoomed in his ears. The sounds sank into the pores of his sweaty skin. His wife sweated, too. The bed was soft, so she rolled down right against his skin.

Mosquito bites itched him—he scratched his skin until it almost bled, and yet he couldn't stop digging his nails into his own flesh. Selma's sticky skin sent shivers of revulsion throughout his body. He turned onto his right side, away from her, and tried to sleep but managed only to fart in anguish.

From the streets came the buzzing of motorcycles and cars, first low, and then louder, and then low again, only to disappear. Voices of adolescents, cheerful and rude, came in from the streets, carrying the notes of their hopes, talk of soccer and girls; and then followed the buzz of the quiet, and then the echoes of steps of a solitary passerby, and again the voices of the same adolescents and the same frogs, and if they were not the same, they sounded the same. The Japanese alarm clock emitted a hiss as minutes rolled over each other. Ivan looked at the fluorescing green digits: 1:10. 1:11.

His wife began to snore. Then she stopped.

All of a sudden the terror of death pierced through his skin, permeating his blood like cobra's poison. He smelled the incense of death, an acrid sensation in his nostrils.

He remembered all the burials he had seen, now somehow unified into one: his. He saw himself in a coffin, in a black suit, with his purple head propped up, giving him a permanent thoughtful air as becomes someone who is contemplating being and nothingness. And he felt pangs of shame, shame that stank of old socks and shriveled genitals.

He was terrified that he would die, just suddenly vanish, without having done anything significant in his life, without understanding anything: he had not even had a single thought that could satisfy him aesthetically and fill his soul, if he had one. He had experienced only petty worries and vanity.

Now, out of an additional vanity, of wishing that he could think well of himself, he was worried that he had lived vainly.

In empty darkness, all his misery fell upon him. The hairs stood up on his arms and legs. His falling naked onto the pavement amidst a roar of laughter re-created itself in his head fluorescently, through a pinkish tint, with derisive echoes recalling his childhood humiliation: his head's being whacked against the cement after he lost a fight, children jeering.

His stomach convulsed with nausea; heartburn climbed in his chest near where a dull pain sharpened with each breath, somewhere along the left edge of his sternum in his rib cage. His heart beat at a strangely slow pace, leaving between each two beats an abyss, an emptiness he felt he was falling through.

His heart had waited too long for the next beat; would it strike? He did not dare draw another breath, because it could press against the heart and choke it. Even a breath of air could annihilate him.

Death horrified him, and the image of walking out into the streets again alarmed him. He wished he'd never have to move again and yet to live, to be neither dead nor alive.

And as though to fulfill his desire, his heart lingered, without a beat, and then a hysterical attack gripped him, convulsed him with powerful luminous electricity, freezing him. And when the electricity ceased, he was paralyzed. He could not move. His eyes stayed open and he could not close them.

Who could blame him now for not solving his problems? How could he? He could not move a single muscle of his body.

At first he was exhilarated to be in this new state. There was something coldly solemn about it: something extraordinary, with a *mysterium tremendum,* something horrifying. Now, instead of despising himself, he began to pity himself. Through the pity he rose to the heights of respecting himself—nay, loving himself.

He continued breathing involuntarily, as though somebody else rather than he was doing it somewhere in him. His heart beat imperceptibly in long intervals, with much sensation of emptiness. He wondered whether he could feel his heart beat, where he usually did, in his ears, in his neck, in his sore tooth, but he did not feel the beat and did not know whether there was a beat.

21

Try it on a death certificate

Upon getting up early in the morning, Selma went to the bathroom without looking at Ivan, washed her face and brushed her teeth in the old way—left and right, not up and down—and then she shouted: "Ivan, get up! It's nearly five in the morning. You'll be late for work. You'll be fired, that's all we need!"

Then she touched up her eyebrows, though in principle she was against makeup—she merely strengthened them so deftly that you wouldn't notice anything artificial about them. She wondered whether her eyelashes were long enough. She took up a small mirror and examined her semi-profile against a mirror above the sink and then penciled her eyelashes—it wouldn't interfere with her nature and would make her eyes look deeper.

Seeing that she did not have much of a husband, she had become interested in herself again. In her middle age she was dignified, self-confident, and sexually, sensually powerful, yet vulnerable and insecure about her appearance. After rolling the pencils into her purse, she drew the curtain aside to look out into the street. Slow rain drizzled in the dim dawn.

She walked to the bedroom, wondering what color to wear. She was leaning toward red, because in the gray of the cold day the warm color would be cheering. She opened her chest of drawers and routinely shouted, "Ivan, get up! Time to go to work!" These types of exclamations Ivan hated from the depths of his soul, if he had any soul and any depths thereof.

When he didn't snarl back in his usual way—"Can't a man have peace in his own bed?! Get lost!"—she turned to see what the new style was about.

Ivan's eyes were glassy and bloodshot, glaringly wide open.

She ran to his bed and touched his arms. They were cold and stiff. Selma screamed. Ivan did not move at all.

Hearing the shrieking, a pale child, her eyes enlarged, appeared at the bedroom door. Selma searched for his pulse and heartbeat, but all she felt was his cold skin. She cried again and would have sobbed had she not noticed her daughter in the doorway. She led her to her bedroom, saying, "Everything is all right, nothing happened, go back to sleep, you didn't see anything, everything will be all right." She was saying all this so quickly that she scared Tanya even more. Tanya didn't dare move out of her bedroom again. Did Dad beat Mom? No, it couldn't be. She was leaning over him. Did she hit him? No, he was so calm. What was it?

Selma had to run through the wet streets to the emergency room eight blocks away, because the phone did not work, which was pretty usual in the postwar mess after heavy rains.

A yawning nurse informed her that the doctor was playing cards at the Hunter's Horn. Selma hated all the bars, but now she had no choice. The doctor had just left the tavern where there were only a couple of drunks, sleeping on the floors. The room stank of spilled, sugary, red wine.

Selma ran to another tavern that stayed open all night long, the Cellar. It was not supposed to stay open, according to the law, but since the police—and nearly everybody else—needed to drink in the wee hours, some bars stayed unofficially open.

And the doctor was there—a cigarette dangling from his lips, cards in his hands, a bottle of yellowish slivovitz on the table—surrounded by several yellow drunks.

The doctor was clearly ill-suited for his profession, good for nothing except the tavern. He had passed his university exams with the lowest passable grades and it had taken him more than a decade to get his degree, since his interests lay in tavern activities: drinking, cards, women, and, now and then, a brawl (though he brawled less and less frequently with his advancing age, but made up for that by whoring more and more routinely at the spa facilities). At the cardiology exam, he had cheated (his look-alike cousin took the exams for him), thus now his assistance to Ivan didn't promise much.

Dr. Rozic walked to Ivan's body. He touched Ivan's wrist and, finding no pulse there, quickly began to feel for it on Ivan's chest, and then, even more quickly, on his neck.

He put his stethoscope around his chin and osculated, sliding the cool mechanism beneath Ivan's shirt, around his nipple, and close to the sternum. The doctor tried to open Ivan's mouth to examine his tongue, but couldn't. He squeezed a thermometer into Ivan's mouth sideways, where a tooth was missing.

"Doctor, is there any hope?" Selma asked as the doctor waited for the temperature to register.

"There's always hope," replied the doctor.

The temperature was around ninety-two degrees Fahrenheit.

The doctor's thin flashlight shone into Ivan's eyes, and his hands slid Ivan's eyelids over them. He took off the stethoscope from his head slowly and dropped it onto his bag. He let his blue double chin rest on his collarbones. He had the dignified air of a general who has just received the news of his army's defeat. Clearly, the doctor had wasted his life; he would have done much better in the theater business, for there his talents lay—actually, he was attracted to taverns because they were theaters of sorts. The impression his acting made was devastating. Selma did not need to ask whether Ivan was dead: if a dignified physician like that reported he was dead, he must be. The physician pronounced his diagnosis—"He is dead"—in a deep and sonorous voice that shook Selma, and her skin tingled. She sobbed.

The doctor pulled out a form and routinely began to scratch out a death report in his jerky handwriting—a sine qua non feature of his profession—in a couple of copies, one for the customer, one for his records. "Died of unidentified causes." He laid Selma's copy onto the table. Selma's eyes were moist and her eyeballs pink. She bit her lower lip as if struggling to repress a stronger expression of her emotions. Seeing that, the doctor embraced her, paternally tapping her on her shoulder blades.

Suddenly he seemed to wake up from his routine performance, for he was very sensitive to female warmth. Under the guise of further solace, while saying, "Everything's gonna be all right," he began to touch the back of her neck and press her against his body.

In near delirium Selma hadn't paid any attention at first to the doctor's reassurances. Then shivers of fear began to mix with some warm streams. Quite freely she leaned her head on the physician's chest, and the physician began to rub his stubbly cheek against her hair, making her scalp shiver. He slid his hands down her back, "Everything's gonna be fine, fine," in his baritone. He buzzed these words into her ears, his breath sending a stream of voluptuous fire into the base of her brain, so that she lost her senses momentarily, and just at that moment, the doctor pressed his fingers into her flesh beneath her skirt, sliding his palms up the back of her cool thighs.

Selma began to gasp. The doctor pressed her against the table, and she sat right on the crumpling death certificate, which rustled most disapprovingly. The doctor's hand kneaded her thighs, and his fingers went into the foreign terrain, where beneath shrubbery they found some moist clay, which gave way, and the fingers searched the source of mossy delights. She moaned as if she were falling. The doctor kissed her. The mixture of tobacco and bacon with cognac in her nostrils and on her tongue triggered her senses back into full awareness. She pushed him away. "How did that happen? Aren't you ashamed?"

When the doctor moved aside, she saw her startled daughter in the doorway. "Go to your room, Daddy is ill, Uncle Doctor is going to cure him! He leaned over to consult with me in a whisper."

She despondently sat in the armchair and the doctor began to touch her gently. Selma stood up. "I must attend to him now—I must order a coffin, buy him a lot at the graveyard, call all the relatives, oh, so much all at once!"

"Hum," the doctor said cheerfully. "You could use my phone—or I could call the undertakers and ask about a lot." He was one of the first people in the town to have a Nokia. He didn't give out the number to the hospital because he didn't want to be disturbed when he was on call.

Selma walked out, woke up her mother, and asked her to take Tanya to the matinee of Disney cartoons at the cinema so Selma would have enough time to decide how to break the news to everyone.

The old woman began to wail. "Poor Ivan. Such a young man and to die of a heart attack!"

"Stroke I think it was," said Selma.

Selma ran to the post office—an old building in orange-yellow, the color of the deceased Hapsburg Empire—and filled out cablegrams with the shocking report.

Selma and her mother busied themselves, choosing the right shirt for Ivan to be buried in, the right shoes, and, as he had no black shoes, the mother suggested they should buy him a sturdy new pair. Selma was reluctant to spend money so impractically, so she painted his worn brown shoes black with their daughter's oil paints. The oil stayed wet for a long time.

Selma and her mother turned Ivan as they washed him with warm water and alcohol. They forced his stiff legs into his best underwear (business underwear) and his Sunday best as if he were about to undergo a very important interview. Tears fell from Selma's eyes onto his face. The mother-in-law muttered under her breath all kinds of sighs and statements about the difficulty of living and the unpleasantness of dying.

22

On the decline of bedside manners

Ivan had hoped the doctor would notice his shallow breathing and hear his heart beating. Ivan fixed his gaze on the blue ceiling. He could not change his focus. The blue pulsated in fluorescent concentric circles, oscillating between yellow and light purple.

After the doctor had come in, Ivan tried desperately to move, to make his breath deeper, and his heartbeat faster and stronger. When the doctor's hand touched his, Ivan was comforted; and when the doctor felt his forehead, even more so. Warm and paternal, the touch claimed that he was in good and strong hands.

The smooth cool metal surface of the stethoscope on Ivan's chest tickled him and inspired bursts of silent laughter in his mind, but his skin did not convulse, nor did a single muscle move. Although he strained his brain as much as he could to move his tongue and shout, his muscles did not stir. Maybe I've had a stroke?

The hazy circles on the ceiling pulsed, engulfed by spreading darkness. Suddenly the doctor's head appeared through the mist of blue: a big, unshaven chin, bloodshot eyes, dark and sagging eye-bags, a red nose with capillaries breaking into tiny purple creeks that curved around little greasy prominences with a little black spot atop each. The doctor's disinterested eyes revealed absentmindedness rather than the objectivity that he probably wished to express.

He is only pretending to look into my eyes! He's just waiting for some time to elapse to put Selma at ease!

The doctor's statement "He is dead!" reverberated in Ivan's head as if his skull were a big hallway from whose walls the sounds rebounded, furnishing exclamation to the statement and distorting the timing: "He is dead! dead eheheeheahaha-heeeesssssssss deadededededeeeess deade heee deaeadeeeeee!" He could make out the echoes into "he is dead, dead he is, he dead is." But in none of the permutations could he find "Is he dead?" The derisive "heheheheaheaaa" began to dominate and metamorphose into a laughter rising in frequency into a high-pitched "ehhhhhh." Ivan's mind was like a telecommunication receiver with speakers out of control, as if receiving some cosmic message from another galaxy: the galaxy of the DEAD.

And through the echoes, he heard Selma and the doctor pant with lust. Ivan was mortified with jealousy. How dare she—on his deathbed! But when Selma refused further advances from the doctor, he was more lenient. After all, let them, who cares!

Selma and Tanya came to see him. "Daddy is asleep, and he won't wake up anymore," said Selma.

Tanya shrieked.

Ivan was happy. "My daughter loves me! Who would have suspected it?"

His enthusiasm slackened as he, against his will, thought that she had screamed out of fright, not because of losing him. You can feel the terrifying reality of death when somebody close dies, not necessarily somebody you love but somebody you are used to as a part of your experience. When a part of your experience vanishes from life through death into a thing (to become nothing), you feel that just as that part of your experience vanishes, the totality of your experience—you yourself—will vanish into nothingness. So Tanya may have screamed for herself.

Selma, too, cried now, and said, "Ivan, Ivan, why are you leaving us?"

Maybe I am wrong, thought Ivan. Maybe they do feel sorry for me. They are sure I am dead. But what if I am dead? Maybe everybody is like this after death—sensing and thinking before disintegrating. What proof of being alive do I have? He panicked at the thought, yet his body retained the same imperturbability.

As Selma and her mother dressed Ivan, twisting his limbs, he suffered great pains. But the warm wet sponge wiping his skin soothed him. The hot tears that fell from Selma's eyes on his face sent shivers of warmth through Ivan. While Selma wiped the tears with her hair, Ivan felt loved as never before, and he loved, and suffered that he could not show it. He forgave her getting sexually excited with the doctor. Aren't Eros and Thanatos two sides of the same coin? "Orgasm is a little death"—death is a big orgasm. The way Selma behaved was natural. As far as big orgasms were concerned, however, he had yet to feel any pleasure from dying, if he was dying.

His brother, Bruno—who'd just flown in from West Germany—and his friend Nenad carried him out of his bed. Selma flung the door against the wall to open the way to the "living" room. Ivan thought they had dropped him onto a hard surface, a casket, judging by his shoulders banging against wood. He could smell the wood juices. Fir! Couldn't she buy at least an oak coffin? A fiberglass coffin or a hard plastic one would be far better, because it wouldn't rot. Damn Selma! She is saving on my death. The warm sensation of love crawled out of him through his cold nose and frosted nasal hairs.

Bruno and Nenad stared at the pale corpse, yawned, walked into the next room, and played chess, while Selma served them Turkish coffee and baked pies for the wake. The whiffs of coffee smelled good, enticing, and Ivan wished he could have a sip; he craved it, but to no avail, though he did feel a little more alert than before, out of sheer lack of fulfillment of his maddening desire. The players banged the pieces on the hollow board, and Ivan's coffin and body resonated with the bangs, as though he, too, were hollow. The players walked back to the living room, took the casket off the dining table—a Ping-Pong table—and put the casket on two chairs next to the window. Bruno and Nenad played Ping-Pong for a couple of hours, the balls now and then falling into the casket, hitting Ivan's nose and earlobe, which hurt, but he couldn't do much about it. The window was half open, and the wind tossed the curtains back and forth, tickling Ivan's nose, lips, and forehead, driving him crazy, or, rather, crazier than he already was. The men competed, sweated, swore, and quarreled about the score.

"Twenty–nineteen," Bruno said.

"No, it's twenty–twenty!" exclaimed Nenad.

"It was twenty–eighteen last time, remember, I served a topspin backhand, and you missed."

"That was the time before last. Your memory is going."

"You never had it, that's why you imagine."

"Let's play the point over again!"

"So, you admit it. But I am in a good mood, considering I trounced you in chess."

"We should play by the new rules, up to eleven, and I was ahead at eleven. Your playing is so boring that I can't concentrate up to twenty-one. And look, you are using the old-regulation balls, and I'm not used to that, don't you know that the balls are now larger, two millimeters more in diameter."

"Excuse me, no excuses! Be a good sport, a good loser."

Ivan winced in his coffin—mentally, that is; physically he couldn't move. I am dead, and my brother's in a good mood!

"The first three games were a warm-up, but when it really counted, I showed you," Nenad said.

"I beat you three to two. So, I have the generosity to let you replay a lost point."

And the ball continued bouncing and the men panting.

"Touched!" Bruno shouted.

"No, it didn't."

"I saw. You were out of position, below the table."

"You are nearsighted."

"Your mother's nearsighted."

"Don't touch my dead mother!"

"I wouldn't be the first."

"*Ustasha* pig!"

"Chetnik!"

The childhood friends reverted to childhood and broke into a fistfight, cutting their lips and knocking out porcelain tooth-caps (well, that part was an improvement on childhood), which they then looked for, in a temporary truce, on all fours in the floor cracks.

After finding the teeth—none had fallen into Ivan's nostrils or shirt collar—the men readjusted the caps on solidified silver posts, clacked with their tongues loudly to test the teeth, and, while exchanging further insults, carried the casket back to the table; the casket slid from their sweaty palms and hit the sofa, without cracking. Ivan's head hurt from being banged against the casket wood.

They treat me like some kind of clutter, Ivan thought. They worry about dead mothers! Shouldn't it be *my* day?

As though the players heard him, they took a look at him.

"He looks pretty good, doesn't he?" Nenad said. "He's not bloating up or stinking too bad. I mean, no more than usual."

"These intellectuals," Bruno said. "When alive, they look dead, and when they're dead they look alive."

When Selma placed two lit candles near Ivan's head, he felt solace from the flames—and Selma's warm breath on his cheeks.

The warm signs of life seemed so simple that he wished he could live. He would know how to enjoy the simple pleasures of life. Now he could love, too. And while making love, he would spend more time on foreplay and afterplay than on the coitus itself.

He felt a strange, stinging substance placed into his nostrils and his ears. His face was lubricated with something that smelled of death and murder. Everything living in him, even his bacteria, was being exterminated. Panic and despair permeated the marrow of his bones, assuming the two moods could go together despite panic being more optimistic in outlook than despair.

He grew used to the chemicals and soon couldn't smell them. Since you can't panic for long, he no longer panicked, and weariness and even boredom set in. Intoxicated by his shallow breathing, Ivan slumbered.

Something crashed on the floor—perhaps the coffee cup Bruno had drained—and woke him up. Tanya whispered. Ivan wondered whether she grieved for him. Will the house seem empty to her when she comes back from the funeral?

He was surprised that the love of his child mattered to him so much now. But since he was rid of vanities, he could acknowledge that love was what he cared about. He regretted that his kid had not come close; she whispered low to Selma as if afraid to "wake" him, make him alive again—would not that be terrifying? It's sometimes frightening to wake up a sleeping person, and it would be even more so to wake up a dead one.

Then Tanya sobbed so softly and sweetly that Ivan's heart fluttered.

The wood creaked in various frequencies. Many people gathered in the room, whispering. The hissing of the whispers terrified Ivan as if a giant octopus's limbs were engulfing him. Some whispers were no whispers, since some people were incapable of whispering. "When did he die? How?"

"Heart attack."

"Stroke."

"Cirrhosis of the liver, I heard."

"Could be, he did drink too much."

"That's how his father died, too. Runs in the genes."

"Not only his. The whole nation is dying of liver problems, I'm telling you."

"No, it's the war. Hell, more people have died of the post-traumatic stress–related diseases than from bullets."

"Nonsense. Pretraumatic stress is what it is—because the country and all its citizens are bankrupt, and are preoccupied with what will happen to them two years from now, they don't see the curve in the road right ahead of them, and bang, they're gone."

"If he'd kept drinking slivovitz, he'd still be all right, I am sure. The trouble with vodka is that it doesn't feel like anything, so you can drink a whole bottle without vomiting or your throat burning. Slivovitz won't let you do that—when you drink it, you know you are drinking."

"You are right about that. After two glasses, your stomach is on fire, and after three, you are vomiting. That's a good safety check built right into the drink. God's wisdom is in the plums— that's how He takes care of us. You don't have to worry about self-control there. Oh good, where did you get that? *Na zdravlje!*"

The sound of glass clicking and gulping ensued.

"That's wonderful! *Na zdravlje!*"

Then people moved on into the dining room, and their murmur reflected a communal relief at being away from the corpse. Ivan could make out some words now and then, "Vacation . . . to Trieste? . . . Opel Corsa is no match for Vectra . . . Suker should have scored again . . . wool . . . the black market rate . . . convertible currency . . . Hungarian pork chops." Glasses clanked; the aroma of slivovitz wafted past Ivan's nose out the window, and the steam of walnut strudels seeped through the cotton into his nose, filling his sticky throat with saliva. It hurt Ivan that his death was an excuse for a cocktail party to which he was not invited.

He thought that around him, out of respect for death, the visitors wouldn't say anything embarrassing—and honest— about him. Too bad I can't hear what they really think. Still, aren't I lucky? Most men after dying couldn't hear their wives and kids cry for them—either for love or terror. And I've heard mine. But I do hate hearing that people think I was a drunk. Sure, I'd love a drink of wine right now but who wouldn't, in my place? Actually, a shot of cognac would be much better, since my mouth feels sticky.

Ivan recalled his childhood daydreams about how it would be if he died right then, how sorry his friends would feel for him. He had thought that suicide was worth committing just to elicit compassion from his friends. The desire for suicide stemmed from a vague impression that after death you could be present at a gathering of your lamenting friends; their sorrow would beautifully uplift you into the oceanic infinity. If you knew that you would be missed among the living, life would become lovable, and so would death. As a boy, Ivan had known that that line of thought about suicide was grounded in bad faith. You have to be actually alive to hear and to believe—there's no postmortem experiencing.

And now Ivan did hear people's reactions to his death. It was fantastic. His life had been worth living just for this moment! And so what if they had a good time? Better so than misery.

The visitors left, and after them remained a macabre silence. Fumes of wax filled the dark. Ivan's bliss dissolved into a consolation that he had been loved, and the consolation decayed into melancholy. From the boiling wax and human breath that lingered, and perhaps from his condition, he got hot flashes in his scalp and forehead.

The candles glimmered. His visual screen was changing through all the nuances of brown, nuances of the soil out of which he was made, and it seemed that the art of dying, in dusty pastel hues, was being enacted right there—dust was turning to dust, in this beautiful and hazy and horrifying preview. The browns were becoming dustier and dustier, less and less substantial. He was turning into dust, which would be blown over the horizon unless it was contained in a good coffin.

23

It is never too late for theology

Before your death, you are supposed to see your life played out as a movie. And now, Ivan saw no rerun, though he wanted to. Maybe the death has to be sudden and convincing, for a mental show like that. He could not re-create pictures in his mind, and when he finally did form some vague outlines, they appeared dark and brown, like photographs from the time of great-grandfathers, with long, rolled mustaches and enormous trousers. Some pictures appeared on an empty screen, as though on a photographic plate bathed in the right chemicals, but as the vague outlines appeared, they quickly darkened. He could not take the photographic paper out of the developer, and so the picture faded into the dark brown, and the forms vanished. If only he could improve his focus! He tried to visualize.

Maybe there's something to the power of positive thinking. His pictures were improving. He saw Selma's eyes from the time of their first meeting: large black pupils surrounded by a hazel flame. The light brown fire would not burn him but could warm him. He now tried to jump through the wreath of hazel fire, through the broadening blackness of her pupils, into her soul. He would have to be a tiger from the circus of love to be able to jump into the black beyond of love. He had never been the tiger, not even now.

How strange that I am seeing her eyes! I haven't looked into her eyes for years. She had seemed so ubiquitous, so banal; he had gladly looked into the eyes of other women, no matter how little they looked into his, but into hers? For minutes he recalled her eyes, so beautiful and sad, and, besides, so . . . so elemental, so indifferent . . . so . . . and the reminiscence vanished, leaving him more dispirited than before.

Ivan thought that the last day of his life had come—the last chance to think something essential. He now had leisure and no distractions, no worries about how to make ends meet (his ends would meet soon enough). Now he could think honestly. He did not need to worry about whether his thoughts were presentable, clever. No need to worry about politics anymore. What a relief! His death would be his own and nobody else's—a private event outside the scope of socializing and nationalizing. In his coffin there would be no spying, intimidation, balkanization, propaganda, ideology, war taxation—nobody could disturb him. He was free to think about what really mattered—death, eternal life, soul, God.

If my body dies, will I be able to exist on the basis of the soul that I neither know nor feel? What is the soul? What is thinking in me? Is my body's biochemistry running this verbal flux and awareness of "I"? Or is there a spiritual, totally insubstantial, soul? Or is the soul made of some fine particles and electromagnetic waves that don't depend on the blood and the heart and the body at all, but which initiate thought and are made of thought and ideas? If the soul is made of something different from the body, when the body rots, the soul might fare differently—live on?

But this is not thinking. I am only asking questions and venturing no answers. Well, let me try again. Where was I? Well, where am I, and, for that matter, where will I be? Some people believe that the soul lives many lives, and that almost all of us have already lived before. If I had lived before, am I now the same I as the I in a previous life? I remember nothing of my previous life. Since I remember nothing and know nothing of it, I cannot care about it. So what difference would a future life make to me, if the future-I couldn't remember the present-I and the present-I's life? Well, the point is not to worry, but to be consoled—or con-souled? Am I consoled?

Pleased that he had thought for at least a couple of seconds, though not pleased with the vague result of his thinking, Ivan relaxed, and he wasn't sure whether he was awake or asleep when he heard some voices: Dr. Rozic's baritone and his wife's contralto. Good deal, he thought. They haven't given up on me!

The doctor and Selma closed the door. "Oh, it's so hard," Selma said.

Poor Selma, she's suffering without me.

"Harder," she gasped.

Doctor Rozic panted and lifted her onto the table. The same inaccurate death certificate rustled. She ripped his pants and tore his shorts. She climbed him; he carried her, her legs intertwined behind his back, and knocked her against the cupboards, the wood cracking, family albums and documents falling from the top, flying and gliding as though an airplane had tossed leaflets with instructions on how to surrender to an invading army. A paper brushed Ivan's nose, upsetting a couple of hairs that stuck out so that they itched him. Is that my birth certificate? Ivan wondered. Selma pushed the doctor to the floor, and sat on him, riding him and squealing as though in a Slavonian dance, while Rozic yelled filthy curses, since his tailbone was being banged on the floor. Then she sat leaning against the coffin and Rozic shook against her. They groaned when they came, pushing the coffin, which fell on the floor.

Ivan's head once again hit the coffin wood above his pillow; he felt as though his skull had cracked in half; his shoulder, ribs, and hips felt broken. The lovers lifted his coffin, their hands smelling of blood, sperm, and sweat, and slid it back on the table. Ivan raged, but all too quietly, and then he wasn't sure whether he was awake or not—his pain left him, and he was alone.

Don't I need God now? God is famous for helping in bed—deathbed.

As an adult, for the most part, Ivan had not believed in God because he couldn't imagine Him. (Sometimes, when fear over-came him, for example during the war, he had become religious and he found that prayer could soothe him.) Now he thought that even if there was God, whether Ivan Dolinar—an insignifi-cant human being—believed should be a matter of total indif-ference to God—unless He was in the same predicament as Ivan: hankering for any trace of love and faith to give Him the sensation of being alive in the face of empty eternity.

I would be happy if a cat or a mouse or a fly were scared of me. That would tell me that I was alive! If a mosquito believed I was alive and wanted to bite me, that would mean so much to me!

Maybe for God, too, it would suffice if a mosquito truly believed in His existence and tried to bite Him! That might be all He is looking for.

Suddenly he felt sympathy for God.

I wish I had read more of the Bible after my childhood. Maybe some insight would have come to me—I could try to understand something from the text if I could remember it word for word. But I do remember my favorite verses from Ecclesiastes: "For that which befalleth the sons of men befalleth beasts; even one thing befalleth them: as the one dieth, so dieth the other; yea, they have all one breath; so that a man hath no preeminence above a beast: for all is vanity. All go unto one place; all are of the dust, and all turn to dust again. Who knoweth the spirit of man that goeth upward, and the spirit of the beast that goeth downward to the earth?" If the Bible writ-ers could not believe in the soul of man, how could I, as igno-rant as I am, be brazen to believe more than they, that I have a soul? And if men had no soul then, they certainly would not have it now, since the world is in constant moral decay, accord-ing to the Bible, and according to Socrates as well.

What is Christianity? A tool for controlling the masses or a soul-saving revelation? Why should there be Jesus, if there was already God? God & Son, Inc. God is too old, so his son runs the business. The son runs the business by appearing to be terri-bly poor, while He is the owner or one of the major shareholders of the universe. He arouses further sympathy, to win votes, by dying, though He is eternal, a cocreator and upholder of the universe. How can I believe in this stuff? In politics, if I saw the richest man in the world walking in rags and running for an office, I'd be extremely suspicious about his plans. And isn't the Bible full of contradictions? To what peoples could have Cain gone, if he was a member, a son, of the first family on earth?

He concentrated on Something, a bright circle. Soon, however, he grew scared that he could be condemned as an idolater, worshiping the sun god Ra. He lost the strength to imagine bright circles. He ceased imagining God, but only conceived of Him as of something unimaginable, like the imaginary number, which, he thought, nobody could imagine.

He could not conceive of God.

It occurred to him to utter some basic credo anyway. Ivan prayed and chanted—mentally, since he could not move his lips—"I believe in God, I believe in God, I believe in God, and whoever believes in God shall be saved." Then, after a silence, his effort struck him as horribly futile.

24

A drunken band looks for the
right pitch of a funeral dirge

Ivan heard the Japanese clock hiss over and over again, slowly and inexorably. The candles had gone out. The darkness scared him even more than when he was a child. He would have screamed if he could have.

He could neither fall asleep nor stay alert. It seemed to him that he had thought about God as much as he could, even beyond his capabilities, without any profit to his soul, but if there was God, the One would have to be satisfied with his endeavor. The religious reflections vanished into an amorphous haze, a chaos, beyond thought.

Wild animals leaped at him from the dark. A leopard treed him. Many hissing snakes chased him up a steep hill; he stumbled over stones. The snakes crept after him relentlessly.

Ivan recoiled from the nightmares and sank into another one. A bluish light like a welding fire illuminated his mind, and his body tingled as if he were a part of an electrical stream. He shivered in fear, or dreamed that he shivers.

A violent hammering in the wood broke Ivan's nightmares. The lid of his coffin was being nailed shut. The sounds of hammering, contained, thundered as if the nails were being hammered directly into his ears.

The hammering over, he heard sobbing. He was not sure that it was not yet another nightmare, and wished it were.

After a while he had a sensation of being lifted and swayed.

Then he was keeled into a steep angle and shaken abruptly. They are carrying me down the stairs!

A screeching sound indicated to him that his coffin was sliding on the hearse floor. He heard a neighing and the murmur of a crowd. Horses and their hooves had always made him uncomfortable, as messengers of death—and now they were.

Soon there was rough movement. His casket popped up an inch or so and slammed back onto the carriage floor. The wheels ground the gravel on the road, reminding him of placing stones on the railroad tracks to derail trains and of the glassy dust after the trains—he had enjoyed squeezing the larger stone particles into his skin until it bled. And now he was a passenger on a derailed coach.

He heard the brass band making saddening mixtures of tones. The music seemed to be in the twelve-tonal system—many superfluous sounds roamed and hesitated, looking for their homes. The nomadic tones now and then all got together in a rally, blasting out the most spine-chilling harmony. Then, the tones retreated into deep, empty, aspirated and exasperated blowing, to emerge into moans. Ivan visualized the musicians' rounded faces—red from wine and abstinence from breathing, veins protruding on their foreheads, amidst green uniforms. The rhythm was being broken and reestablished in the same breath; the tones lost one another, and then rushed back lest they should be left behind and lost. Unintentional jazz.

Fond of brass music in their Germanized tradition, the old Czechs blessed Ivan's wish to have jazz at his funeral. In taverns Ivan had often proclaimed that he would like to have jazz at his funeral, and there it was—albeit slow—improvised and thoughtful. What beatitude! He could listen to his own funeral music!

When the musicians took a break, he again heard the grinding of stones below the carriage wheels. As the wheels shook, he felt the wood outside and his bones inside. The wood and the bones squeezed his mortified flesh mercilessly. In a jolt, his body jumped up a dozen millimeters from the bottom of the coffin and freely fell while the coffin rebounded from the cart.

Each place that the coach had passed was behind him, dead to him. Only as much of the town and of his life remained as the distance between him and his grave pit. He wanted to jump out and run in the streets and climb trees like a child. He should try to end his hysterical state now that he had no reason to fear life. If he succeeded, could he scream? Wasn't he too self-conscious even now to scream? Wouldn't that be beautiful? Shrieks coming right out of the casket! The superstitious crowd's hearts would burst.

He cheered up a little at the thought that the procession had to swallow the dirt-road dust, and he wished that those absent from the procession would swallow even more dust. Maybe some dust came from the human corpses that had died thousands of years ago? Or even from the living? He had read that most dust in city rooms comes from people's shedding layers of their skin. It struck him as wonderful that dust on unread crumbling Bibles came from humans. Dust to the dust-touting book.

When the coffin ceased to shake, Ivan guessed that the hearse had reached the asphalted Lenin Street, renamed Tudjman Boulevard. He felt like a voyager on a ship that passes from a stormy sea into a bay calmed with spilled oil, where all waves are choked—a kind of Persian Gulf, the "serenity" of the region spilling gently over into the sea. Ivan doubted that he had any chance of becoming a uniform black liquid, useful for precisely the functions at which he had failed—work and mobility.

Ivan thought that his head was closer to the horses than were his feet; the head would enter the graveyard first and the feet last—like a runner jumping through the finishing line.

Blood flowed into his head, so pressure built up in his ears. We are going downhill, and my head is lower than my feet, I was right about that. The school park is on my left. He recalled the fights he used to have on the grass, how he had tried to squeeze his opponents' necks enough to weaken them so they wouldn't recover right away once he let them go—otherwise, they'd try to strangle him.

We are passing by the gym. Ivan used to suffer there, twisting his body into an array of geometric shapes on various stretchers that looked as though they belonged to the Spanish Inquisition. The phys-ed teacher piously read manuals on gymnastics before ordering children to turn upside down, stand on their heads, swing on the parallel bars. Each exercise demonstrated the truth—that the children were heretics to the Holy Discipline of Obedience.

On the right side Ivan envisioned a long building of the textile factory—rows and rows of sad women behind long machines. Ivan used to peep through the window down into the overheated factory basement at the sight of horror, communal labor.

The coffin continued to shake steadily in little jerks, the iron-belted wheels rasping on the Roman-style gray-blue cobbles. The Roman Catholic church stood where the cobbles began. Ivan used to visit the cave of God to shake with the eerie organ vibrations that mercilessly shook the pillars and the benches to portray the horror-inspiring mercy of the Lord.

And a block down the street stood a yellow Orthodox church, where on Saint Stephen's day elderly, silver-toothed Serbs in the churchyard had let him dip bread in the fat that had dripped from roasting pigs. He chewed the heavy, salty bread with charcoal blood, enjoying the melting of bread and blood on his tongue. In a few minutes, he grew queasy, and he leaned against the cool wall of the church and vomited. In his passing out, the yellow clouds flew quickly past the rusty steeple so that he had the impression that the church was falling onto him, about to crush him. He felt nauseated and dizzy even now, in his coffin.

But he also had good recollections from the churchyard. A deep well nursed water colder than ice—impossible, but that's what it felt like. Moss padded the bricks, and far down you could see liquid blackness with sporadic silvery flickers. Ivan used to let the bucket drop into the water and sink deep, and then he'd turn the spindle wheel until the thick rope lifted the fresh bucket within his reach. Tightened and coiled, the rope made crunching sounds like the grinding of teeth. Ivan dipped his face in the water and gulped the coolness, his eyes open, gazing at the aged wood's grains made larger, clearer, and closer through the water. Now Ivan grew thirsty in the coffin.

The empty church—as Communists, most Serbs didn't want religion to compromise them—had its own, wooden smell. Your eyes closed, you felt you were in the woods and not in a building. Burning candles twisted and melted in the heat, like a group of emaciated old men and women in white, dripping tears on the snowy ground; the flames, like the Pentacost tongues, licked the low sky, gulping its oxygen, and uttered silence.

On his right was now the library, a long building, where Ivan had once noticed a Hungarian girl with a long, flowery mouth and deep, emerald eyes. She lived in an annex of a desolate Lutheran church full of bats, cobwebs, rats, broken furniture, and sultry darkness. Her grandfather used to be a minister, but after the war no Lutherans remained in the town, except for him. To feed his family in the postwar famine, he hid in the steeple, catching shitty pigeons with his bare hands. Her lips always shone so smoothly that Ivan could nearly see his image on them, turned upside down; anyhow, her lips had turned his wits upside down. Near the library Ivan had a sudden yearning to impress her. He jumped onto the high wall along the library and ran to the tall end, at nearly two meters high. Ivan planned to jump, his hands in his pockets, and continue running on the ground in the same way. He timed everything perfectly. On the run, he whistled a spaghetti-Western tune nonchalantly. He didn't notice a rusty piece of metal sticking out of the concrete wall, which, like most things in Constructive Socialism, was not quite finished. He tripped and flew. While trying to free his hands from his pockets, he couldn't pay enough attention to balancing himself in the air. He fell straight on his head. But it's never too late. Ivan sprang up from the ground, his hands still in his pockets, and ran off, whistling the same tune. If he'd missed the opportunity to show what tremendous control his brain exercised over his body, at least he had shown that his skull was hard indeed.

A month later he had seen the Hungarian girl kissing a policeman three times her age behind a large beech in the park. Thus Ivan's hatred for the police had started early.

Now he wondered whether there were any policemen at his funeral.

In the coffin, the ride became smooth—asphalt again. We are in the Marshal Tito Square—well, it used to be called that. What was it now? He couldn't remember; he never paid attention to how the new politicians changed the nomenclature. On his left, Ivan felt the presence of the county offices where clerks drank smudgy coffee, shuffled cards, gossiped, and stared through the windows, while the public waited and coughed in the cement corridors littered with spittoons, next to which, usually, some old tubercular smoker dripped yellow spittle from his cracked mouth.

Ivan visualized: white stripes came down the county building from swallows' nests; faces from his past drifted by; people leaned against traffic posts with their hands in their pockets; bony drunks, their flies unzipped, staggered along a wall, singing ditties to Tito and the Party; a wedding party climbed into horse-drawn carriages—accordion and tambourine music, and sturdy horses lift their tails to drop smoking, green dung on the pavement, and the flushed, tomato-faced bride and the pale, egg-faced bridegroom ride home to lie with each other and live.

And I ride in a smaller cart, to lie in wedlock with maggots and die.

The hearse hit cobblestones again—Nikola Tesla Street. Ivan saw in his mind the blue house of the chief of police, the steps where he'd fallen naked. He was ashamed even now. The policeman should be even more ashamed, that after becoming a murderer he should run for a political office—on the other hand, what better qualification for politics should one have than a proof that he's willing to commit murder?

On the left stretched a redbrick building with thick doors, Cinema of May First, where Ivan had seen his first movie: a black train rushed headlong, larger and larger. Ivan, terrified that the train would crash into the audience, rushed out. He was surprised that he saw no hole on the outside of the building where the train had entered.

Later, he used to break into the cinema through the basement, climbing over firewood; through the back of the canvas screen he stared at the reversed images. A short-tempered, chain-smoking janitor—who was dried up like a salted herring—watched out for him, trying to catch him before he would run off into the audience in the dark.

The town park followed, with hot springs where he used to take baths, once per month, in large, Turkish oval pools. Ivan used to insert his penis into the tub holes so the whirling water would give him dizzying orgasms. With his softened thumbnails he scratched holes in the thick window paint so that later he could peep at the naked female bathers from the outside. And there were many lonely female bathers coming to town for the mineral baths, to cure their infertility.

On his left the town market murmured: peasants and artisans sold their live chickens, geese, rabbits, turkeys, garlic, watermelons, wool socks, rugs, clogs, brass pots, sheepskin jackets; people swarmed, scrutinizing the merchandise, argued loudly for a lower price, tapped one another on the shoulders, shook hands, unfolded bills, clicked coins.

Ivan slumbered. A bang startled him. The hearse passed over the railroad tracks in four jolts. He remembered how his bicycle wheel got crumpled when he hit the tracks at high speed after a downhill run—he'd flown off and scraped skin off his elbows and knees and forehead and nose.

The Czech band played the sad music again, capturing the essence of grief and missing everything else. Sorrow gripped Ivan, supplanting the fear, as if somebody else were to be buried, and he listened to the muffled trumpet grunts.

But his sorrow was more a torpor than an emotion. He had exhausted his emotional life. That he could not be passionate anymore was one more reason to grow even sadder, but he stayed melancholy.

The horses drew the carriage up a steep incline, so that Ivan's corpse-to-be slid, his feet pressing against the wood. When the balance changed and Ivan's head hit the wood on the other end, Ivan knew that he had passed over the top of the hill. Brakes screeched against the wheels, wood against the metal frame.

25

Mud to mud

The carriage squeaked and trembled on the uneven approach to the cemetery. It was stuffy in the coffin, although his wife and the doctor had cracked the coffin during their violent sex. Ivan heard dull moans. Even if the people wept in fear of their own deaths and of the grave pit, he liked their weeping. He was not jealous of their self-pity. After all, the grave would be his home, and soon his flesh would melt into the mud; the grave and he would be one and the same thing.

The carriage stopped, the coffin slid forward. The horses snorted as if they would be pushed into the hole.

Ivan felt uneven waves. He must be on the shoulders of several men of unequal heights. He wondered who carried him. He had never been a pallbearer himself, but he had carried Peter's fresh, pre–rigor mortis corpse to the ambulance. He felt seasick. Ivan imagined that he had heard wood colliding; his coffin was pushed onto a plank of wood above the grave, and ropes slid beneath his coffin. The space below him emptied all his blood vessels of the last traces of hope. A sucking vacuum of terror began to swallow him into the black hole of his imagination, into antimatter. His guts froze.

The casket was lowered into the pit unsteadily, with a loud buzzing of the ropes, as if a saw were cutting the wood. The sound reverberated through the wood; the wood trembled like his own thick skin. Now one side was higher, now another. Suddenly he felt acceleration in his skin and flesh as when an elevator rushes down, his blood lingering in the upper parts of his body, in his nose, eyes, lips, penis, knees, toes. The casket crashed against the bottom of the grave.

He imagined a shriek from the outside, but he was not sure.

The outside was ceasing to be. After some quiet, clumps show-ered his casket. They bumped against the wood, first loudly and then more and more softly, as the earth thickened above him. Then only a dull thudding of shoveled soil, and then it grew quiet, except for a few choked sounds from above, as if a storm were brewing somewhere far away, and the ground carried the waves of thunder, like a murmur, through the ocean of soil.

And then it was quiet. A grave silence. Not a sound. Nothing.

During the funeral he could see himself as thinly shut off from the world, but in it. Now he had lost all links with the external world. There were no sounds of life outside to deny the death inside, no jolts over railroad tracks to trigger memory chains.

Even if his hysterical paralysis were over, he could not scream for help—anyway, nobody would hear him.

Maybe I am dead. Maybe I've been dead for a long time. I thought it before and did not really believe it. And now how could I believe anymore that I am alive? Maybe the dead go on, never fully believing they are dead. Maybe death is a state of total skepticism. Maybe I will spend my whole eternity hesitat-ing between the two doubted poles, death and life, two versions of one illusion.

It became steamy in the casket. He would have slumbered into death if it hadn't been cold. He would have shivered if his muscles could have moved. He shivered mentally. He felt water at the bottom of the leaking coffin. Ivan damned Selma for buy-ing the cheapest sort of coffin she could find. But maybe the low quality of the casket had prolonged his life—if he was alive. Air had leaked through the cracks, in the procession. But now he would suffocate.

Will a nation of worms creep in and gnaw at me? But could worms live in the cold, wet soil? Worms eating solidly buried corpses is merely a product of morbid imagination. Sure, mag-gots would eat bodies in mud days after battles, and in shallow graves in the summer, but not in the frozen soil. There are no worms here.

That he would rot he could not doubt, however. He had brought along a good supply of homegrown aerobic and anaerobic bacteria. They could feast on him and multiply all over him, from the tip of his nose to the long nails on his toes, from his ears, through the pipes, hoses, and strings of his body—throat, neck, trachea, esophagus, intestines, rectum, blood vessels, white nerves. Water soaked his back. From dust to dust doesn't describe it. From mud to mud.

Would his bones last a millennium? He doubted it. The human skeletons crisscrossed the soft, slippery clay ground, holding the hill from sliding down into the valley, like a system of old tree roots. The hill had grown like a baby with human bones, firmer and firmer. The hill stood above the town, a giant dog, a Charon, crunching bones every afternoon. The bones rotted slowly, unlike those in dry sand and more like the Dead Sea Scrolls, which lasted longer than any culture, language, and even longer than many gods, certainly longer than the Greek gods, who had perished in a theological genocide driven by Byzantium. But these muddy bones in the Pannonian valley would crumble and turn into mud in brief centuries, the way the old western Slavic gods did, so thoroughly that no trace remained of their religion, other than the mud, soil, Slavic soil, and, therefore, gods from the dry regions had to be imported to replace the more perishable Slavonic gods. How could we last and survive for long, he thought, when we couldn't even create gods that would last, and so, for lack of anything better, we believed in dictators, risen to the stature of divinity. Tito was our only god, in my era, and his gangrene, a form of infested rot, best represented the quality of our religiosity, our putrid stigmata.

He regretted now that he had not sold his body to a medical school so that he would have been kept out of the soil—dissected and gently cut by the trembling hands of nervous first-year medical students. They would stand around in stuffy air, silently farting—not glamorous—but Ivan could have used the little money the school would have paid him. He could have, if nothing else, visited a whorehouse in a large city. That might have been better than his seducing—or being seduced by—Svjetlana.

What would come of his bones? He recalled how, as a child in a summer-vacation camp on the coast, he had wandered into a bunker and found several human skulls and hundreds of ribs. He had embraced the skull and run back to the camp, stumbling over bones and stones, his feet mangled, as if the bones remaining behind would piece themselves together and run after him with scythes to cut off his legs, so he would fall on the ground like grass. He had hung the bones at the entrance to his tent, transforming the tent into a boat of pirates. The camp director had expelled him from the camp, for disrespecting the dead and for raising the question of who the skeletons were.

Now the dry skull grinned at him wryly, the jaws clanking, showing brown tooth-holes. The large, empty eye orbits loomed. The skull grew ever larger, gazing stupidly, bringing forth senseless Nothing. Out of the broken ridges of its nose a putrid wind gusted into his lungs. The wind gusts turned around, picked him off the ground, and sucked him into the nasal passages. He crashed against the crooked bones and floated into the darkness through a hole into a big space of the cranium. Weightless and frozen, he was trying to inhale air, hoping there was air. But the space of the cranium was a vacuum. His lungs bloated like a balloon of spongy flesh to dissolve into a tepid yellowish slush. In the putrid dissolution, Ivan was hallucinating and swooning beyond.

26

It's never too early for a dig

Ivan's colleague from work, the jovial joker Paul, staggered into the cemetery. That evening he had been to the Cellar, where the bartender, Nenad, sorrowfully told him the details of Ivan's death.

"Man, can you imagine, his brother from Germany hadn't visited him in two years. And now that capitalist Yugo-Schwaba felt guilty. And what does he do with his guilt? He takes a precious pocket watch from the eighteenth century and puts it in his brother's pants, in the coffin. The watch could tell you the phases of the moon, astrological phases of the sky, the positions of the planets, and Good Lord knows what else. The whole thing is made of gold and rubies. Eh, what a fool his brother is to part with such a precious thing. It must be worth thousands of euros!"

"Come on, quit your bullshit!" People laughed at Nenad because they knew that Nenad spread tall tales for the hell of it. Some drunks were tempted to believe him, but they feared ghosts, and no thought of treasure would entice them to dig up a grave at night, especially not a grave of someone just buried. Going to dig up this grave required one to believe this unlikely story, and not to believe other unlikely stories—ghost stories—which would be a unique mind-set of selective credulousness. Paul's mind was selectively credulous, under the influence of greed and alcohol.

"I thought he'd be buried with his violin."

"I am glad you mentioned it," Nenad said. "You know, none of us thought much of his violin, and he never boasted. I peeped in once and saw a snaky S written inside. I didn't think anything of it then, but now I am sure it stands for Stradivarius. The fact that the violin's neck and head look like an angry snake only confirms that—the snake shares the initial with Stradivarius, *serpentina,* or whatever it is in Italian. So that was another way of signing the signature."

"Incredible! And that he'd never cashed the violin in . . ."

"He may not have known himself what it was."

"Do all the Stradivariuses look like that?"

"No, I think this one was unique. Probably it was made for Paganini or someone else with demonic powers . . . some prince of darkness."

By the time Nenad finished his speech, tears flowing down his cheeks for the treasures buried with his friend, Paul had rushed out of the bar to retrieve the violin and the gold watch. Carried away by his own story, Nenad was tempted to run out, too.

Paul went into his workshop, grabbed a shovel, flashlight, a pair of pliers, a hammer, and a chisel. He drove to the cemetery in his old Yugo.

As he began to dig he whistled. "Green Grass Around My Home" by Tom Jones. In several hours he reached the casket and soon cleared the ground around it enough to open the lid. He hammered the chisel into the wood, cracked the casket open, overthrew the lid, and grabbed Ivan's cold hands.

Cool air streamed into Ivan's nostrils. Warm hands moved his blood. Taking himself to be dead, he had lost the fear of life and the fear of death—the causes of his hysterical paralysis, or, medically more aptly described, his electronic cardiac arrest. He began to draw air in. Paul didn't notice it; his flashlight made him blind to everything that was outside its focus. Paul searched in a frenzy. No watch in any pockets. None on the hands, calves, legs. The only thing he found beneath the pillow was the New Testament. He pulled it out, leafed through the thin flimsy pages, and put it back into the inner jacket pocket. He sat lazily on the side of the coffin and drank slivovitz from a flask.

Ivan was not sure whether what he heard, felt, and saw was a hallucination. He was so numb that he had the sensation of a swarm of ants covering his skin and marching over it and beneath it. His body was asleep.

When Paul lifted him and pushed him around in the coffin, Ivan wished to shout, but had no strength to. He inhaled more and more deeply and stared into the dark clouds—blindingly bright to him. He tried to lift his head and could not do it, tried again and could not do it. He kept trying, because he felt a stirring in his muscles. He managed to raise his right arm a little. That excited him; his heart began to beat perceptibly, he drew breath loudly, raised his arm almost fully. He lifted his head, changing the angle of his vision, and noticed Paul sitting near his legs with a bottle in his mouth. The sight, far from scaring him—for what could scare him, after all?—gave him a warm sensation, a hope. Ha, look at this! A man! Is that a dream or a man? Am I really seeing? Yes, yes, look!

Ecstatically he gazed at the man and, wanting to embrace him, he called out softly, gently, with love—that is, he wished to do it with love—"Brother!" But his superhuman efforts produced only a subhuman hissing and growling that blended into the whistling of the wind and hooting of owls far away.

Uncomfortable with the sounds, Paul climbed out of the grave and slid back into it, and he rushed, trying again, because the sounds were making him more and more uncomfortable. He grabbed a tree root that was sticking out and lifted himself out. Angrily he gulped more slivovitz and then began to shovel the soil back into the grave, not because he feared that his deed would be found out but so that someone else would be disappointed in the same way. He was sure the whole town would line up to dig into the grave for the hidden treasures. That would serve them right. That low-life no-goodnik Nenad, he'll have to pay for this.

A shovelful of soil hit Ivan in the head. His head banged against the wood, and Ivan lost consciousness—by now he was used to it.

27

A taste of soil in the nostrils

When Ivan came to, he tasted soil in his nose and mouth—the shovelful of soil had hit him just as he was opening his mouth to say something.

Moaning from a headache, Ivan tried to crawl out of the coffin. He rolled over the edge and stood up, gradually, first on all fours, and then into a homo erectus bipedal position. He stepped onto the coffin, swearing at his wife because he realized that the coffin was not as cheap as he had earlier imagined. It was varnished and slippery. Repeatedly he slid back into the grave. His hands groped along the edge of the grave and found a root of a powerful fir tree. Ivan seized the root and, strengthened by the physical exertion, managed to pull himself out of the grave, pushing his feet against the coffin.

With courage, though not in the posture of courage, he began to stagger away from the grave toward the town of Nizograd. After the burst of energy stemming from his initial enthusiasm for being among the living—though realistically still more among the dead, considering the neighborhood filled with crosses, flowers, and candles—he grew feeble, and the bipedal posture grew uncomfortable. On all fours he made his way through mud onto the main road of the graveyard. On the way, his palms crushed several worms and snails, and he cut his left knee on a sharp gravel stone. His throat and mouth were dry. But though the ground was wet, he didn't come across a puddle. He crawled to the graveyard fence.

Where should he go? Should he crawl all the way home, a couple of kilometers away? Beyond his strength. And how would his wife react to seeing him alive? Would she believe what she saw, or would she take him for a ghost? Well, what of it?

Maybe I am a ghost? No, ghosts must move more easily than I do. If this is how ghosts move around, with so much pain, I don't recommend the profession. But since in the coffin he rediscovered family values and family love, he decided he would attempt to crawl all the way home, even if he could not make it that far. This was no time for pessimism—he had made it this far against all odds. He thought that everything should be possible to him now, including a crawl of several kilometers.

He came across a house under construction that looked like a bunker, stumbled upon a water pump, and pumped. Water dripped, and he lay beneath it, continuing to tug at the handle of the pump. The water washed his eyes and filled his mouth. He gulped. The cold water hurt his teeth; even his brain somewhere in the back seemed to be freezing from the water, but it felt so good, so invigorating, and he wanted it so much, that he gulped too ambitiously—the water poured into his lungs and he nearly choked on it. Then he grunted, coughed, feeling feverish. But when he touched his forehead, it didn't seem any hotter or colder than his palms. This, however, did not reassure him, because he remembered that his palms couldn't objectively measure temperature, being a part of the subject. Still, it surprised him that his health had held up so well through his dying.

Gradually he felt refreshed enough to crawl out of the bunker-like house. He passed through a garden, through leaves of cabbage. A soft wind with the scent of apples on the ground caressed his face. So late in the year? He ate crunchy apples without washing them. His stomach rumbled as if complaining that it would have to work again.

From behind a street corner stepped a young Croatian policeman in a blue uniform, whom Ivan had never seen before. Since Ivan generally hadn't had good experiences with the police, he was startled, and what surprised him most was that he felt a strong heartbeat in his chest. The policeman's apparition had a medicinal effect on Ivan, like a shot of adrenaline to a victim of cardiac arrest. Ivan reminded himself that he had no reason to be excited, having experienced dying and death as thoroughly as one could possibly wish.

Patrolling the streets, the cop noticed Ivan's strange appearance—a suit and tie and hair all covered with mud. Ivan looked like the imitation of a human being fashioned out of clay, like an Adam half finished, as though God had forgotten to breathe the spirit into the fashioned clay.

"Stop!" shouted the youngster in the uniform. "Why are you crawling?"

"Why wouldn't I? It's not illegal to crawl, is it?"

"Are you drunk? Are you hurt? Did a car run over you?" The cop sounded ready to help.

Maybe I could hitch a ride home with him. But he'd most likely take me to the hospital. I don't feel like going there. And so, Ivan answered, "None of the above."

"So, what are you doing at this time of night? Are you insane?"

"Mental health is a subject far too slippery for either of us to get into. What do you think I'm doing? I'm walking—in a manner of speaking—home from the cemetery."

"Stand up when you talk with the law."

"I didn't know you were the law. OK, I'll stand up."

"And what were you doing there? Stealing from the new graves?"

"No, I was dying. I was buried alive by mistake."

"By mistake?" said the policeman, and took a step back to examine the bizarre man. "Buried?"

"How do you think I got to look like this?" asked Ivan.

"There's been reports of people digging . . . and you are drunk, aren't you?"

Ivan leaned against the building. "No, just tired from sleeping in the coffin. If you are tempted to get away from it all for a while—noise, family, job, politics, police, and so on—I still don't recommend coffins. They are stiff, stuffy, very unrelaxing."

"Maybe it makes sense, it's cool there when it's hot outside and warm inside when it's cold outside. Not a bad trick for a bum. Why would you be so muddy, though?"

"I guess someone dug out my grave, opened the lid, rummaged through my pockets, and left, and he hadn't even torn the golden crowns out of my mouth. Now that's the amazingly lucky part. I remember, during the war, we all used to do that."

"You talk a lot of nonsense."

"Nonsense? You just mentioned stealing from graves," said Ivan calmly. Generally he felt calm, enjoying a distance from life and death. He added, "I have no time to quibble with you over trivial matters and syllogisms, seeing that neither one of us is capable of setting them up. I'm glad to be alive, and I'm on my way home. I have a wife to gratify, a child to educate, music to play, Bibles to read—in fact, there's a lot of work ahead of me!" And Ivan began to walk off. The cop grabbed his forearm.

"Your ID, please!"

Ivan searched his pockets and found only a New Testament. He pulled it out and showed it.

"Oh, that's who you are, one of those new believers, sectarians, who allow Serbs to hide and plot against us. Let me tell you, I've had my share of dealing with you bullies. So what were you really doing in the cemetery?"

He shoved his gun into Ivan's neck, handcuffed him, searched his pockets. "Where's your ID?"

"In a small town like this, you don't need one. Nearly everybody knows me at least by sight. Clearly, you're a newcomer?"

"No ID? It's against the law not to . . ."

"Maggots don't need your ID to start gnawing at you, do they?"

"You crack political jokes and you have no ID. Come with me to the station!"

And he grabbed Ivan by his biceps and shoved him into a blue Volkswagen police car. Ivan was too weak to resist.

—

The cop dragged Ivan through glass doors, wooden doors, and finally metal doors. A couple of policemen, their legs on the table, played cards. When Ivan walked through the door, the card players shrieked out. They sprang up from their tables and jumped through the glass windows from the second floor.

"Now what was that?" asked the young policeman, frightened by his colleagues' behavior.

"See, they think I'm a dead man walking about!" said Ivan proudly.

The policemen screamed for help from the pavement below.

The young colleague rushed out and gave them a ride to the emergency room where they could be fitted into casts.

Half an hour later, Chief Vukic, sleepy, knuckling his eye bags, appeared at the police station.

He was startled by Ivan's appearance. Ivan's hair had turned completely white during his tribulations, so that he did look ghostlike.

"But you are dead, you cannot be here!" Vukic said. "What the hell is going on?"

"It seems to me I'm alive, though, of course, I could be wrong."

"You can't be alive. You are registered as dead." Turning to the young cop, who was back, Vukic said, "We'll have to return him to the grave. That's all there is to it."

"What do you mean?"

"What I mean is, he belongs in a grave."

"You mean, we should kill him?"

"No, no, you can't kill the dead, that wouldn't be necessary. Let's just put him back where he was. That would be the correct thing to do, and it should be easy, since all the paper-work is done already; he's registered as dead. God, I hate paper-work!"

"But I am alive!" protested Ivan, who did not like the thrust of the conversation.

"Shut up!" Vukic rubbed his eye bags. "Hm, I'm going crazy. I should never drink ouzo again."

"You can't drag me back there," said Ivan. "I'm alive and will stay alive. Actually, we should start an investigation. I sus-pect that my wife and the doctor conspired in my death. You, too, may be involved—you remember, your wife and all that. The doctor must've given my wife some sort of drug that para-lyzed me—and he wrote the death certificate. I know it, I heard them making out on top of my death certificate. I want an investigation right away."

"There will be no investigation. We'll put you back where you belong. Plus, don't remind me of that whore."

"My wife is no whore. She may have moments of weakness . . ."

"I mean *my* wife, you moron. And yes, you are a moron if you trust your wife."

"Wouldn't you like a game of chess?" asked Ivan. "If I win, you let me go."

"No, I don't want to play. I had enough of your chess, you . . ." Vukic inserted some indecent word that has to do with inserting.

"But it's a big tradition. You play chess with death, haven't you seen *The Seventh Seal*? Remember the scene when Death cheats the knight—as though he could beat Death otherwise. Well, I did beat it! And now I am gonna beat you! Hahaha!"

Ivan wept from laughter, his tears wetting the mud on his upper lip. All that clay melting on him reminded him of his sculpting days, when his busts of Julius Caesar melted in the rain to look like a bunch of Ciceros.

Chief Vukic swore again. "I hate foreign movies. What do those Germans know anyway that we don't?"

"It's a Swedish film."

"Swedes . . . OK, at least they make some good pornography."

"Anyway, remember the scene when the knight asks Death, 'What's there, after death?' And Death turns around slowly, stares at him, and says calmly, 'Nothing,' and walks away. Isn't that marvelous?" Ivan was getting carried away, shouting, standing up, enacting the scene, and—mud-caked, grisly, and pale—he was perfect for the role, far better than any actor of Bergman's. At any rate, Ivan put more feeling into the scene.

The young cop, clearly convinced that he had an explanation for the prisoner's strange behavior, said, "Chief, this is what I found in his pockets." He pulled out of his pocket a muddy New Testament, a small black book with silky pages, red on the edges.

The chief wouldn't touch it. He was beginning to believe that he was seeing a ghost, and that what Calvinists and all sorts of sectarians talked about, the resurrection from the dead, was what had just taken place.

Seeing the pallor of Vukic's face, and feeling superior to him because of defeating him in chess and not inferior on account of being physically weaker, Ivan embarked on another approach: "Now then, if you have me buried alive, I will rise again, or I will haunt your house. You know, I have some connections in the spirit world and, for your information, even in this one. Have you heard of the Freemasons?"

Like many other people who read popular nationalist newspapers, Vukic believed that Freemasons controlled most of the world, that the pope, Clinton, Bush, Putin, and most Western heads of states were Freemasons. It was rumored that Freemasons financed the Calvinists and the Adventists in the town to build new churches and to reorganize the pan-Slavic Balkan federation—in other words, Yugoslavia. Ivan's self-confidence in threatening only confirmed Vukic's suspicions. He still asked, in a shaky voice, "Tell me, are you really a Freemason?"

"Yes, of the thirtieth rank. Gorbachev, my old friend, is of the thirty-first rank, the pope is of the thirty-third, and Bobby Fischer is of the thirty-fourth," replied Ivan.

"I can't let you go," sighed the chief.

"Well, in that case . . ." Ivan raised his hands and began to pray. "Hearken unto me, you Most High Almighty . . ."

"Stop! Praying is not ah . . . allowed here!" the chief stammered.

"I know better. It was not allowed in the old regime, but it is desirable in the new. Have you forgotten your regimes? Have you skipped the Sunday mass?"

Vukic walked to the cabinet and, with twitching lips, sucked vodka, his Adam's apple loudly click-clocking, like a chess clock in speed chess. "You can't utter pagan prayers here."

"Could I have some spirits, too?" Ivan said. After all he'd been through, he felt he needed a stiff one.

"No, the dead don't drink," Vukic said, but handed the bottle over to Ivan, as if no longer in control of his will.

"Good, at least you know that much." Ivan, sighing, refused it. "I was only joking. But now I am not joking. Uncuff my hands. Write me a passport—you can do it—and give me a ride to the Zagreb train station! Give me two thousand German marks so I can reach my brethren Masons in Vienna."

Vukic walked up and down the room, smoking a Honduran cigar and staring at Ivan. Ivan talked about the all-pervasive power of Freemasons—how they would irradiate Vukic's head and orchestrate an electromagnetic takeover of his brain through his metal tooth-fillings . . . Bobby Fischer, who specialized in this, would personally be in charge of turning Vukic into a robot. Vukic as a robot would, for the rest of his life, clean Masonic bathrooms in Vienna, scrubbing away the ceremonial sperm and urine from the tiles, on all fours.

Vukic had another drink, and poured another shot, his hand trembling, and soon afterward he passed out from drunkenness and exhaustion. Ivan felt forlorn; in the middle of a conversation, he'd lost his listener. He realized he'd been sociable—he had talked up a storm simply out of desire for communication. Maybe he'd have to come back if he wanted the passport. So, he walked out of the police station, passing by the front desk where a policeman slept, his face sideways on the table, blue cap with the red-

and-white chess-set emblem of Croatia next to his nose. What did the chess set symbolize? Ivan was tempted to lift the cap—it might warm him up out there, plus it would give him the kind of authority he'd never had, the authority of the state apparatus. Well, perhaps if he didn't look the way he did, so earthy and ghastly. Where should he go next? To the people's clinic? Perhaps, after all this, a good heart examination would be in order— EKG with a stress test—and, for that matter, a CAT scan would make sense. He wondered how much brain damage he must have had with all that oxygen-deprivation.

He realized that medicine had become privatized, and the tests would be expensive. Moreover, there would be no doctors in the ER this time of night. He'd be more likely to find doctors at home, having sex with his wife. That would be quite convenient, to meet everybody he needed, in one bed. No, he was not jealous. He could pretend that he was resurrected and open a clinic. He could become a doctor yet, with better qualifications than a diploma: overcoming death; his soiled certificate—even if it did bear a crack-print—could work as a majestic diploma. Maybe he could do well as a minister in the church, although people might think it was too imitative and derivative to die, be dead for three days, and come back to life. A whimsical thought that he might be Jesus crossed his mind, and he laughed at that. Twenty percent of madmen think they are Jesus. Having a thought like that might indicate that he was mad indeed. Nevertheless, madmen are sometimes right. How many madmen manage to get out of the grave after death? So, his claim would be quite a bit better than the average. If he were Jesus, that indeed would be silly. No, that couldn't be the case. If he were, he'd probably be more intelligent, and he'd be able to talk to God, but then again, who knows whether Jesus did that kind of thing. And why would I believe now, now that I don't need religion?

28

Ivan avoids recognition in the streets of his lyrical hometown

Yearning for a draft of yeasty beer, Ivan aimed to stop by the Cellar. Mindful of appearances, he first visited the hot-springs tap in a pit below a blue, fortlike structure in the park. He washed his face in the sulfurous, steaming water flowing out of rusty pipes, melting all the remnants of soil in his nostrils. The rusty water smelled wonderfully oily; he drank some through his nose, and sneezed. The steam cleared his sinuses, and, while he walked up the stairs, he inhaled the piney air so deeply that his impression that he was among the living gained validity.

The moon was coldly licking the town, and wherever it couldn't reach, black shadows loomed. Ivan walked close to the houses that lined the streets, on the shadowy sides, feeling extraordinarily shy. When he touched a swollen wall, he heard sand hissing inside, in the spacing between the outside mortar and the bricks. Houses were still pockmarked. By now the town could have stuccoed the wounded walls, but the citizens wished to remember the war and to feel like martyrs. He had a vague sense of not belonging and of the impropriety of taking a walk after such a long burial. Of course, he had always had a sense of not belonging and of not wanting to be recognized; he had walked in this manner many times before.

The streets were dim; the new regime was no more prosperous than the old, and the town was subjected to a partial blackout. When he got close to the tavern, he saw Nenad standing outside the door, leaning forward, apparently locking it up. Ivan shouted, but his voice didn't carry—he couldn't even hear himself properly, either.

Nenad's silhouette moved away from the door, across the cobbled street—and straight into his silvery, moonlit BMW. The tires smoked on the pavement even before Ivan could hear the engine, and Nenad drove by in all his imported technological glory. It struck Ivan as strange that Nenad and many other people seemed so much more prosperous than he; after all, Ivan had thought he was the most intelligent man, but here, the old question mark of doubt arose—If you are so smart, why aren't you rich? On the other hand, what would he want a sleek car for? Well, now, for instance, he could be driving to his old home. But it must have been after two in the morning . . . appearing at home now would be quite shocking to the family. During the day Selma would see him so clearly that she couldn't doubt his being there regardless of whether she thought that he had risen from the dead or merely recovered from the false diagnosis, in which she took a big part.

To his mind, he seemed much improved by the ordeal of dying. Previously, he would have hated her, would have thought it a matter of honor to be furious and vengeful, but now he was pacific. He walked back into the park. The cool smell of mossy soil mixed beautifully with the aroma of trampled, dusty oak leaves and sulfur from the hot springs. The moonlight cast the shapes of conical cypresses onto the graveled pathways, in black and blue. He walked across the railway tracks resting on wood ties, doused in fresh tar and oil. He didn't have any light to guide him beneath the huge oaks and beeches—they had certainly grown in the last forty years. That was the only beauty in getting older, that the trees he knew in his youth were now giants, and while the town and the people deteriorated, the park grew more and more upright and majestic.

He navigated to the bunker by the peculiar smell of cement, rot, and dankness that flowed out of it. He fumbled in, felt the rugged walls, fearful of the fragments of river shells that stuck out of the concrete and could cut him like razors. He inched forward deeper inside, to the back-wall concrete bench. So this is what it's like to be blind—you poke at everything gently with your fingers, in constant trepidation. As he felt around, he pricked his finger on a needle. With the other hand he examined the shape of the needle—it was a syringe. He assumed some drug addicts must have used it. He had no idea the youth of his town was quite that progressive. What if they had HIV? Will I get AIDS? Ivan wondered. What if I do? It'll take some fifteen years to take effect, and then a few years to die, and then I'd die at the age of seventy. That's more than I imagine I could live under the best of circumstances. For a while, the war was credited with stopping the spread of the disease—because German and American sex tourists quit coming to the coast. But then, the UN was far busier setting up—or at least frequenting—bordellos than safe havens, and the UN soldiery and staff were quite an international medley of young hormones and viruses, and add to that Moldavian and Ukrainian prostitutes who'd never heard of condoms, and yes, whatever virus and bacterium there was in the world to be transmitted—that could live outside the body in a bit of blood—could have just been transmitted to me in this little prick. How could I claim that I am lonely? I am now in company of the world's finest: the effort of millions of people has just been communicated to me. The poetry of sex- and drug-induced ecstasy goes straight into my blood and bones, and now, for years to come, it can be decoded and read throughout my body.

And who's to say that Nizograd is provincial? Look at the condoms and syringes. Now it's part of the global village. My life of refusal to travel out of the country has just been vindicated.

Still, maybe some boys picked up that syringe from the hospital dump site and played with it, pretending to be drug addicts, and the little prick delivered nothing to me, other than a bit of rust, and I'm sitting not on top of a chain of edgy excitement but in a dreary dungeon. Maybe old-fashioned tetanus is all I'll get.

Ivan stretched out on a blanket he found on the bench and let his hands probe the floor, touching bullet shells, soft chicken bones, a rotted boot, and a cigarette lighter, which he grabbed and tried to light. His fingers were a little stiffer than he'd imagined. Still, after a few tries, he flicked a flame, and soon, aided by its light, found a whole cigarette. He lit it; he smoked and sighed with sorrow.

Ivan slept from dawn till nightfall. Not even the cargo trains that clanked on the tracks some twenty yards down the hill disturbed his dreamless sleep. Upon waking up, he was stiff all over. He had a hip ache, a shoulder ache, and a backache—most of his pain was skeletal. He suddenly recalled his father, who had kept the bones of his leg and arm in a potato sack. What happened to those bones? Are they still in my basement somewhere? Or, if there's a doomsday and a general resurrection, my father will rise from the dead not on the cemetery slopes but in my basement, assembled in the potato sack, and he'll have to tear out of the sack.

A vague moonlight passed through the clouds, enough to make the path to the hot-springs fountain visible. He washed his face and drank the water—not terribly hot, just like tea cut with milk; this tea was made from iron and sulfur, a kind of doomsday tea or the tea from the creation of the earth; perhaps it was a bit of sweat that fell from God's brows and stayed restless in the earth.

Applying his usual stealth technique, Ivan walked toward the bar. By now there were some people in the street, but not like there used to be. Before the war, most townspeople promenaded before going home to sleep. During the war, because of frequent shelling, people lost the habit. Now, you could see TV lights flickering behind the curtains from many houses. In some, the flickers were quite rhythmic in orange shades, with lots of light, little light, lots of light, little light—probably some highly imaginative pornography. You could deem the speed of fornication by how quickly the light and dark alternated. And if you heard lovemaking cries from an open window, those more likely came from a movie than from actual, local lovemaking. And if by any chance the locals cried sexually, the loud style was novel to the region and highly imitative of the Western style of lovemaking. Sex used to be a form of relaxation, and, therefore, mostly quiet, except perhaps at the very end, but the Western style created the mania of acting out the panic of pleasure throughout. Plus, the locals were satisfied with doing it a few minutes at a time, and now these moans went on for hours, as though the locals had started using cocaine, morphine, and some other drugs that would make that kind of marathon approach to sex feasible. At any rate, Ivan was pleased that the wholesome, pedestrian culture had vanished. People still went places, to and fro, and sometimes they didn't know why they were going anywhere, but they were going—in cars, making practically a traffic jam in the main streets. He took side streets and emerged at the Cellar. The place was crowded, but he found a chair at a small table in the corner.

He recognized nobody. The war was partly to blame—many Serbs had constituted the bar scene, and most of them were now gone—some had left to ethnically cleanse the Croats and now couldn't return, or some were ethnically cleansed by the Croats, and so now Ivan was in a cleansed bar, and, of course, it was a filthy one, with many incontinent drunks. After the war, so many Bosnian Croats moved into town, nearly all bony and tall—you'd think they were concentration-camp inmates, but many of them simply grew up like that in the mountains, with all that goat milk and giardia and tobacco and sometimes TB. On the other hand, some of the Bosnian new-comers may have indeed been survivors of Serbian concentra-tion camps, such as Omarska.

Soon Nenad and Bruno appeared and walked down the stairs without glancing over toward Ivan's corner. They looked far more cheerful than when Ivan had been around. Maybe the whole damned country would all of a sudden turn out to be an optimistic place, like Italy or Fiji, with people making quaint conversation, all nice and chummy? It was entirely possible. Oh no, it was not possible. At that moment, the patrons shrieked. A large TV set was broadcasting a soccer match between his beloved Hajduk, Split, and not beloved Dinamo, Zagreb. The Dinamo fans were burning Hajduk flags. Ivan couldn't follow what was going on in the game, because of the thick smoke both at the stadium and in the bar and of the occasional bursts of glasses on the bar walls. A few fathers with young sons, who had come in to watch the match, grew scared and walked out. During the intermission, the Splitters threw several cars with Zagreb license plates into the Adriatic. Ivan thought that now that the Croats had no Serbian teams to play, and the inland Croats hated the Croatian clubs from the coast, and vice versa, if things continued this way, pretty soon there would be another soccer war that would result in several new banana republics—Dalmatia, Slavonia, Istria, Independent Republic of Dubrovnik, and so on; they would be so small that one should call them fig-leaf republics. At this point Ivan didn't care whether Croatia would splinter into five tiny countries or whether it would unite—well, who would it unite with? The times of uniting were over. Ivan merely wanted to get some attention from a pale waitress with brown eye-bags and nicotine-stained teeth, but the strange thing was that when he tried to speak, his voice was gone. Did he catch a cold?

Once Dinamo scored, a peasant paid for a round of beer for the whole bar; one mug landed on Ivan's table. *Starocesko pivo,* he'd learned from a local beer technologist, was the only live-yeast beer in the country. The yeast was strong indeed; it made him burp and his stomach rise, as though he were a loaf in the oven. His flesh was rising, he thought jovially; maybe yeast was a necessary ingredient in the resurrection recipe?

Soon, the game was over. Machine-gun fire and grenade explosions resounded in the streets—merely a celebration.

When the bar quieted down, Ivan overheard two men at a neighboring table:

"Crazy town! My neighbor says that a dead man went to the police station last night."

"That doesn't sound crazy. After the war, all sorts of weird things have been happening. Many victims of atrocities wander around at night."

"They show up as visions to people who killed them. That's guilty conscience, nightmares, that's not real."

"It's real. It's more real than the soccer we saw. All those dandies in shorts get bribed—it's like pro-wrestling. It's just supposed to look like they are tough."

"Only the murderer sees the ghost, nobody else."

"That's not true. Anyway, like tonight, there were probably quite a few murderers here, so they could have all seen ghosts."

"Well, have you ever seen a ghost?"

"No. But I've never hurt nobody, either."

"Don't say that too loudly around here. Weren't you in the Croatian army?"

"Sure, but all I did was play cards, drink beer, and ride in trucks from one safe area to another."

"Don't tell anybody. Say you are a traumatized war veteran and ask for a pension."

"I asked, and they say I'll get one when I'm sixty. And it won't be much of one, not even enough to cover my beer expenses."

"I am not surprised—two engineers' salaries couldn't do that. Well, let's get another round. Nenad, my man, more beer!"

"Don't you need to drive home?" said Nenad.

"I drive much better when I am drunk. My nerves are calmer, so I don't swerve if I see a black cat on the road."

Nenad fetched two brown bottles of beer and click-clocked the contents into the mugs on the table.

Ivan walked to the bar and cleared his throat. He tried to speak, and out came a strange hissing sound, as though Ivan had been a goose in the previous life, or in this life.

Nenad was talking to Bruno, who was drinking Johnny Walker, red label, on the rocks.

"All the town drunks have heard the story of your brother's ghost bothering the police. Even Paul believed Ivan was buried with treasures, so he went digging. Was he actually buried with anything worthwhile?"

"Maybe just a good pair of shoes. Maybe Indira Gandhi's fan. I never believed his story about the fan."

"Was it made of gold and rubies?"

"It's some gaudy piece of junk. Anyway, my friend, can't you give me a few more ice cubes? I wanted it on the rocks."

"Isn't one piece of ice enough? Aren't you afraid you'll catch a cold, get strep, or something like that?"

"In this country, I can't get Scotch on the rocks, I don't know when you people will get it that ice is fine—actually that's the only way to drink if you don't want a headache."

"As you wish." Nenad walked over to the refrigerator, passing by Ivan, not noticing him, and brought a glassful of ice. "So there, but don't complain about your throat tomorrow."

"*Es tut gut!*" Bruno crunched an ice cube between his molars.

"You know," said Nenad, "I heard that the men who killed a lot of people in the war can't be buried right. Their coffins float up during heavy rains, caskets crack open, and their bodies wash up somewhere in the fields where ravens pluck their eyes and drink their brains through the eye sockets. Or there's a landslide, and just their coffins come out, or there's an earthquake, and the same thing happens, and then these war criminals' bodies roll around the country, and peasants sometimes prop them up in the fields as scarecrows, and once in a blue moon one of these scarecrows begins to walk and the whole village goes wild from horror, and people start burning the fields to make sure all the scarecrows are gone."

"Where did you hear that shit?"

"Right here, a man from Babina Greda told me."

"Of course you hear all sorts of tall tales here with the drunks who drink slivovitz. If they drank Scotch, they wouldn't hallucinate like that."

"Maybe your brother's coffin got opened and he fell out

and . . . you know, he's been down there in Bosnia, who knows what the hell he actually did."

"My brother wouldn't have killed anybody. Well, as a kid he was cruel, but he was squeamish—he couldn't even touch a frog."

"He did kill, he told me when he drank."

"Depends on what he drank. You know, the damned thing is that those who killed don't talk about it, and those who didn't spin tales."

"Well, well, you never know what will roll off a man's tongue, and sometimes even the truth does."

"Why don't you close the bar and we can . . ."

Ivan was in the meantime trying to get their attention, hissing, asking for a beer, protesting that he was alive—in fact, giving whole speeches on his medical history, explaining there was no such thing as resurrection, only false diagnosis and coming back to senses and out . . . but none of it apparently came across, so, he grabbed an empty glass and shattered it on the floor. He was afraid that even that behavior wouldn't be noticed since on that day so many glasses were shattered that it would appear that merely one more Dinamo fan was going crazy.

Nenad was startled. He looked to Ivan's side of the bar and went pale.

Bruno didn't turn his head but took advantage of the lull in the conversation to gulp another shot.

"Hey, is this . . . it can't be!" Nenad shouted. "Look, your brother's ghost!"

"Come on, all that soccer and ghost talk got to you. Sober up."

"But look, there he is, sitting just a few stools down . . ."

"Where?" Bruno looked in Ivan's direction; his eyes were crisscrossed from too much whiskey and he didn't appear to notice Ivan.

"This . . . right here . . ." Nenad was running away from the bar, knocking down glasses and shattering them on the floor.

Bruno did a double take, finally noticed his brother, and he jumped up and tripped over a chair's leg. As he fell, he cut his hand on shattered glass on the floor, cursed—*Scheise!*—and ran out.

The two peasants were alarmed by the communal fright that launched the owner and his friend out of the bar. They looked at Ivan and evidently found his appearance to be more convincingly otherworldly than worldly; they rushed out, too, but not quite as fast, because the supernatural occasionally occurred, or at least was to be expected, in their village.

Ivan walked to the door and saw several people running in the streets. Nenad unlocked his BMW, and both Bruno and he jumped into it, and the car roared off. Ivan shook his head. This was ghastly behavior on the part of his townspeople. Quite indecent.

Ivan remained alone in the bar. He would have been depressed if he hadn't been more than depressed before, and any depression would qualify as veritable cheer, comparatively speaking. Yes, it was a bummer to deal with such a superstitious population. Those guys—why didn't they read philosophy, Descartes, or even the married sociologist, Marx, to get rid of their superstitions? Now, a man couldn't even come back after a severe illness. Shouldn't they be happy to see him well enough to drink? And supposing that he was a ghost, Bruno and Nenad and the patrons should have celebrated their communal ESP experience, and they should all be now drinking merrily.

Ivan walked behind the bar and had a glass of sweet red wine. He opened a drawer and found a bundle of money. During soccer games, people were reckless with their money, as though they were in a bordello. It occurred to him that he should go grocery shopping. He hadn't eaten in a while, and, although he didn't feel hungry, some cold cuts would do him good. Ivan stuffed his pockets. He was merely borrowing money from a friend. He would return it when things got back to normal.

29

No more chamomile tea, please!

He hadn't seen his mother in a long time, and now was as good an occasion as he would ever get. In fact, that was one bad thing about his death—that he wouldn't see his mother again. It would be terrible to leave this life without ever having had a good conversation with a parent.

Moreover, visiting Opatija to stroll along the Adriatic on the old promenade built for Austrian and Hungarian officers and their wives might do him some good. Salty air, sunshine, seagull calls, they all might chase away the last vestiges of death out of him—the pallor, the numbness, the general slowness, and the morbid imaginings.

Once he got to the coast by train, in Rijeka, he took a cab to the hills above Opatija. The view was beautiful, Bruno was right. He stood and admired the blues of the sea and the sky and the islands. He remembered that da Vinci had observed that all the objects in the distance tend to appear blue. Of course, the islands were mostly gray—from the rocks—and brown, and green, but now they looked dark blue. If he were a painter . . . well, forget it. It's good enough to see the world. He rang the bell at his mother's house. No answer. He rang again, and, when he got no answer, he opened the door and walked in. His mother was watching a Mexican soap opera on TV.

"Hello, how come you don't open the door?"

"Ah, at my age, what do I have to look forward to? It could be a beggar, it could be a mailman, what do I care who could be at the door?"

"Still, it could be me, you know."

"I didn't think about that."

"Well, aren't you glad to see me?"

"Yes, son, I am."

"Not surprised, like everybody else?"

"Why should I be surprised? But yes, this is the first time you deigned to visit us at the coast. All right, I am surprised."

"But not just that. You know, I was supposed to be dead, there was a funeral."

"I know. I went to it."

"Well, isn't it strange?"

"So they were wrong, you aren't dead, and they opened the coffin, and here you are, what's so odd about that?"

"It's nice to have an accepting mother who takes you for what you are. I wish you'd been like that when I was a kid."

"True, true. I was tense then, I had obligations."

"I'm not accusing. I'm marveling. Still, isn't it strange that I'm here?"

"I've been trying to die for years now, and it's not that easy. Why should it be easy for you? If it were, I'd be terribly jealous. Of course, there's always suicide, but I am not going to do that. You'd think that after a heart attack, a stroke, diabetes, and all that, I could just go, but it's not happening, not yet, I have no idea why. Anyway, you are too young to worry about nonsense like that. Would you like some tea?"

"Only if it's not that awful chamomile that you've been drinking all your life."

"It is chamomile."

"Then I'd rather not."

"Suit yourself. You know, it's very good for your nerves."

"Sure, like everything else that's boring. It puts you to sleep."

"I do have some Turkish coffee."

Ivan went to the cupboard and rummaged, and found the coffee and sniffed it. "How old is it? You call it Turkish? Is it something left over from the Ottoman days?"

"I see you are as prickly as ever. I do have some whiskey. Bruno always brings that along."

"Oh, let me guess, could it be Johnny Walker?"

"I don't know what it is, but I have a sip every day. It works very well as a mouthwash."

"Great, let's have a toast!"

Ivan poured her a glass and one for himself.

Her hand trembled, but she managed to pour whiskey into her mouth. She moved her cheeks, blew them, and Ivan could hear the liquid squeezing through and around her dentures.

"You want a cup to spit?"

She swallowed the liquid. "Oh no, I don't do that. The stuff is too expensive to just spit out. Plus, it's good for it to go down and burn around in my system for a while. I have all sorts of bacteria there, and if it can get some, praise the Lord."

Ivan said *"Zivili"* and gulped his drink. He took a look at his mother—she was quite ashen, her skin sallow, her hair white, but her small eyes still shone with intelligence.

She was looking at her son critically. "You don't look that hot, son. I recommend that you go down to the beach and swim a little, take a look at the topless Austrian women, have a drink with one of them."

"Are you recommending adultery? I've tried that—it hasn't worked that well for me."

"No, nothing that crass, but do go out into the world, flirt a little, warm up your blood. And try walking, take up hiking, climb the mountain. Mount Ucka is quite a hike, you go from the sea level to fifteen hundred meters."

"That sounds too strenuous. Besides, there are too many copperheads and other snakes there. All right, if we are at the stage of giving wisdom to each other, let me tell you that I think you shouldn't live alone."

"I don't. Bruno comes here nearly every weekend from Germany, and his in-laws are just next door. They come in and check on me."

"That doesn't count—it all sounds cold and distant. I mean, you should have a little organism milling about, sleeping with you, giving you creature comfort: a cat."

"I don't think so. Cats stink."

"Everything that's good stinks. Look at the whiskey. How about French cheese?"

Ivan walked out. It took him three minutes to find a stray kitten. It was a tabby—purry, licky. He went back to Branka Dolinar, and put the tabby in her lap.

"That is silly of you," she said, but her hands apparently liked the furry creature. She petted the kitten, and the kitten rubbed its head against her wrists.

The cat seemed to understand that this was a very important interview, on which her future depended—if she didn't appear charming, she'd remain an alley cat. She purred loudly right into Branka Dolinar's ear.

"She's a charmer, isn't she?" Ivan said.

"I hope she doesn't give me fleas."

Ivan stood up, kissed his mother on the cheek that wasn't occupied by the cat, and said good-bye.

He felt great about having visited. He had finally done something good—given mother an engine of creature comfort, the cat.

He went down to the promenade and made one lap. He'd read in a short story by Chekhov—who had come here in search of good air to recover from TB—that there was no more dreary resort than Opatija, that the town amounted to one dismal street. It hasn't changed much in the century that had passed since, thought Ivan, except there's no grumpy Chekhov sitting on a bench and staring at seagulls and ladies with petticoats and lapdogs.

Ivan took a cab to Rijeka—old Fiume, that is—and a train back to Zagreb and Nizograd. On the train, he read *Vecernji List*, the Croatian somewhat right-wing daily. He was surprised to read a report from Nizograd that a man who was pretending to be a ghost of a recently deceased local schoolteacher managed to scare the patrons of the old Cellar tavern, and once the patrons ran out of the bar, the man stole ten thousand kunas. The police were looking for the man-at-large.

Ivan laughed as he read the report, and he was proud. Now

he did have enough money to dress nicely, so in Zagreb he bought a black blazer, a pair of the finest Italian shoes, imported razor blades, and he went to the bathroom of Hotel Dubrovnik in the center of the city. When he saw himself in the mirror, he was shocked to see how pale—almost blue—he was. He shaved, which got rid of the blue tinge, and the massage returned some color to his skin. He went out and got a haircut.

Now, though he didn't look fresh, he looked sharp and gentlemanly. He got off the train in the evening and walked slowly home.

As he was passing by the apartment complex where Chief Vukic lived, Ivan couldn't resist the temptation to visit Svjetlana. The door was unlocked, and he walked in quietly.

He found Svjetlana alone, drinking whiskey and listening to the *Symphonie Fantastique* by Berlioz. He had no idea that she harbored secret tastes in classical music. His favorite part resounded, the dance with the funeral march. The bells tolled, while double basses tugged at one's grief centers in the brain. Her eyes were closed, and she sighed and had another sip. She stood up unsteadily and stumbled to the bedroom. Ivan didn't know what it was about that woman's body; maybe all that voluptuous flesh, like a retired Laura Antonelli, brought a sense that he was back in his youth, in his erotic dreams and yearnings, and that it still was not too late to relive them, that it was never, in fact, too late.

She did not notice him and walked to her bed, undressed, and lay on it. Her breasts spread out softly, with stretch marks but still substantial, and obviously even softer than before. She did not resemble a *femme fatale*—with her flaccid flesh she seemed very unlikely for the role, but the fatale part should benefit from the unexpected. She was entirely naked and still had plenty of pubic hair. Apparently she hadn't yielded to the new western ways of hair animosity and excessive shaving. Pretty soon she seemed to be asleep; her mouth was open, and

she breathed heavily. Her lips were red—she must have put lipstick on just before Ivan visited. Perhaps it was a ritual listening
to the *Symphonie Fantastique*? Did she by any chance grieve for
him? Was that his funeral she was celebrating?

Ivan tiptoed and gently stroked her belly. Svjetlana moaned
but apparently didn't wake up. Ivan lay down with her, and they
made love. She must have been awake—she was certainly very
active. At one point she fumbled for her glass of whiskey and
finished it. They made love vigorously, nearly doing the entire
cycle of Kama Sutra, whereupon, exhausted, Svjetlana definitely
fell asleep and even snored. Actually, Ivan grew bored with the
whole thing in the middle of it, and continued more out of a
sense of decency and gentlemanly obligation than out of pleasure. He wondered why he used to think that sex was something
to write home about. It occurred to him: Maybe most ghosts
are good lovers? Maybe that's why the creaking furniture is such
an inevitable cliché—sooner or later they get laid, and when
they do, they do it as enthusiastically, at least for a while, as
though it were the last time. Anyway, that didn't concern him,
for he didn't believe that he was a ghost, and he didn't care
whether it was the last time, and, in a way, he hoped that it
was—that would simplify things.

While Ivan went to the bathroom, he heard the door open,
and Vukic shouted, "Svyeta, I am home. Where is my supper?
Grilled pork, I hope?"

She didn't answer. He walked into the bedroom and
shouted, "How can you sleep so early? Oh, you are drunk! You
must go into rehab."

He shook her and woke her up, and she said, "I had the
most amazing dreams. You know, I heard all that talk about
Ivan's ghost, and thought, how come everybody gets to see
him, and I don't? There's something not right in that. And so I
listened to all the funeral march music I could find, and imagined him, and so I fell asleep, and you know what, it worked."

"What do you mean, it worked? What nonsense is that?"

"I was making love to Ivan's ghost. It was just wonderful, I never . . ."

"I am not surprised, the whole town is having similar dreams."

"Oh, no, not like that. It was very vivid. I even had multiple orgasms."

"Oh, don't tell me about it. I know that masturbation can do wonders."

"My dear, maybe I wouldn't have such wild dreams if we did it more often. We should do it at least once a month."

"Now, now, don't be so ambitious."

"Come, let's give it a try."

And they went at it, doggy-style. When Ivan looked on, he chuckled. Sex was a ridiculous thing indeed. Why had he wasted so much time on it—well, not really on it, but on daydreaming about it? That was sorrowful. If he got to live as a normal citizen again, he'd never bother with it.

The chief grunted very soon.

"Is that it?" she said.

"I am tired, what can I say. We'll do it better next month."

"The ghost did it much better—what stamina, imagination, what a subtle touch . . . mmm . . . that was something. I sure hope he comes back."

"Don't mention that bastard."

"If you didn't watch so much pornography, and masturbation didn't do wonders, you'd do better."

"I don't watch it."

"Oh, you think I am that naive? I found your whole *Private* stash."

"Where is it?"

"I threw it into the garbage."

"My God, how could you do it? It's very expensive, finest French . . ."

"Finest, my ass. Such disgusting filth, no wonder you can't do it."

The couple began to quarrel in earnest, and Ivan walked out quietly, leaving the doors open, so that all the way down the stairway he heard the insults exchanged between the couple. Pretty soon plates and glasses were being smashed against the walls. It's best to leave them to their devices, Ivan thought. He stood near the center of town, sniffing the smell of chestnut trees. When he snapped out of it, he saw Vukic rummaging through bags of garbage on the sidewalk. Ivan was tempted to offer him a few words of solace about the tedium of sex, but felt shy and walked away along the wall.

30

A damned owl hoots too much

Now it was time to go home. Ivan expected that the doors would be unlocked. That is one peculiar thing about the town, that it could go through wars, and it still remained safe, so safe that most people rarely locked their doors. Well, the doors were locked, but the key was hanging in the familiar spot—on the nail.

Ivan unlocked it and walked into the living room. He was nervous. This was the place where his troublesome death had started.

Tanya was sitting alone in the armchair and watching a *Madeline* tape, a bunch of girls dancing.

"Hello, my girl, how are you?"

"Hi, Dad! Where have you been?"

"I traveled to many places. Even went to the coast to see Grandma."

"Why didn't you tell me, I would've come along!"

"Next time, when it gets warmer, then we can swim. Where is Mom?"

"She went to town to buy some milk and stuff."

"And she left you alone?"

"Why not?"

True, Ivan thought. Why not? It's a safe town. "Aren't you tired of watching the same tape over and over again?"

"No, but you can tell me stories, like you used to."

"All right, I'll tell you a true story."

"Oh, no, that would be a drag. Make one up."

"So one day I went to the Slovenian Alps, and I climbed the tallest mountain, sliced a little cloud . . ."

"How cruel of you!"

"No, clouds don't have veins, they don't bleed, you know.

Each cloud can be split into many little clouds, and my cloud was the cutest. It spoke Austrian and told me many jokes. I stored it in a matchbox."

"Was it a girl cloud?"

"Yes, it was a beautiful girl cloud. Anyway, one day I opened the box too much, and our cat pounced on the cloud and ate it."

"That's terrible."

"So we chased the cat and tried to gag her so the cloudich could come out, but it didn't work. We were sad indeed, but then a strange thing began to happen to the cat. The cat got bloated more and more and gradually turned into a balloon, and the balloon floated up. We tried to catch her but couldn't. And the balloon grew and grew, until it turned into a cloud that looked like a gray cat with stripes. It was the ghost of our cat. And then it rained, and the whole countryside turned green. The raindrops bounced high from the ground. And the surprising thing was that it wasn't real raindrops, but tiny frogs. The town and the hills nearby were covered with tiny leaping frogs. It was beautiful."

"But what happened to the cloud?"

"Oh, clouds live forever, one cloud becomes another, and they keep floating in the sky."

"And what happened to the cat?"

"Well, the cat became a ghost."

"What's a ghost?"

"It's a soul which doesn't need a body."

"What's the difference between a ghost and a soul?"

"I don't know."

"You must know."

"All right, soul is the real you in your body, and it makes you live, and it is also what remains of you after you die, and it's free to go to heaven . . . or hell . . . and ghost is what remains of you after you die, when you are not free to leave the earth or even your town. Then the ghost stays around, usually in the attic, and it loves to move the furniture around." Here Ivan was suddenly reminded of Aldo and Aldo's passion to move furniture all around the room whenever he was left alone. What possessed him?

"Are ghosts scary?"

"Not at all. Many of them are beautiful, silky creatures, who move around in streaks of smoke. If you just wave your hand in front of your eyes, they leave, but often you wouldn't want them to leave."

"Are there ghost ballerinas?"

"Yes."

"I'd like to see one. Could you make me one?"

"Oh, no, I don't control that. I can make up a story where one comes here and dances for us."

"I don't need it in a story, I'd like a real ghost."

Tanya was sitting on Ivan's knee, and he was bouncing her up and down. She leaned her head on his shoulder. And he felt happy. He relaxed. That was a wonderful sensation. Now his life was complete. He got the ultimate creature comfort, that of a parent with his child, his flesh, which will continue his life in a better, younger, happier form. He wouldn't even need to hover around as a ghost. He could be a free soul.

"Daddy, do you want to see my drawings?"

"Definitely."

She showed him a drawing of many striped cats, turtles, ballerinas, a wonderful cosmos of a child, full of life and song.

"All right, draw some more, I'll go check out the attic."

"Why, to see whether we have ghosts?"

"Yes, and to tell them to buzz off."

"If you see one, let me know, I'd like to see one, too."

And so Ivan went to the attic and wondered whether he could live there. Suppose that Selma never accepted him as alive, he could still live upstairs, modestly, as long as he didn't make too much noise. That should probably be all right. They kept an old armchair there, and he moved it closer to the window, so he would have a view of the street. And then, on an old, rickety bookshelf, he noticed Gandhi's fan. He brought it downstairs. "Tanya, look, this is a very special present that a woman who is now the ghost of India gave me. Just keep it, and whenever it gets hot, flap it in front of your face, like this, see? You'll feel cooler. And if there are any ghosts that show up and you feel scared, just flap a few times, and the ghosts will fall apart, like smoke, and the smoke will fly out the window, into the sky, and it will rain."

"Will it rain frogs?"

"No, only tears. So, when it rains, go out and stick your tongue out, and you'll see that the drops are salty. Tears are salty, you know that."

"Yes, I know. That's why I like to cry—because I can lick the salt off my upper lip."

"You are just like a little goat, my kid!"

He hugged her, and a few of his tears fell down on her cheek. She licked the tears off her cheek. "That's nice, Dad. You didn't use to be so nice."

"I know. That's why we grow older—to learn, to become good, to do good at least for a few hours before the end."

"Why would the ghosts be crying in the sky?"

"I don't know. Maybe because they can't ride bicycles anymore?"

"That's silly. If I see one, I'll ask it why it's crying."

"I'll come back some evening, and we'll chat more. Now, let me see what else is there upstairs." And Ivan walked up the creaky staircase.

Soon Selma was back, opening the door and carrying in the groceries. Doctor Rozhic followed her.

"Mommy, guess what? Daddy is here."

"Really? I don't believe it. He went far away, and he wouldn't come back so fast."

"You don't have to believe."

"Where is he now?"

"Up in the attic. He's looking for his maps of Ancient Egypt. If you stay quiet, you'll hear him."

From upstairs came the rumbling of furniture.

"That is just too weird for words," Rozhic said.

"Don't tell me you believe in ghosts?" Selma said.

Now everything grew quiet.

"I believe in ghosts," said Tanya. "They are souls who are not free to leave the earth. I'd like to see one."

"For now, it's your bedtime. Should I read you a little booky before you fall asleep?"

"Yes, please."

"Darling, can you wait, watch TV or something, I'll be right out," said Selma, and the doctor sat in the chair and poured himself a shot of gin. Ivan went down the stairs creakily and wanted to go through the back-room window, but then he thought, Well, let's be reasonable about that. These people can't be superstitious like everybody else. At least a doctor and my wife should accept me, and so he strode bravely into the living room and asked for a glass of gin for a toast.

When Doctor Rozhic saw him, he gasped out of sheer fright. His glass and bottle fell from his hands onto the carpet. And after them fell the doctor, holding his chest. His throat made strange creaking sounds. Blood trickled from the side of his mouth. He was dying of a massive heart attack.

Ivan didn't know what to do. He felt the man's pulse. It wasn't there. To pump his chest, do artificial respiration? No, thank you. That part of medicine never appealed to him. Moreover, what would the poor man think when he came back to life, if he did: a ghost kissing him and blowing air into him? It would be appropriate for ghosts to do that, of course—that might be the best kind of employment for them. But if it was the fear of one to begin with, such a sight would finish him off. As for chest-pumping, he'd read a study that showed that the results were inconclusive—many people's hearts resume work after the initial shock, and if the pumping is done, it might appear that the action produced the resumption of the heart's activity, while in fact it's a matter of a spontaneous resumption that would have probably occurred anyhow.

Ivan stared for a moment at the contorting face of a dying man, and he didn't feel particularly grief-stricken, nor triumphant.

He walked out the door slowly and quietly. When he was down the stairs, and out in the street, he heard Selma's shriek. Well, she'd been through something like that earlier, she'll know how to handle that. She even had a Nokia. Now she could call a doctor, a better one than before, no doubt; she could get an ambulance, and let's see what luck she has. Oh, that's all right, I don't have to hang around for that.

Ivan concluded that it might be a little too awkward for him to go back to the attic. Selma might not accept him—it seemed only children and very old people could accept him. Everybody else found him terrifying. So, out of consideration, he went back to his bunker. He was tired, but since it was such an eventful and exciting evening, he couldn't fall asleep easily, but when he did, he slept for two entire days.

Upon waking up, he had a peculiar desire to see his own grave. For that matter, he might stop by a shop, where probably nobody would know him among all the newcomers, and buy a shovel. He should dig into the grave and see what the hell was going on. Is there a body in it? If there is, I am just some damned astral projection. Of course, there is no body in it.

He walked through the woods and past the old brickyard. When he saw clay, he couldn't resist the temptation, and he spent hours fashioning—with his bare hands—his own image. There's a certain stage where you might be interested in your looks not just out of sheer vanity but out of a quest for your own soul—who am I, what do I know, what can I hope to know, and, actually, it could be simplified, Am I? Even Rembrandt kept fashioning his self-portraits, not only because he couldn't manage his budget very well (thus, he was not often able to afford a model), but out of a soulful quest, looking for spirit in his decaying face. There's more intrigue in Rembrandt's several facial creases than in one hundred and one of Titian's ass curvatures, and, at the moment, Ivan found more intrigue in his own sagging lips than in a dozen of Svjetlana's thighs.

He didn't need to wait for rain to wash his clay busts out and to make his image elongated and weepy-looking; he would make it right away like that, give it an El Greco spiritual kind of dimension, elongated gloom. It must have been Sunday, he thought—there was nobody in the brickyard.

As he got closer to the cemetery, he realized why the town was empty. Everybody was attending the doctor's funeral. Rozhic was being buried not very far from Ivan's grave. Ivan walked closer, shielded from the funeral by a row of evergreens, and, anyhow, people were too preoccupied to analyze everybody's features—Ivan had no need to worry about being recognized. It was a weepy crowd. Ivan never knew the town was that emotional and humane. Dr. Rozhic was having a French-style funeral. Next to the casket was his wife and his two nearly adult children; and then the mistress, Selma, and even Tanya was there. Tanya wasn't crying. She was whispering something to her mother—Ivan could guess some kind of soul-and-ghost question, and Selma shushed her.

Ivan couldn't complain. This funeral was a great improvement over his own. He had no reason to hate anybody or to envy anybody. He felt good. He drew a deep breath, full of chamomile aroma, and quite happily he walked to his own grave.

The grave was all covered, there was no gaping hole, and there was a lot of white gravel over the mound, and healthy flowers—some of the varieties he'd never seen before—framed the area. Well, he was never a flower buff anyhow. Several candles were burning with straight flames. The flames weren't flickering and hesitating as they usually do on the graves of the unhappy dead. They were straight, going up like an honest cat's tail. The grave looked completely undisturbed, self-sufficient, kind of peaceful and perfect, so perfect, in fact, that he wished he were in there. The image of the perfection of his grave shook him up. Who would have put the soil back over the grave and kept it up so neatly? Did someone come back to his grave and cover it? Did Paul do it? He had started to cover the grave even when Ivan was there. Maybe he had come back to finish it.

Now, the fact that the grave looked so good didn't mean that Ivan shouldn't dig into it. Ivan walked back to the brickyard to get a shovel, but along the way he got tired. His stamina wasn't what it used to be. Maybe he would leave digging his own grave for later. If the coffin was empty, as it should be, he could perhaps go there and lie down. Maybe he should make another entrance to his grave, perhaps through his father's grave? He could live modestly, mortgage-free, in his own grave. He would sleep there undisturbed, better than anywhere else, in total silence and darkness. In this modern day and age, when you can't get a wink of sleep because there's always some engine buzzing somewhere or something or other exploding, total silence is worth more than happiness. And now and then, when he got tired, he would walk out and stroll through the town—at night, so as not to scare anybody—and he would drink the mineral water, enjoying the taste of rust and sulfur, his doomsday tea.

But what if instead of finding an empty coffin he found his own body there, already in a somewhat advanced stage of decay? That thought, though he at first deemed it to be merely a fantasy, gave him a chill. What if indeed he were solidly dead, and all this roaming around was just a spasm of his imagination? Maybe a hallucination so vivid that it's impossible to doubt it?

Oh, nonsense, he thought, but still, he went to the spring, drank some mineral water—it was warm and delicious. He hadn't realized how chilly he had been, so he splashed the water over his face and massaged his hands until he got some warmth going. He walked over the train tracks, and when he got to the bunker, there was his old cat, the Russian blue-fur. Delightedly, he petted her, and she walked with him into the bunker, and as he stood in the dark, waiting for his eyes to get accustomed to it, the blue-fur rubbed her arched back against his ankles.

Now that was months ago. Since then, there have been reports of Ivan Dolinar sightings. Some say that he goes to his own gravesite at night, lights candles, and digs into the soil with his bare hands, and makes busts of himself. They are wonderfully expressive busts, even with tears streaming down his cheeks, and he looks a little bit like Cicero.

Others report that they have seen him lying down on the train tracks at night, and even after the cargo trains have rolled by, he is still there, sleeping peacefully. And he has supposedly been sighted near the bunker. In fact, the rumors about the bunker have gained most force, so at night nobody dares approach the bunker—no lovers are quite that desperate for privacy. The only person who claims to see him frequently is Tanya. She says he comes at dusk, and each time he has a different story to tell, and they are all beautiful stories about frogs, cats, and snakes. According to her, Ivan likes to read *War and Peace* in the original, in the attic—and the book makes him so restless that he keeps looking for a better position in the armchair, and he moves it all around the attic, and then the chair creaks melodiously. They turn off the lights, and he tries to scare her, like a ghost, with all his creaking. Sometimes he stays overnight and makes very few, slight sounds. It does seem to rain more often when he stays over—but he may be merely urinating through the window because he's too shy to come downstairs to use Selma's bathroom. Selma doesn't like all those sounds that come from the attic, usually on Saturday nights, and she has put up the house for sale, but nobody wants to buy it. Nobody who has visited the Dolinars, however, has heard those sounds and can confirm the story.

As for the grave, more and more people visit it, and not only from Nizograd, but even from as far away as Novi Sad, and, at the moment, it seems that Ivan is getting a sort of cult following . . . many people who are usually very pale but have very red lips come to the grave and move their lips. Now, whether they are praying or just chilly and trembling, that is hard to tell.

During the day, only brave boys come to the bunker entrance but don't go farther, and they report that one can often smell fine Cuban-cigar smoke there. And indeed, sometimes, at early dawn, willowy blue smoke comes out of the bunker and floats silkily. And if you strain your ears, you might hear a sorrowful sigh accompanying the smoke, but you can never be sure, because some damned owl nearby tends to hoot around that time from the county's largest oak.